The Magic Carpet

THROUGH space to the most distant corners of the universe in the twinkling of an eye! When Scheherazade told her Sultan the tales that make up *The Arabian Nights Entertainments,* she told him of a Magic Carpet that flew through the sky and carried its human cargo to distant countries with the speed of thought.

The MAGIC CARPET Magazine, like the carpet of Scheherazade, carries its readers out of the humdrum life of our modern civilization to lands of romance, adventure, mystery and glamor. You can hear the shouts of the sorely beleaguered defenders of Vienna when the Turkish host of Suleiman the Magnificent was thrown back; you can see the beauty of the wicked Queen Semiramis of Babylon; you can thrust aside the hangings of Oriental harems and enter the forbidden rooms of the women's baths; you can exult with Kurdish tribesmen as they ride down their enemies in bloody battle; you can experience the mystery of India, stalk through tiger-infested jungles; or fly to distant planets and perilous adventures among the strange beings that inhabit them.

The MAGIC CARPET goes places and those who ride upon it see things hidden to most eyes, and feel to the full the glamor of far places. This is the magazine you have been waiting for all your life—*the supreme magazine,* in which you can experience as nowhere else the thrill and witchery of adventure and romance in distant lands. A panorama of exotic fiction with the whole universe as its setting will unroll before your gaze as you speed onward upon the MAGIC CARPET.

The Editors.

THE MAGIC CARPET MAGAZINE

with which is combined ORIENTAL STORIES

| Volume 3 | CONTENTS FOR APRIL, 1933 | Number 2 |

Published quarterly by the Popular Fiction Publishing Company, 2457 E. Washington Street, Indianapolis, Ind. Entered as second-class matter, September 8, 1930, at the postoffice at Indianapolis, Indiana, under Act of March 3, 1879. Single copies, 15 cents. Subscription, 60 cents a year in the United States, $1.20 a year in Canada, 80 cents in other countries. English office: Charles Lavell, 13, Serjeant's Inn, Fleet St., E. C. 4, London. The publishers are not responsible for the loss of unsolicited manuscripts, although every care will be taken of such material while in their possession. The contents of this magazine are fully protected by copyright and must not be reproduced either wholly or in part without permission from the publishers. All manuscripts and communications should be addressed to the publisher's Chicago office at 840 North Michigan Avenue, Chicago, Ill.   FARNSWORTH WRIGHT, Editor.

The Vagabond-at-Arms

By SEABURY QUINN

"Immediately he was under my guard, stabbing at me with his poniard."

A swashbuckling mediaeval adventurer, Carlos de la Muerte, tells the story of his exciting and perilous career—a story of thrilling events and romantic dangers

1. How I Became a Vagabond

MY MOTHER was called Ayeshah, the beautiful, for her Christian parents baptized her Mary, star of the sea, and in the Arabic tongue that name is rendered Ayeshah. Sometimes she was called Mabrouka, the fortunate, although, God wot, there was little enough of fortune in the poor lady's life, save, perhaps, that which was of an evil sort. How she was surnamed I do not know, for though she told me much of myself and of that far-off England where she was born and reared to womanhood, there was much she either dared not or could not tell, because of very grief and

131

shame that she, a Christian woman, should have taken the veil and religion of the Prophet of Islam.

My father I never knew, for he died with sword in hand and defiance on lips when the man whose bounty fed and clothed me during the days of my youth assaulted the ship on which he and my mother voyaged from England to Africa.

Of the circumstances of my birth and of my mother's coming to Algiers I learned at her knee as I played in the women's apartments of Sidi Ibrahim ben Ozman's palace near the Street of the Silversmiths, for it was in that house of green and red tiles that I first saw the light, and there I lived until evil fortune removed me to the house of Si Ibrahim's brother, an aged man who had lost an eye fighting against the Spaniards in the olden days and distilled so much of the vitriol of hatred of all things Christian in his nature that there was no room left for the milk of human kindness inside his withered bosom.

While my mother was yet but a bride, my father, who lived by the sword, was granted a commission to command the armed guard of a ship voyaging out of England to Africa, and with him he took his wife. She was of a delicate constitution, and as the humor of the Mediterranean was mild at that season of the year they thought the voyage would aid her health, for I had lain beneath her heart for some three months, and it was my father's hope that she be strong and hale when the fullness of her time was come.

While the tall ship stood powerless for lack of wind between the Iberian peninsula and the shore of Africa—for she carried no rowing slaves—a corsair galley beset her, and after a shrewd fight all who had not been slain in the encounter yielded themselves to Si Ibrahim's arms, though in doing so they bought safety from the sword at the price of a lifetime's slavery at the oar. Howbeit, life is sweet, and even to labor on the galley bench is rather to be preferred to welcoming the kiss of Azrael, the Death Angel; besides, there was always hope of a rescue, or perchance, of ransom, though the rescue was likely to be at the hands of the Spaniards, which meant only trading Moorish chains for Christian fetters, and the chances of a poor seaman's ransom were but slight.

Several women fell into the corsairs' hands together with my mother, and the better favored of these were sent to Constantinople, where women of the West brought better price than in Algiers, while those not comely of face or figure were taken to the Algerian market to be sold as household drudges.

But when the Moorish captain looked upon my mother's face it was fair and pleasing in his sight, and he ransomed her forthwith with gold from his own purse and made her a fair offer of marriage if she would acknowledge the Prophet, promising, the while, that when her child was delivered, if it were a boy it should be treated as his own first-born, and if a girl, provided with suitable dowry when marriageable age should have been reached. And so, upon the deck still wet with her wedded husband's life-blood, my mother bowed her head and recited the *Allah Akbar*, acknowledging that there is no God but God, and Mohammed is His Prophet. Poor lady! Who shall blame her if for the freedom of her unborn child she turned from Lord Christ with her lips, so long as she kept Him in her heart? For well she knew that had she stubbornly refused homage to Islam, both she and the babe would have tasted the bitterness of slavery.

As for Ibrahim ben Ozman, he kept his promise to the letter, for he was a knightly gentleman, and when they laid me on my mother's breast for the first time he recited the *Fatahah* as fervently as though in truth I had been the child of his own house, and gave great praise to Allah and much charity to the needy for that his wife had come safely through her travail.

Me they called Mohammed, to the greater glory of God's Prophet, and to this name my mother added al Kamel, signifying the perfect, for to a woman her first man-child is ever without spot or blemish, either of soul or body, though he be ill-favored as a monkey and vicious as a scorpion.

Thereafter my education was that of a Moorish lad of good family. In the school of the mosque I learned to read and write and to recite whole chapters of the Koran from memory. Slaves taught me to ride and swim and wrestle right cunningly, and my foster-father's men-at-arms instructed me in skill with the arbalest, the pistolet, the lance and the harquebus, for as yet the musket had not come into general use along the shores of Africa. Also there was a Greek from the Golden Horn, a captive of war who had bought freedom and preferment at the price of apostasy, who was more cunning with the sword than any man in all the city, and to him Si Ibrahim sent me for instruction; so that before I had reached my fourteenth year there were few of my age, or even my seniors, who could stand against my swordsmanship, and those who could better me with either saber or rapier were fewer still.

Meantime, in the sanctity of the harem my mother schooled me in the English tongue and taught me of Christ our Lord and of His Maid-Mother, so that I in the innocence of my childish heart was wont to recite *Our Father* in addition to the glorification of the Prophet at morning, noon and evening, believing

that by praising both I was securing favor from each.

When my sixteenth birthday arrived I was permitted to join Si Ibrahim's ship and sally forth to attack the infidels, for it had long been decided that I, as first-born male of the house, should carry on the honorable profession of harrying the Prophet's enemies when my second father should have become too old to lead in the fight.

Well do I remember when first I spilled Spanish blood—the first of much I was to let loose before the tale was ended. In the arrogance of my youth and ignorance I had thought the Nazarene dogs would quail and tremble at sound of the Prophet's battle-cry, and great was my astonishment when they met us breast to breast and blade to blade, right cut, left cut, thrust and parry, with such good will that I was like to have yielded up my spirit in the first of the fight had not a beetle-browed seaman missed the blow he aimed at my head and succeeded only in gashing open my cheek. The pain of the wound maddened me. Crying, *"Din, ed-din!"* with the loudest of them, I sallied into the fray, swinging my simitar with such fury and skill that even their mailed men-at-arms gave ground before me, and more than one of them tasted of my steel, and, tasting it, tasted nothing thereafter.

When all was done and the prisoners whose hurts would not incapacitate them from labor were stowed between decks (the badly wounded we threw into the sea, for there was small profit in feeding helpless Christians whose market price would not repay their keep), old Aben Alahmar, the ship's surgeon, bound up my wound with healing herbs and praised me to my face for the part I had borne in the action. *"Wallah,"* he told my father, "our little cockerel has sharp spurs! A few more brushes with the infidel and he will be worthy to carry thy pennon into battle while thou remainest home to count the spoil!" And Ibrahim ben Ozman, who loved me with a father's love for all that I bore no blood of his within my veins, smiled on me and patted my wounded cheek, declaring that never had such skill or valor been shown by one so young. Truly, the praise of the elders is like the taste of honey on the tongue, even the Grecian honey which sells for half its weight in silver.

So PASSED the days of my youth, and, though I knew myself to be happy, I understood not how happy I was, for he who has never suffered thirst knows not the sweetness of water. The house of Si Ibrahim was a home of joy, for the restrictions of the harem, never so harshly applied by the western Moors as by their brethren of the east, were scarcely enforced at all, and I was free to wander as I chose within the women's apartments, and, though my mother gave him no children, her husband loved her tenderly and refused either to put her away or take other wives from among his own people, though he had several offspring by the lesser women of the establishment.

My eighteenth year arrived and with it the plans for a suitable marriage, for Si Ibrahim would have me established in a house of mine own before he handed over the command of his sea-rovers to my grasp. Gifts had been exchanged and negotiations were speeding toward my nuptials when word came from our sea scouts that a great flotilla of Spanish merchantmen had been sighted and that much rich spoil might be obtained by a foray.

I pleaded to go upon the quest, but since the treaty of my marriage had begun my father would not hear of my exposing myself to danger; so I remained behind to govern the house in his absence. Alas! The terror of the inland sea who had ever been a gentle and indulgent father to the fatherless Englishwoman's son returned no more to his pleasant house with its gardens of melon plants and almond trees. Instead, upon the fourth day following his departure a small boat from his ship limped into port bearing the sole survivors of the disastrous raid. Perfidiously, the Spaniards had mingled disguised ships of war with their trading-vessels, and when the corsairs swooped down upon them they were met with such a hail of lead and iron as sank most of their ships outright while the greater portion of their men perished in futile attempts to board the war-galleys. Of all the Moorish fleet only eight men survived, and I was doubly fatherless.

My father's elder brother, an ill-favored man whose lust for gold was equaled only by his hatred of all things foreign, assumed charge of our household, selling many of our most valued possessions and most beloved servants. My mother and me he gave shelter, as he was bound to do; but my days of happiness were over, for the one-eyed curmudgeon who filled my second sire's place imposed a rigid embargo upon the harem and I was no longer free to visit with my mother except in the presence of one of my stepfather's detestable eunuchs, and then only if she were veiled.

Nature had denied the aged rogue offspring, for evil living had blasted his vitality; but instead of treating me as his son-in-law he chose to regard me as an usurper in the household, and, as far as lay within his power, made life a misery to me. Si Ibrahim's fortune, which was no small one, was mine by right of inheritance; yet my uncle doled me out such pitiful driblets of money that any one would have thought me heir to a beggar's heritage.

Two months had passed since Ibrahim ben Ozman's death, and I was fretting mightily beneath the restraint of his successor when release came unexpectedly. Together with several companions I had been to a house of love; for, though I found small pleasure in the company of dancing-women, having seen performers better than any who danced for public hire in the house of Si Ibrahim, the time hung heavy on my hands, and the company of other youths was oftener to be found in the house of the dance than elsewhere. I was returning to my bed when, as I passed through the Street of the Silversmiths, I descried a figure huddled in a corner of the house wall.

"In the name of Allah, the merciful, the compassionate!" I challenged, laying my hand upon my dagger; for, though there was much money in the town, there was also much poverty, and those who took by force what they could not beg were frequently encountered after night-fall. And:

"In Allah's name, is it thou, my little cockerel?" cried the voice of Aben Alahmar, the surgeon who had bound up my wounds after my first taste of battle.

"Truly, my father, it is I," I returned, replacing my dagger in its sheath, "but why dost thou accost me in this manner?"

"Praise be to Allah that I am able to accost thee at all, my son," the old man replied, taking me by the arm and drawing me into the shadow of the wall. "There be evil things abroad this night, son of my friend. Thy mother, the lady Ayeshah, passed into paradise about the sixth hour this night—some say because of poison; and thy uncle, unworthy wretch that he is, has even now taken possession of thine inheritance. Wert thou to return home thou wouldst be murdered before thine outcry could be heard; for verily, he purposes to destroy thee, that he may possess thy property."

"*Bismillah!*" I cried, seizing my dagger afresh. "This shall not be! Am I a Jewish dog to whine and cringe beneath the lash? By the beard of the Prophet, I shall apply to the Bey for justice!"

"Nay, my son," the old man counseled, "there is no justice for thee in this city. Already thine uncle—may the dogs bite him!—suborns false witnesses against thee, charging thee with treason and apostasy to the creed of the Nazarenes. By morning the Bey's janizaries will seek thee with lance and sword. Thine only safety is to put the sea between thee and them."

Now at these words I became sore afraid, so that my right knee was like to have exchanged greetings with its fellow; for though I feared no man in fair fight, the power of the Bey was a mighty thing, and my uncle's treachery had swept the world away from under my feet. "What, then, am I to do?" I demanded; for though I was a grown man in stature, I was but a lad in years.

"Behold, my son," the old physician answered, displaying a bundle on the pavement at his feet. "What I can do for thee I will. Allah knows 'tis little enough, yet it is better than letting the jackals eat thee."

From the bundle he produced a shirt of fine chain-mail, close-knit and well-nigh as light as cloth, capable of turning a crossbow bolt and fending off the stoutest thrust of sword or dagger. "Wear this, my little one," he bade. "More than once it has saved my life in battles with the Roumi, but what should I, who am too old to give and receive blows, do with the armor of a man? Here, too, is that which will make thy faring forth easier," and he handed me the simitar and dagger which he had worn on half a thousand sea-forays.

They were beautiful weapons, the product of the cleverest armorers in Damascus, so finely tempered that they could shear through plate mail well-nigh as easily as through a leather jerkin, and so cunningly balanced that whether the swordsman struck with point or edge their penetration was twice as great as any other weapons wielded with double the force. Each had a handle fashioned like a gerfalcon's head and a cross-guard formed by extended lion's paws, and on the blade of each was a legend in ancient Chaldean letters which I could not read, but which I had been told proclaimed: *"Who Feels My Kiss Fears Death No More."* Often had I seen the old man striking about him with those twin dealers of mortality and often had I envied him their possession, but their like was not to be had in all of Barbary, and as for offering money for them—as soon would I have dared offer gold for Aben Alahmar's hope of paradise.

While I was yet at a loss to thank the kindly old doctor for his gift, he pressed a purse of woven silver on me, saying, "A hundred gold pieces, lad; 'twas all I could command at such short notice, but 'twill more than pay thy passage into Europe. After that, Allah be with thee."

"Nay, my father," I replied, very near to tears, "if I must go among the Roumi as a fugitive, 'twill be but for a short time; for surely I shall return when my uncle has gone to dwell with Shitan, and claim my bride and my inheritance."

"Eiwa!" he laughed in his beard. "Those be brave words, young cockerel, but the eagle's child is no less an eagle for having been fledged in the nest with the hawks, nor yet does the hawk become an eagle because he hatched among the crags. When thou hast returned to thy father's folk we shall see thee no more, and, belike, thou wilt take up the religion of thy fathers as well. It matters not, my son, what god thou callest on in thy prayers, so long as thou followest a religion of justice and truth.

"And now be off," he ordered, almost gruffly. "The call to prayer will sound shortly, and thine enemies will seek thee as soon as there is light enough to guide their knife-thrusts." Once more he pressed me to his breast and kissed me on each cheek, then turned and lost himself in the shadows of the street.

Holy old man; may he remember me from his happy place! Though he was a sea-robber and an infidel to boot, surely he has not gone to that abode of burning of which the priests seem so certain; for, from a long lifetime spent among men of many religions—and none—I know his words to be true: it matters not overmuch what religion a man professes, so long as he practises one of justice.

A Levantin shipmaster who was beholden to me for some small favors in the past gave me shelter aboard his craft that night, and—for half my store of gold pieces—obtained me a disguise of European doublet and hosen and conveyed me safely to the Port of Malaga.

Thus ended my pleasant youth and began a manhood of toil, danger and strife such as few—thanks be to God!—have known.

2. How "Carlos de la Muerte" Was Born

Now, of the things which befell me in the city of Malaga I do not purpose to tell at length; for though they were many, and of some small importance, the veteran of many battles keeps no tail of the shots he has heard fired, and were I to set down all that which I have done, the supply of paper in all the world would scarce suffice for the chronicle.

One or two events fell out, however, which go to prove that ignorance, coupled with luck, may stand a man in greater stead than all the learning of the school-men.

My upbringing was like to have proved my undoing on the first day I wandered through the streets; for, though my mother had told me much of the underlying truths of the Christian religion, of its outward forms and ceremonies she had taught me nothing at all. Also, be it remembered, I had paid devotion to Mahound since the earliest days of my youth; therefore, upon the first noon of my stay in the city, when bells began ringing from all the spires at once, I turned me toward Mekka and had already bowed my forehead toward the earth, reciting, as a parrot does, without thought upon the words:

> *"Allah akbar,*
> *Ayah salat . . ."*

when I bethought me that my Muslim days were done, and had the wit to make as though bending to recover my cap, which had fallen in the dust as I leant forward, and to stand with lowered head and moving lips until the city's business was resumed at the conclusion of the Angelus. Even so, I was glad to walk hastily from the spot when the prayer was finished, for more than one unwashed citizen of the town had cast glances of angry suspicion in my direction, and I had no mind to be arrested as a Morisco. Indeed, had I fallen into the clutches of the law at that time my shrift would have been short; for, though I was fairly proficient in the Latin tongue, having learned much of it from an unfrocked priest who had fled to Algiers for sanctuary, I knew no word of the prescribed prayers, and the briefest examination would have exposed me to conviction as a Moorish spy, of which there were many in southern Spain at that time, as the sons of Islam had not yet abandoned hope of recapturing the lost provinces.

Howbeit, my luck held, and I escaped further suspicion for some days.

Everywhere I found reason for offense. The dwellers in the city were vilely dirty, for washing was no part of their religion, and the smell of their unbathed bodies was well-nigh as distasteful to me as the odor from the benches where the sweating, unwashed slaves toiled at the oars beneath the boatswain's lash. Too, the inn where I stayed was but a filthy hovel and the bed on which I slept was alive with vermin; so that I spent what time I could in the open air of the streets. On my second night at the *posada* some thieving rascal stole most of my remaining money, so that I was like to have starved had not my ignorance led me into the way of obtaining fresh supplies.

My money being nearly gone, I was wandering aimlessly through the streets when I chanced to pass a church. The heat of the afternoon was excessive and the building's interior looked cool and inviting; so, doffing my cap, I entered the sacred edifice and sank to rest in a corner of the wall hard by a tiny wooden booth which reminded me of the sentry boxes maintained on the battlements for shelter of the night watch during inclement weather.

IT MIGHT have been the sun tired me more than I realized, perhaps the wine I had drunk at breakfast made me drowsy, for wine-drinking was a new thing to me, who had been reared in the total abstinence enjoined on faithful followers of Mohammed; whatever the reason, I was soon asleep and dreaming of my mother, my happy African home and the brave fighting I should do against the Spaniards, when the droning of two voices close beside me brought me up wide awake.

Some one was whispering to some one else inside the sentry box by which I slept, and though the conversation had begun while I was fast in sleep, I quickly caught the drift of it.

"——and who was it thou slewest, my son?" asked a voice as smooth and unctuous as oil of olives poured from an earthen jug.

" 'Twas Lopez, the *escribano,* father," returned another whisper which reminded me of the vinegar men make from soured wine.

"Why didst thou do it?"

"Because he was a lawyer, therefore a robber of the poor, and because he had much wealth in his house."

"And who were thy companions in this evil deed?"

"Pedro the muleteer and Manuel the porter, and none others."

"None others?"

"Nay, father, we three and no more. We entered his house two hours before the Angelus and killed him in his bed. His body we hid in the well of his patio, while such of his wealth as we could lay hands on we bore away and buried in the old cemetery of the Jews. Some little of it we kept, but most of it we buried for fear our sudden possession of too much unexplained gold might bring suspicion."

What more was said within the little box I do not know, for I had already heard enough to know a foul killing had been done and one of the murderers was near. Rising very quietly to my feet I crept to the entrance of the church, where I remained kneeling, as though over-long at my devotions, and watched patiently for a movement of the curtain which veiled the booth's entrance. Anon the curtains parted and a big-nosed, loutish fellow with a hangdog face crept forth and made for the open air with never a backward look.

I rose and followed him, and as he left the building I heard him murmur: "Give myself up to the Alcalde? Not I! Though twenty absolutions hung upon my surrender I would not do it. Am I to have the trouble of murder only to be cheated of its rewards by the hangman's noose? Give myself up, forsooth!"

Carefully, treading softly on the thin-worn soles of my ancient boots, I trailed the fellow at a distance, taking care not to excite his suspicion, but always keeping him in view. As we neared a principal thoroughfare I heard the ruffle of a drum and a loud and formal crying in the street. It was a herald from the Alcalde's palace declaring that Quesada de Lopez, the lawyer, had been murdered and robbed the night before and that five hundred maravedis would be paid as reward to any one giving information concerning the identity of the killers, a like amount to him who found the notary's body, and another similar amount to the person who disclosed the hiding-place of the loot.

Now I had thought to follow the self-confessed robber until he led me to the spot where his plunder was buried, but another plan formed in my mind as I heard the herald's proclamation. Taking counsel with myself, I turned aside and wandered through the byways until I had gone some considerable distance, then, accosting a passer-by, doffed my ragged cap politely and explained to him I was a traveler but newly come to Malaga and desired to learn the location of the old Jewish cemetery.

He looked at me shrewdly, desiring to know whether I were a new Christian—

as they called the baptized Hebrews—or no, but I informed him I was as good a Christian as I was on the day of my birth, which was true, and that I wished to go to the burying-place because there was buried there a certain Abarbanel who had bested my father's father in a business transaction, and I desired to spit upon his grave.

The apparent Christian-like reason for my desire to visit the cemetery commended me highly to my companion, and he obligingly gave me full directions how to find the place, even going out of his way to accompany me on my quest.

At length I found the ruinous remains of the place where the sons of Moses had aforetime been buried, and made short work of searching every foot of it for a spot where the earth had been newly turned. Beside the wreck of what had once been a headstone I found the place, and exhumed three leathern bags, the contents of which I spread out before me on the sun-dried grass. Two of the bags contained broad gold pieces, and these I returned to their place, since the gold was bulky and not easily to be carried, but in the third I found a number of precious stones of excellent water, and these I pried from their settings and hid in the hem of my doublet, then replaced the earth above the treasure's grave and hastened to the house of the Alcalde.

The officer of the guard was for denying me admission at first, but when he learned I bore news of the murderers for whom the whole town was searching he led me before the magistrate, to whom I told a cock-and-bull story of having seen three villainous-looking fellows skulking from the house of the dead notary early that morning. Pressed further for details, I said I could not name the men, for the light was poor, but that I would undertake to lay them by the heels if he would

give me three men-at-arms to go with me as escort.

Together with the trio of soldiers I made the rounds of the city's cheaper wine-shops, eventually finding the man I had seen in church that day drinking prodigious drafts of port with two companions as ill-favored as himself.

"There they be," I exclaimed, pointing to my quarry; "seize them before they can make off!"

To my surprize the three culprits made little resistance when the soldiers swooped down upon them, and though they at first stoutly denied all guilt, it took but half a dozen lusty blows with the flat of a sword to force them to confess.

WITH the prisoners firmly bound we made our way toward the Alcalde's house once more, and I was beginning to think that Malaga was no very evil place after all; since, though thieves stole my money while I slept, more was easily to be made in its stead, when a remark by one of the soldiers set my fears alive. "What think you his Excellency will do to the informer?" he asked in a low voice.

"Oh, belike he will torture him until he discloses the hiding-place of the loot," the other replied carelessly, "or perhaps he will only fling him into a dungeon as a suspect Moorish spy and leave him there to starve."

Now neither of these contingencies was greatly to my liking, and I commenced straightway to make plans whereby I might circumvent the Alcalde; for well I knew that if he ordered me into custody and his servants searched my clothes they would find the hidden jewels, and then I should most certainly taste the rack or the water-torture until I confessed to any crime with which my captors might wish to charge me. Therefore:

"Companions," said I as we passed a

dimly lighted wine-shop, "let us enter here and drink to our good fortune in finding the knaves who did the estimable lawyer to death."

Nothing loth, and grinning broadly at each other for that the gull whom they were taking into custody should offer to treat them, the soldiers dismounted and entered the vintner's with me, and I bade the wench who served us bring four bottles of her best claret for us and carry three more to the poor wretches who stayed bound without the door. "Belike it will be long enough before their gullets taste good wine again," I added in explanation of my charity, whereat the soldiers laughed loud and long, and winked at each other with what they thought a hidden meaning.

"Friend," said one of them as he poured a second goblet of the wine from the sturdy bottle the serving slattern set before him, "thou drinkest not. Is not our company good enough for thee?"

Now this was the very thing for which I had wished, and, indeed, I had been seeking some means of forcing a quarrel on them when the half-tipsy fellow saved me the trouble.

Even better was my luck when one of his companions blurted out between hiccups: "What may be thy name, Master Informer?"

"Carlos," I answered, giving the first Spanish name to flash into my mind.

"Carlos what?" he persisted.

"Carlos Francisco," I replied, thinking to satisfy him, but:

"Carlos Francisco, forsooth!" he laughed scornfully. "Hast thou no family name, or art thou one of those who may claim none? Faith, none but *bastardos* and heretics lack surnames!"

"Have it as thou wilt, then," I replied. "Let my name be de la Muerte, signifying Death!" and I snatched the dagger from my belt and struck him in the throat midway 'twixt chin and gorget.

He sprawled forward across the table, his red blood mingling with the spilt red wine, and his two companions were on me in an instant, their long swords flashing in the dim torchlight.

But though they were both of greater stature than I, their knowledge of the fence was such as is learned in the *baracca,* not in the armory of a finished master such as had trained me.

Nicholaides, the Greek who taught me the science of the sword, used no fencing-masks, and to that fact I owed my life's salvation that night; for the first of my opponents lunged directly at my face, and had I fought as the Spaniards do, his point would surely have struck through my eye. But I fenced with my head well back, and as his steel slipped past my cheek I shortened my sword, then drove it gently forward as his body lurched against mine, and, scarcely thrusting at all, ran the keen blade through his breast so that he fell writhing at my feet with an inch-long wound in his bosom and a slit half that length in his back.

Loosening my blade from the dying man's chest I turned to engage his companion, but the fellow had no stomach for the fight.

"Help, help, a man lies murdered!" he bawled as he ran from out the shop, stopping not even long enough to let his metal cross mine.

There were few wayfarers abroad at that hour of night, and the tavern where we fought had been deserted (a fact which had led me to invite the soldiers to it); so, although the cowardly mongrel bellowed for help at the top of his lungs, none came to his assistance, and I left the place unmolested.

From one of the dead men-at-arms I took a steel cap, cloak and jerkin, and from another his boots, for I should need fresh clothing on my journey, and mine own was in a woful state of disrepair. Only a moment was required to hamstring two of the troopers' three horses and serve the poor brutes which bore the prisoners in the same way; for though I hated the cruelty, I well knew my own safety depended on distancing pursuit in the early hours of the chase.

So, astride the remaining cavalry steed and equipped like a member of the Alcalde's mounted guard, I dashed through the night, carrying on the fleeing soldier's cry: "Help, help, a man lies murdered!"

On my way from the city I bethought me of the Jewish cemetery and halted long enough to exhume the remaining bags of gold, then set forth for Granada, knowing full well that whatever fortune lay before me I was not like to acquire so much gold for so little work as I had in that night's business.

Thus ended my first visit to the Port of Malaga.

3. How I Met the Beggar Princess

NONE accosted me or offered me let or obstacle as I clattered along the highway toward the old Moorish capital, for I made a brave show in my burnished morion, my red cloak and my high boots of new cordovan leather as I bestrode the tall cavalry horse. Moreover, the first wound I ever received in battle had left a long crescent-shaped scar athwart my right cheek, and this gave to my countenance a singularly sinister expression at times, and the long sword clanking and clinking against my rowels warned the over-curious that I was an excellent man to leave alone as he rode about his business. And so I made my way by leisurely stages, stopping at such inns as proved inviting to my inspection, drinking spar-

ingly, gaming not at all with the idlers in the common rooms and swearing as little as I could without arousing suspicion, for the Spaniards were much given to strange oaths and the filthiness of their profanity disgusted me.

Now it was on a Sunday morning, very early in the day, when I neared the outskirts of the city which was my destination, and my surprize was great to see a mighty throng of people passing in the same direction, as though there were some fair or festival toward. Many of the peasants, too, were in their holiday attire; so that I was moved to ask a caballero who galloped past, as though he were afraid of missing some show, "What means the concourse of people, friend? Is it a pageant they go to?"

He looked at me narrowly from under his black brows and asked with what I thought a tone of suspicion, "Whence come you, that you ask such a question this day?"

"*José y Maria*, comrade," I replied, using the mildest oath I could think of, "I come from the African coast, where I have been fighting with the infidel!" which was true enough, though I neglected to say that all my blows had been struck on the infidels' side. Seeing that he still looked doubtful, I added meaningly, "There were men there who could give stout blows, as well as take them, and my arm grows numb for want of action these many days. Would you, perchance, care to——"

But it appeared he would not, for he crossed himself hastily and set spurs to his horse, riding rapidly away from me in the direction of the city gate.

Further questions were unnecessary, for the procession of boors and esquires, knights and ladies, serving-wenches and pot-washers set all in one way, and I had but to drift with the human tide to find myself presently overlooking a plaza, or open square, in the center of which two tall stands of benches, like flights of monster stairs, had been built facing each other, with a little space of cleared ground between. I bestrode my charger wonderingly, for though all seemed ready for a play of some kind, I saw neither mimes nor actors, though a great press of audience was already assembled.

Presently, however, there came a blaring peal of trumpets, and immediately thereafter the melancholy chanting of a psalm-tune, and a procession the like of which I had never seen before filed solemnly into the square. A company of swart-faced fellows in black doublet and hose, white crosses blazoned on their tunics and cloaks, marched first, glittering halberts carried at the shoulder. Before them, like a standard-bearer, marched a friar in habit of black and white carrying a green cross swathed in veilings of black, and behind the pikemen there marched, or rather shuffled, a company of what I first took to be mountebanks, so grotesque was their dress. Each wore a short, smock-like garment of brilliant yellow cloth on which was painted in blue the X-shaped cross of St. Andrew, while over all were daubed crude representations of flickering tongues of flame and figures of djinns, dragons and devils such as the story-tellers in Algiers were wont to tell of in the evenings when the seamen gathered in the houses of entertainment to while the hours of the night away. In addition, each of these people had a twin-peaked cap like a bishop's miter on his head, and about his neck was loosely drawn a noose, the ends of which hung down in front, pinioning his wrists together before him. In his hands each carried an unlighted candle of green wax, and all walked in their bare feet with legs uncovered to the knee.

Now, I was at first for laughing at the idiotic show these mummers made of themselves, but past experience had taught me caution, and before I burst into a guffaw I looked about me under lowered lids and beheld there was little enough of laughter on the faces of the crowd. Rather, it seemed to me, there was a look of fright on many a countenance, and many more showed sorrow, while those afoot bent the knee and beat their breasts as the procession passed them by and those who were mounted bared their heads and bowed them low upon their bosoms. Therefore, not being minded to cause remark, I did likewise, but watched shrewdly what was toward from beneath my brows. And behold, I saw a great company of shaven-headed friars in habits of black and white pass by, and after them, marching beneath a canopy of red and gold with such show of pomp and pride as the Bey would hardly have made as he passed through the streets of Algiers, there came a priest in full sacerdotal robes, and before him tripped a little boy with a staff of bells in his hand, and as he rang the chimes the multitude bent lower and lower, as though it were a signal for utter self-abasement.

Onward the strange parade wound its way to the wooden benches at the center of the square, and here the priestly marchers disposed themselves on one side, while the buffoons in yellow cap and gown were seated on the other.

Followed the celebration of the mass, and tears of admiration ran down my cheeks as I heard for the first time that wondrous mingling of beauteous words with stately music; but anon a man in a notary's robe arose and read from a parchment scroll a great list of trivial offenses which seemed to have been committed by the clowns in yellow.

"Truly," thought I as I watched this

strange proceeding, "the Spaniards are over-harsh in their judgments, for even the strictest *maula* in all Algiers would not humiliate a man guilty of such insignificant faults as these by obliging him to appear in public in such outlandish garb." But my wonder turned to loathing and my eyes went wide with horror as the notary gave place to another man who announced that the poor wretches were to be taken thence to an adjoining field and there burnt alive at the stake!

Scarce could I keep my stomach from retching as I turned my horse about and rode from that place of infamy, that spot accursed of God and man, where those who bore the sign and seal of the gentle Christ of whom my mother had told me doomed their fellows to death by hideous torture for no greater crime (in some instances) than that of giving a drink of water or a crust of bread to a starving Hebrew!

THE day was nearly spent and shadows had begun to take ever-changing shape in the streets before I could bring myself to think of food again, for ever and anon throughout the hours of daylight I fancied I could detect the scent of burning flesh which hung above the city like the odor of incense from some satanic festival.

But youth is ever quick to put behind it the thought and memory of things unpleasant, and by the hour of the evening Angelus my body, which was hale and stout as a young brute's, was crying out in anguish for nourishment; therefore I turned my footsteps toward mine inn, treading carefully, for as yet the town was strange to me and I scarce knew which way to turn to find the place I sought.

And as I walked along I brought up suddenly with a malediction, for the twistings and turnings of the lane I followed had brought me back again to a place I had left some minutes before, and I stood at the junction of two tall walls, arguing with myself whether I would do better to turn me to my right or to my left, when the sound of flying footsteps and a woman's scream drove all thought of myself and my difficulties from me.

Very beautiful she was to behold as she ran toward me, her arms outstretched, her golden hair streaming in the breeze of her flight. Her face was long and oval-shaped and of a white-skinned pallor which minded me of the alabaster from which the lamps of Si Ibrahim's palace had been carved. Her eyes were large and blue, and of such depth and beauty that my heart melted to water at sight of them, and as for her form—women in plenty had I seen, but never one like her. Lightly clad in a sleeveless gown of some crude and dirty cotton stuff, her little feet, white as lilies o'erspecked with violet veins, bruised and bleeding from contact with the sharp-edged flints of the roadway, she seemed to me like a being from some other world—a houri from the Prophet's paradise, perhaps, or belike one of the holy angels who sang the good tidings of great joy above the fields of Judea on Christ our Lord his birth-night.

Howbeit, I was soon to know she was no angel, but a mortal woman fast held in mortal terror, for piteously she held forth her ivory hands to me and pitifully she cried, "Good friend, for Mary's sake, succor me; defend me; hide me—they come! They come!"

Now, till that moment women had meant little in my life, for I could have had my pick of any of a hundred fair-faced dancing-girls in my father's house, and many were the women of the kashbah who looked on me—or, perchance, upon my purse—with the soft eyes of love; but trading blows with sword and lance had ever been more to my liking than bartering kiss for kiss, and so I stood tonguetied before the maiden what time she ran the length of the little alley and flung herself despairingly to her knees before me, holding me by the feet and imploring me to befriend her.

But finally the beating of my heart subsided enough to let me find my voice—though the breath still came hot and fluttering in my throat—and I raised the virgin in my arms and spoke her civilly, beseeching her but to tell me how I could serve her, and I would be her faithful slave till death, and much more such senseless things I said, the like of which young lads have ever declared when first love drives his dart into their vitals. What more I would have babbled I know not, for no man is master of his words when Eros holds the reins of his heart, but interruption came quickly to break my speech asunder.

Adown the narrow street, their eyes and teeth gleaming horribly, like those of wild and savage beasts when they quest their prey, there came two black-garbed men with crosses of white upon their ebon doublets, long halberts flashing in their hands and triumph on their faces.

"Heretic, devil's child, abandoned of God!" screamed one as he distanced his fellow and rushed toward the maid and me. "We have thee in a trap!" Whereat the damsel in my arms began to tremble violently and would have swooned had I not supported her against my bosom.

"How now, friend," I asked mildly, addressing the hangman-faced man who leveled his weapon at us, "what wouldst thou with the little maid?"

But the fellow seemed beside himself with a kind of frenzy, gnashing his teeth together as though he would tear his own lips to tatters and screaming at me: "Judaizer! Heretic dog, paramour of the abandoned, obstructer of the hand of God! Turn loose the devil's brat and yield thyself to the authority of the Holy Office!"

"Nay, friend," I temporized, putting the maiden behind me and speaking softly still, for I had no wish to close in battle with two spearmen at once, "indeed, I am no heretic, but as good a churchman as any in the place from whence I came, and as for turning loose the damsel, as soon would I yield up my spirit."

"Have then thy wish, accursed of God!" the fellow shrieked, and made at me with his pike.

Then did I thank my guardian angel right heartily that I had learned to swing the sword in the armory of one whose masters in the fence were few; for as the villain attacked me I whipped my blade from out its scabbard and drew it quickly to the right in a single upward motion, and so keen and true was the good steel that it sheared the iron head from off the halbert staff, leaving mine enemy with naught in hand but a four-foot stave of wood.

Meantime, with my left hand I snatched the dagger from my girdle and struck right manfully at his breast, but the steel bent nearly double in my grasp; for under his doublet of black stuff he wore a shirt of mail, and had my hanger been less finely tempered, it would have surely broken in my hand.

Immediately the caitiff was under my guard, stabbing at me with his poniard, and had not the good steel shirt I wore beneath my tunic turned his point I had given up the ghost then and there.

But the tablets of my fate did not decree that I should die at the hands of such as he, and before he could recover his footing I had tripped him up with a wrestler's trick and driven my good

O. S.—1

sword's point into his mouth as he lay back-down upon the pavement, so that my steel and his filthy blood mingled with the curses he spewed at me even as his soul sped forth to Satan, its lord.

His companion rogue, who had been vainly endeavoring to strike me with his pike, but feared to thrust too swiftly for fear of hitting his brother in crime, now closed with me, and would have made short work of it had not my secret mail stood me in good stead again. For, though his heavy iron lance-head bruised and pommeled my ribs like the kickings of a vicious mule, the point could not win through the forged links about my body, and I had recourse to a trick learned in the early days of my youth when rough and tumble fighting had been more to my taste than the cool science of the fencing floor. Pretending to be stricken unto death, I fell upon my back, spreading my arms out crosswise, and lay there, breathing heavily. Over me leaped my opponent, shortening his pike to strike me through the gullet; then from right and left I brought my two blades upward at once, like the arms of a pair of scissors, cutting through the tendons of both his legs and dropping him to the pavement beside me as though he had been shot with a crossbow quarrel. Thereafter I slew him at my convenience.

I was for going through my fallen adversaries' pockets; for, though they looked a scrawny enough pair of catchpolls, there was some small chance I might find that upon them which would repay me for the trouble I had been at in killing them. Howbeit, I was deterred in my quest by an exclamation from the fainting virgin behind me. *"Santa Maria, Señor,"* she cried as she recovered her senses, "have you killed them both?"

"Aye," I replied with no little show of

O. S.—2

vainglory, for the man who would not shine before the woman of his heart is but a sorry sort of fellow. "Aye, my beautiful one, they will hound thee through the streets no more. Already they drink the drafts prepared in hell for such as they."

I turned upon her, expecting full meed of laud and praise for my heroism, but to my amazement the little maid burst into a torrent of weeping. *"Ay di mi!"* she sobbed. "Alas, we are undone!"

"How so?" I demanded right testily; for it seemed to me our troubles had been greatly lessened by the dispatch of our assailants.

"Knowest thou not whom thou slewest?" she queried between deep-drawn sobs. "Alas, they were of the Militia Christi—familiars of the Holy Office— and who hurts or hinders them would better have had a millstone hung round his neck and been cast into the sea!"

"Say you so?" I answered, looking with no greatly increased respect upon the relics of my conquered adversaries. "Why should that be? Methinks they fought no better than other men, not so well as some I have met."

"Ah, *Señor,* you knew not what you did when you opposed them," she responded. "They carry with them the whole dreadful power of the Inquisition. Men have been tortured and burned for less than this night's business. I myself was taken in their custody for no greater fault than that I did refuse a piece of pork, which I hate, and thus became suspect of Judaizing. They were conveying me to their prison, which is hard by this spot, when I broke from them. Tomorrow I was to have been questioned, perhaps with torture, and anon they would have burned me. Oh, wo is me that in my weakness I called on you for succor, and wo are you that you accorded it to me, for I have assuredly dragged you down to death and torture with me."

"By the bones of St. Jude," I answered, using one of my new-found Christian oaths, "do you tell me so? Fair maiden, have you no home to which I may convey you? Do but tell me where you would go, and Carlos de la Muerte will see you safely there in despite of all the shark-faced familiars of the Holy Office; aye, and of the Grand Inquisitor himself!"

"Hush, oh, hush!" she implored, signing herself with the cross fearfully and glancing about as though the very walls could hear my boasting. "I have a father who mourns me as lost, and, could I reach him, perhaps I might be safe from those birds of prey; but how can we make our way through the city beset with these dreadful servants of the Inquisition?"

"Sayest thou the populace fears these fellows?" I asked in my turn, stirring one of the bodies before me with the toe of my boot, for a thought had already taken form inside my mind, and needed but her assurance to be translated into action.

"Yes, Señor, there is none in all Granada, from the Governor General down, who would dare raise a finger to hinder one of them. Surely you are a stranger in our midst, or you would have run away and left me to my fate."

"A stranger I am, verily," I replied, "and as to what I might have done had I possessed more knowledge of your ways, we need say nothing at this time. The fact remains that the people fear these night-birds, and to that fact we shall owe our safe conduct through the streets."

So saying I stooped and possessed myself of one of the militiamen's black cloaks, spreading it over my own scarlet cape and drawing it about me until I was muffled in its sable folds from throat to calf. "Do you likewise, Señorita," I commanded, handing her the other vulture's garment and loosening the shoes from off his feet. "Array yourself in his cloak, cap and shoon, and go boldly through the streets with me. Should any stop us, we will say we go upon an urgent quest for the Holy Office, and methinks few will ask us further questions. For those whose curiosity goes deeper"— I struck the hilt of my simitar—"I have this to argue our cause. Come, let us be off."

And so, disguised in the raiment of the little maid's late captors, we marched openly through the darkening streets, and I could have shouted aloud with laughter to see how the few passengers we encountered bared their heads and louted low at sight of the white crosses on our sable cloaks.

"How came it such a gentle dove as thou wert in the clutches of those hawks?" I asked as we pursued our way through the quiet streets.

"'Twas jealousy, Don Carlos," she answered, giving me the Spanish title of nobility, whereat my heart beat faster and puffed with pride inside my breast. "Yesterday morn I did repair with other maidens to wash my hair at the fountain, and a certain girl, a gipsy-blooded wench named Sanchica, reviled me for that my hair was yellow, instead of black, like hers. 'Thou'rt no true daughter of Spain,' she taunted me, 'for only the heretics of the north or the bastard brood of Andalusia have light hair and eyes.' Whereat I became enraged and replied, 'At least no light-complexioned maid need fear suspicion of having blackamoors for ancestors.'

"At this she screamed and bit her thumbs, for there was much talk of black blood flowing in her family. Natheless, that evening she appeared to have forgiven me, and came to me and kissed me on the mouth and made me the offer of a great piece of roasted pork, a meat which sickens me whenever I attempt to eat it.

"I thanked her civilly for her present, but declined to eat of it, whereat she went straightway and informed against me to the Holy Office, and when the officers apprehended me this morning there was a great concourse of women who testified that I had publicly refused to eat the pig's flesh, which rendered me suspect of Judaizing. They took my silken robe from off me and clothed me in the shift of one foredoomed to torture. Tonight they conveyed me from one prison to another, and I broke from them and fled. The rest you know, Don Carlos."

ANON my fair companion led me through a succession of mean thoroughfares to an ancient Moorish house which had been all but demolished by the earthquakes with which the city had been plagued in former days. Brushes grew rank and wild before its gateway and spiders had spun their snares from post to post of its portal, so that it bore the signs of having been long deserted, but the little maid turned sharply to the right, stooped suddenly till she almost knelt upon the paving blocks, and slipped through a rift in the wall, signaling me to do likewise. I obeyed her wordless summons, crept through a jagged cleft in the house side, clambered over the broken shafts of fallen pillars and avoided breaking my bones against the fragments of ruined masonry by the narrowest of luck more than once before I found myself in the patio of the house, open to the sky and dimly lighted by a fire of dung burning on the marble pavement near the central well.

"Who comes there?" a hoarse voice challenged as we crept through the fissure in the wall and stepped into the patio. A villainous-looking cutthroat armed with a stout pole ax loomed suddenly from the darkness and barred our way. "*Santo Redentor!*" he cried sharply at glimpse of the cross on my companion's cloak, and would have struck her down without more ado had she not cried out:

"Sancho, it is I, Jacinta!"

"Praised be all the holy saints of heaven!" the fellow answered, lowering his weapon and doing a sort of grotesque dance for very happiness. "Our little one has come back to us. *Por Dios*, little princess, we had given thee up for lost!"

A great man in black with tattered cloak of purple, bearded like a Franciscan and swaggering like a man-at-arms, strode forward through the gloom and clipped the little maid to his broad bosom. "By'r Lady, *niñita mia*," he cried, while his great belly shook and bobbed with sobs like a wine-skin tossed and bounced upon the back of a capering mule, "I can scarce believe mine eyes! Hast thou really come back from that place where only the hope-abandoned go? How comes it? Tell me not they found no fault in thee; for, by San Luis, those dogs would prove heresy in the Archangel Michael himself were he haled before them!"

"Nay, father mine," the maid replied, turning from stroking the man's hairy cheeks to cast a glance of gratitude on me, "this good, brave gentleman saved me from their clutches. Aye, but he did slay the two who had me in charge, and it was in their clothes we made our way safely through the midst of their fellows to thee." Thereafter, when we had seated ourselves by the fire and been refreshed with great platters of savory stew and many a stoop of strong, sweet wine, she told the tale of her escape and rescue, taking care that my reputation suffered none in the relation.

As for me, I hung my head and appeared as modest as circumstances would allow, albeit now and again I was forced to remind her of this incident or that which she had overlooked, for much of the time she had lain in a swoon, and could not properly recollect all details of the noble fight I had made in her defense.

"Well done, by my crown and throne!" the fat man cried when all had been said. Then, to me: "Young sir, your services this night are highly valued. How would you that I reward you?"

"Truly, *caballero,* I know not what to say," I replied, "for I am a wanderer upon the earth, having been cast off by mine own people and very like to find no hospitality other than that of the grave among these Spaniards." Therewith I told him of my life from the time of my birth in Si Ibrahim's palace to that night when I had wrested his daughter from the clutches of the Holy Office.

He pondered long upon my tale when I had done, nursing his hairy chin in the palm of his thick hand and staring pensively into the fire. At length:

"Spain is too hot to hold thee, for a time, at least," he said, "and such gold as thou left at thine inn is as good as gone, for to return to seek it would be to hand thyself over to the familiars of the Inquisition. Perchance, however, I can give thee that which is better than gold, for I think adventure will be the breath of thy nostrils for some few years to come, though thou wilt win wealth and no little fame before all is done, unless a rope stretch thy neck meantime.

'Know then, young friend, that I am Ruiz, king of the beggars in Granada, and that I rule the clan with a power absolute and unassailable here. In other cities and other lands there be other kings, or, rather, grand masters, of beggars, and to them the word of Ruiz of Granada is as a friendly greeting from another of their family. Take thou this, wear it ever on thy person. Shouldst thou ever be in need of friendship, succor or assistance of any kind, thou hast but to show it to any beggar, wherever he may be, and he is bound by an oath not to be broken to aid thee to the end so long as the probability of helping thee is greater than that of losing his own life."

Into my hand he pressed a heavy golden ring set with a stone of amethyst, and as I regarded it closely I saw the setting was carven with the effigy of Lazarus lying at Dives' door, and so cunningly had the lapidary wrought his work that the very tongues of the curs which licked the beggar's sores could be plainly distinguished, though the entire stone was no greater than the nail of my little finger.

I put the bauble in a secret place within my doublet and thanked King Ruiz honorably for his goodness.

Next morning, attired in a beggar's filthy gown, my face besmeared with grime and a rattling clack-dish at my hempen girdle, I made my way from the ancient city of the Moors.

But underneath my beggar's gabardine I bore three talismans, aye, four: the ring of Lazarus, my good Damascus sword, and a rose plucked new and dewy from its bush that morning and flung to me by the little beggar princess, Jacinta. And in my heart there echoed and re-echoed as I trod the road toward Italy her parting words: "Go with God, Don Carlos, and take with thee my prayers. *Hasta luego*—until we meet again."

In the next adventure Carlos de la Muerte acquires a new name, a new coat, a new companion and several more exciting experiences. Don't fail to read it. It will be published in full in the next issue of the MAGIC CARPET MAGAZINE.

"One of the rukhs lifted me up in its claws and carried me to its nest."

The Truth About Sinbad the Sailor

By ALLAN GOVAN

A tale which tells facts about Sinbad's voyages that do not agree with the story in the "Arabian Nights"

THIS story from the glamorous city of the Califs is really a little sermon on man's natural inclination to toy with facts. Like those that have preceded it, it should, in the language of the *Arabian Nights' Entertainments,* "be a lesson to him who would be admonished." But human nature being what it is, the writer doesn't believe that the story will make any difference; he doesn't expect for a moment that it will be a lesson to anybody. That, however, is by the way.

In the *Arabian Nights' Entertainments*

the stories of his seven really remarkable voyages were told by Sinbad the Sailor (who was a very wealthy man) to a namesake who was a humble porter. What is here disclosed for the first time is that Sinbad never went on those seven voyages at all. Not only that! He never even made up the stories of his alleged travels —he got the stories in all their essentials from a certain Marwan, who was a water-carrier.

MARWAN, a tall thin person of very uncertain age, glared banefully at the little wizened shrimp of a man before him.

"There you sit like an owl without a single idea in your head," he stormed. "You sail down and up the Tigris between here and El-Basrah in that old tub of yours, and you meet all sorts of people and hear all sorts of tales and yet you can't give me one original idea. At El-Basrah you rub shoulders with seamen who have sailed every sea, and when I ask you if you have heard anything that would give me an idea for a yarn to spin to my friend Sinbad, you scratch your coconut-shell head and say, 'No; I don't think I have. No; I can't call anything to mind.' Think, man, think! Haven't you heard any stories about countries where the people walk on their heads, or where the cats have six legs, or where the trees grow downward out of the clouds? For the love of Allah, think!"

Talib tried to think, but the only apparent consequence of his trying was that his features settled themselves into an expression of mild agony.

"No, I'm sorry, Marwan, but I don't seem to remember having heard anything that——"

"And there is Sinbad sitting in his palatial home, waiting with his ears cocked to sop up tales of strange countries over the seas; and perfectly prepared, if I hit on a particularly good lie, to press upon me a gold goblet or some such trifle as a memento of a happy evening."

"When I was in El-Basrah this trip I—did hear a deep-sea sailor say that in Africa there is a bird as tall as a camel."

"What's that?"

"A bird as tall as a camel, and——"

"What's it called?"

"An ostrich. But I don't see that that would help you to——"

"In the name of Et Taghoot stop prattling, and let me think. A bird as tall as a camel! Exaggerate the size of the bird, say, ten times, and we have a bird that could fly off with a man in its talons, and——"

"The sailor said that the ostrich can't fly."

"O Muslims! Will you stop interrupting me! . . . A bird that can carry off a man in its talons, and that lays an egg the size of a camel. It is called the great rukh. One of these rukhs lifted me up in its claws and carried me to its nest as a titbit for its young. But by slaying the young rukhs in the nest I escaped, and——"

Marwan sprang to where his shoes were lying, beside the door.

"I can think out the details and add the embellishments while I'm telling the tale. Through the mercy of Allah (whose perfection be extolled!) I have thought out a corker this time. I'm off to see Sinbad, and if luck favors me, your humble assistance shall be suitably recognized, Talib my friend."

And with that Marwan was gone.

"YOUNG man, be good enough to convey my humble respects to your master." Marwan addressed the tall Nubian who stood on guard at the door of Sinbad's big house.

The Nubian's black brows came together threateningly.

"Where have *you* been these last months? And what are you after now?" he asked.

"That's *my* affair, my ebony friend," Marwan told him insolently. "Just you run along and inform Sinbad that Marwan is without," and having given that instruction, Marwan seated himself with easy grace on the *mastabah* or stone bench near the door.

For a moment the doorkeeper stood looking simitars and javelins at the caller. Then he thought better of whatever he had had in his mind, turned about, and stalked away to carry out the instruction.

Presently Marwan was in the presence of the master of the house.

"Enter in the name of Allah, and welcome back from your voyaging," cried Sinbad heartily. He motioned to the cushions at his side, and asked Marwan whether he would have white or red.

When Marwan's goblet had been emptied and refilled, Sinbad looked at him expectantly.

"Allah (whose name be exalted!) has brought me safely back to this city of Baghdad, after I have again visited many strange lands and met with adventures which, if they were written, would excite wonder and astonishment," Marwan observed.

"A-a-ah!" said Sinbad, and motioned to a slave to fill Marwan's goblet once more. Having done that, he needed to throw out only a very few hints to induce Marwan to plunge into the tale of his latest adventures.

The story was a long one, and from beginning to end it held Sinbad breathless with excitement and wonder.

When he got his breath again, Sinbad said: "I've got an idea. It's a scheme for making money."

"Making money—eh?" said Marwan, deeply interested immediately. He glanced at the slaves loafing about here and there. "If the scheme has something to do with money——"

"Oh, well, perhaps it might be better," Sinbad admitted. "I'll clap when I want you," he told his retinue, and next moment he and Marwan were alone.

Now, as has already been said, Sinbad was a very wealthy man. But when a man is wealthy he doesn't necessarily cease to be interested in schemes for making money. Indeed he is usually all the more interested, and that explains why the capitalist system has been such a marked success throughout the ages.

Marwan understood this perfectly; his only wonder was as to the nature of a scheme which a wealthy man such as Sinbad should think fit to expound to a wayfarer like himself. He summed up his thoughts by asking himself: "What in the name of all the tribe of Sheytan is this compound of cunning and credulity up to now?"

"During your adventurous career you have visited many very interesting places?"

"I have," said Marwan.

"Isn't it to be supposed that others would find them equally interesting?"

"Undoubtedly. But I don't quite——"

Sinbad bent toward the globe-trotter. *"Why not organize pleasure excursions to these places?"*

His lungs completely deflated by the shock of the suggestion, Marwan stared at Sinbad.

"Pleasure excursions!" he managed at last to say in a dazed kind of way.

"Conducted tours, run on good lines," said Sinbad.

Marwan could only continue to stare at his friend. His mind refused to focus on anything at all very clearly.

But at last out of the jumble of his

thinking there emerged the words: "My friend, I am of opinion that you have hit upon an idea destined to lead to very interesting developments."

"I tell you, the citizens would eat it," said Sinbad. "Think of the advertisements! 'A pleasure trip to the land of the great rukh—the bird which feeds its young on elephants.' 'See the mighty rhinoceros which lifts a bullock on its horn and continues to graze without being aware that the bullock is there, and the bullock's fat, melting in the heat of the sun, flows into the eyes of the rhinoceros and blinds it.' 'Visit the land of the black giants who are as tall as palm-trees, who have tusks like the wild boar and nails like the claws of the lion, who eat a man or an ox at every meal.' 'Don't miss this trip to the valley where the pebbles are diamonds and jacinths and pearls!' 'Come with us on the wonder trip of the age!'"

"As I said before, I can see interesting possibilities in the idea," said Marwan, his eyes dancing strangely.

"If we did everything in really good style we'd be booked up every trip," Sinbad asserted. "With the blessing of Allah we would get our capital back almost at once."

"I could, if desired, accompany the parties as dragoman," Marwan suggested, feeling that he ought to enter into the spirit of the thing.

"I had that in mind, naturally," said Sinbad. "We could get out a few really splashing advertisements, mentioning the tonic effect of the sea air, and we'd not forget to work in about the tropical moonlight on the dancing water."

"I know an island ruled by an Efreet," Marwan observed, entering still further into the spirit of the thing. "It might be possible to come to some arrangement with him to appear while our ship hove to for ten minutes or so."

"One of my wives—Budoor—is on very friendly terms with the lady Zubeydeh, the Calif's favorite," Sinbad hurried on enthusiastically. "If we went about the thing in the right way it might be possible to get the Calif to send the ladies of his harem in batches of, say, fifty at a time."

"That would popularize the scheme right away," Marwan assured him.

Sinbad finally suggested that, before going to any actual expense, he would arrange an interview with the Calif, and would do his best to interest the Prince of the Faithful in the scheme.

As MARWAN was passing the doorkeeper on his way out he poked that functionary playfully in the ribs; and the sight of the Nubian's furious expression caused Marwan to give vent to the guffaw that had been so long suppressed. He guffawed at regular intervals all the way home.

"Well——?" said Talib hopefully when Marwan got back to the suite of one room and two beds which the friends shared.

Quite suddenly Marwan realized that all this was most unlikely to benefit him in any possible way.

"Talib my friend," he said solemnly, "I am possessed of the fatal gift of making people believe that I am speaking the truth."

"Who is secure from affliction?" said Talib.

"Sinbad," Marwan explained, "has taken me only too literally;" and he told Talib of the scheme which Sinbad had worked out, and mentioned that Sinbad's thoughts had been so preoccupied that he hadn't offered a single souvenir.

"The Calif will very likely swish off

old Sinbad's head for putting up such a mad proposition to him, so you'll get no more souvenirs—ever," Talib commented unkindly.

"This is a very hard, unsympathetic world, Talib," said Marwan sadly. "A very hard world indeed!" And on that dismal note Marwan crept off to his humble couch.

THROUGH the efforts of his wife Budoor and the lady Zubeydeh, Sinbad got his interview with the Calif.

Haroun al Rashid was so interested in the wonders which the mariner Marwan had seen that he made Sinbad tell the story of that adventurer's voyages right from beginning to end.

When the tale was done the Calif commented to his boon companions Jaafar the Wezeer and Mesroor the Executioner: "Verily, I have never known the like of that which hath happened to this mariner."

"Nor have I, by Ham the son of Nooh (on both of whom be peace!)," said Jaafar.

"Nor me either," said Mesroor.

"It occurred to me, O Calif of the Age," Sinbad began insinuatingly, "that it would interest others to see these sights——"

"What got me," interrupted the Calif, "was that account of the gigantic bird—what did you call it?"

"The rukh," said Sinbad. "It occurred to me, O Prince of the Faithful, that pleasure trips run on good——"

"I see possibilities in this mariner's discovery. What size is this bird's egg?"

"The size of a camel, O Refuge of the Poor. . . . As I was saying, if——"

"How many people do you think one of these eggs would feed, Jaafar?"

"A hundred or two, I should imagine."

"That's what I calculate myself. M'm!"

"O happy King, if we ran excursions and catered——"

"I believe that, in accordance with the will of Allah (extolled be his perfection!), this mariner has stumbled on a discovery which will be a blessing to the sons of Adam." The Calif turned to Sinbad. "Some of us, O Sinbad, have fairly large establishments to maintain. Myself, I have some three hundred ladies on the other side of those curtains. Work it out for yourself—two eggs each every morning for seven days a week—and you will arrive at the vast number of eggs required in this household. Now if we had a few of these rukhs——"

"That would simplify your catering arrangements considerably, O Calif," said Jaafar.

Mesroor gave vent to a sound between a grunt and a sniff, but the Calif ignored him. He instructed Sinbad:

"You are commanded to set forth immediately. You will capture a number of the young of these rukhs—of both sexes—and return with them to Baghdad as speedily as Allah wills. I will provide a ship," he added when he saw that Sinbad was looking blank.

"But what I actually came to suggest to your Magnificence——"

"The interview is over," said Jaafar warningly.

"If I may be allowed to say just one word more, O Calif——"

Mesroor touched Sinbad on the shoulder, and repeated Jaafar's words, sternly —"The interview is over!"

"I h-h-hear and obey," mumbled Sinbad. He kissed the ground at the Calif's feet, expressed the hope that Haroun would live indefinitely, and allowed himself to be escorted from the presence.

SINBAD found Marwan waiting for him when he got home. He told him what he had been commissioned to do.

"I've never been to sea before," Sinbad said doubtfully.

"You'll love it," Marwan assured him. "The tonic effect of the sea air, the tropical moonlight on the dancing water—see advertisements."

"It was the will of Allah that I should go on this mission," muttered Sinbad, resigned, but not really satisfied that Allah had arranged things for the best.

When he heard about the mission, Talib said: "But there aren't any rukhs! And where do *you* come into this?"

"Come into this, my simple freshwater sailor? I will have a positively gorgeous vacation—oh, how I have longed to see some of the places I have described so often!"

"But when old Sinbad finds out that there are no rukhs?" Talib persisted.

"When the worthy creature begins to suspect that he is on a wild rukh chase I will choose some island such as heretofore I have seen only with my mind's eye. I will quietly desert the ship, and my superior intelligence will enable me to live as a prince amongst the simple natives of the place.

"Oh, think, Talib," Marwan rhapsodized — "think of the island of your dreams. An island cooled by gentle zephyrs. An island where luscious fruits hang heavy on every tree, where the women are like the damsels of Paradise —an island overflowing with maidens tall of stature, smooth of cheek, of perfect form, with eyes like a gazelle's, with mouths like the seal of Suleyman, with brows like——"

Marwan stopped short. His rapt expression changed suddenly to one of apprehension—somebody was hammering at the door!

"B-b-best see who it is," Marwan suggested to Talib.

But just then the decrepit fastenings gave way, and a tall Nubian entered, simitar in hand. Three other Nubians followed.

Marwan instantly recognized the foremost Nubian as the one with whom he had been unnecessarily familiar at the door of Sinbad's house. The man had obviously came to wreak private vengeance for the insults he had suffered! Marwan regretted, now, that he hadn't listened more closely to the warnings of his parents—he could quite easily have been a much better man! His father had prophesied that he would either be hanged or decapitated. The latter prophecy was evidently the one that was going to be fulfilled.

"Bind his hands," said the doorkeeper, "and we'll get along."

For an instant Marwan simply could not believe that he was actually going to leave the room alive.

"What are you—where are you——"

"We are taking you to the house of Sinbad our master, whom you have deceived with your lies," he was informed.

Marwan gave a great sigh. So it was only that! He was able once more to be glad that he hadn't taken his parents' advice. When one takes one's parents' advice the consequence is invariably a somewhat stodgy, humdrum life.

"What about this other rogue?" one of the Nubians inquired.

"Better bring him along," said the leader. "He's probably in the plot too;" and next moment, in spite of his protests, Talib's hands were pinioned, and the two friends were being hustled through the dark, tortuous streets of the Abode of Peace.

WHEN they reached Sinbad's house they were taken to a tiny room where they found Sinbad waiting for them. The tall Nubian shut the door on the inside, and stood guard with his brightly polished simitar at the ready.

It was painfully evident that Sinbad was laboring under great stress of mind. He indicated the Nubian.

"Lutf, here, tells me that he has been making inquiries about you. He maintains that you are not a seaman at all, and says that your stories are a parcel of lies. But I—I can't believe that Lutf is right. I simply can't believe it," Sinbad added, the wish evidently being father to the thought.

"He's a water-carrier," said Lutf.

Marwan admitted it. "I regret that the force of necessity has driven me, only temporarily I hope, to take up that humble occupation."

"And what—were you before you became a water-carrier?" asked Sinbad, and hung on the reply.

Marwan drew himself up with some show of dignity.

"I have filled various positions of more or less importance," he said. "But recently I was employed in the warehouse of a wealthy Baghdad merchant."

"And you ran away with the merchant's spare cash," Lutf suggested.

"I did not run away with the merchant's spare cash," answered Marwan indignantly. "I owned a small shop in the bazar at the same period, and the merchant who employed me accused me of stocking my shop with his goods."

"So!" said Lutf.

"Be quiet, Lutf," Sinbad broke in irritably. "All that matters is whether there is any truth in the stories that the fellow has been telling me."

"There is what might be called a substratum of truth in them."

"The one that now matters, the one about—about the great bird——?" Sinbad's eyes pleaded with Marwan to say that that one was true.

"That story can be said to be based on fact—on the statement of my friend Talib, here."

"I told him that the bird couldn't fly," said Talib. "And I only said it was as big as a camel."

"This will cost me my head," moaned Sinbad.

"There is no reason at all why your head should be severed from your body at this juncture," Marwan assured him.

"No reason! What d'you mean?" A faint glimmer of hope began to illumine Sinbad's darkness.

"Simple!" said Marwan. "You take a dutiful leave of the Prince of the Faithful, go down to El-Basrah . . . and find there your family and your worldly goods, which have been secretly conveyed to the port. You slip on board a different ship altogether—and all the wide world lies before you."

Sinbad gasped his relief. He almost beamed on Marwan. "There are great opportunities for trade in India and China, and one might do worse than——"

He was interrupted. Somebody on the other side of the door was calling wildly, "Sinbad! Sinbad!"

"Open the door, Lutf," cried Sinbad agitatedly.

The Nubian flung open the door, and Sinbad's wife Budoor, throwing the rules of the harem to the winds, dashed in.

"Oh, Sinbad," she cried, "a secret messenger has just come to me from the lady Zubeydeh. Mesroor refused to believe your story about the great bird, and he has persuaded the Calif to have you brought back to the palace—you and the mariner who told you the tale. Mesroor is on his way here now."

There was a tragic silence. Sinbad began to feel tottery about the knees. Marwan's *sang-froid* had left him mysteriously. His face had gone a nasty ashen gray.

"Don't stand there looking like a petrified he-ass," yelled Budoor, and shook her dazed spouse to wake him to action. "Fly, while you've still got——"

There was a loud, peremptory, official sort of rap at the street door.

"Too late!" moaned Sinbad, and went limp.

Budoor dashed past Lutf and bolted into the women's quarters two seconds before the large forbidding form of the Calif's executioner appeared at the door, a small forest of simitars showing behind him.

Mesroor came forward into the middle of the room. "In the name of the Calif (on whom be peace!)," he said, and laid his chill hand on Sinbad's shoulder.

Sinbad's rotund person visibly shrank under the touch. He looked beyond Mesroor to the forest of simitars, and wailed out, "O Allah!"

"Who are these two persons?" asked Mesroor, fixing his vulture-like glance on Marwan and Talib.

Sinbad struggled with a huskiness that was affecting his throat. "This is the— the mariner of whom I spoke to the Calif, and that other one is his friend, another— another mariner."

"That simplifies matters," said Mesroor. He conveyed his instructions to his assistants by means of a jerk of his head in the direction of the mariners, and next moment the three culprits were hustled out into the street.

To ANALYZE the feelings of the prisoners as they were marched to the Calif's palace would be altogether too harrowing. Suffice it to say that during the last hundred yards Talib had to be supported on either side because of the partial paralysis that had affected his lower limbs.

The three were placed in a row in front of Haroun al Rashid—and it was clear to them that the Calif wasn't in a playful mood. He addressed Sinbad.

"Mesroor says that the stories you told me are a pack of lies! Who is the originator of these stories?"

Sinbad looked at Marwan, and Marwan looked at Talib. Talib grasped that it was up to him.

"O Calif of Allah," he began abjectly, "I only said that the bird was——"

"Ahem!" Marwan's cough cut into Talib's disclosure only just in time. "O Calif"—Marwan went on hurriedly— "my shipmate is a poor ignorant seaman, and he is so abashed and overcome by this presence that he can hardly be expected to speak coherently. If I may be allowed to be his spokesman——"

"Who are you?" The Calif roared out the words. He fixed on Marwan a truly terrifying glare. Marwan was, however, so terrified already that the glare couldn't make him more so.

But when a man's throat is threatened with a major operation such as threatened Marwan's, he is sometimes able to rise to heights. Marwan rose.

"I was the mate of the ship in which this man was an ordinary seaman," he lied glibly. "I, too, saw this great bird. Indeed it was I who spoke of it to this merchant." He indicated Sinbad.

"Well, what have *you* got to say about it?"

Marwan had a lot to say. And he said it without once contradicting himself, and so convincingly that the Calif presently began to feel sure that Mesroor's doubts were unfounded. He put questions to Marwan, and Marwan, being a supreme artist, answered them in a way that made Haroun al Rashid more and more sure every minute that Mesroor's doubts were unfounded.

"There you are, Mesroor!" the Calif

cried at last triumphantly. "I told you you were quite wrong."

"Uuuh!" grunted Mesroor.

"This seems to me to be a perfectly honest fellow. And why should he try to deceive me and tell me lies?"

"Why does anybody tell lies?" asked Mesroor, putting a question which to this day still remains unanswered.

"Well, you might have admitted gracefully that you were wrong," said the Calif huffily. He turned to the three prisoners. "You may go now," he told them.

For the moment the prisoners were bereft of the power of acceleration. Their joy was too much for them. They heaved three sighs, and let their thoughts wander to the long lives that again lay before them. Talib told himself that, in future, he would run the moment he heard a deep-sea sailor beginning to talk about his experiences. Sinbad tried to think which he ought to settle in—India or China. Marwan was conscious of a mad, impish desire to sidle up to Mesroor, insert a playful finger under the executioner's armpit and say, "Tickle, tickle!"

But, instead, he and the others bowed their heads in the dust at the Calif's feet, after which they got up and began to look for the exit door.

"O Calif——!" It was the loud, detestable voice of Mesroor that broke into the rapture of that moment.

"Well?" said the Calif, in no very pleased tone.

"I ask a boon," cried Mesroor.

"Oh, ask it, in the name of Allah!" said the Calif grumpily. "We will decide afterward whether it ought to be granted."

Mesroor put his finger right on the spot. "O Calif, if these men are lying, they will sail away—and never come back."

"U'm!" muttered Haroun, "I hadn't thought of that."

"Permit me, O Calif, to go with this expedition—with authority to perform my office on the persons of these three should they fail to find this bird."

The Calif hesitated a moment—and it may have been that he suddenly noted a guilty look on one of the three faces. "You are commanded to do so, Mesroor," he said, and emphasized the word "commanded."

Mesroor was taking no risks. "Bring these fellows this way," he told his assistants—"I'm keeping them under guard until we sail."

The joy of a moment ago had vanished. It was as though it had never been. Three pairs of slippers trailed miserably on the tiled floor in Mesroor's wake.

THE wind had increased steadily from the moment when the ship set sail from El-Basrah. Now, three days out, it was blowing a gale.

Marwan hadn't been at all happy the first day out. Indeed he had been quite unwell. But he had recovered quickly, and was now beginning to feel that he could risk sniffing at the smell that came from the cook's galley.

Sinbad, to his own amazement, had taken to the sea like a sailor born. The more the ship rolled, the better he liked it.

But there was one member of the expedition who had not yet got acclimatized—Mesroor the Executioner. Mesroor—who until now had never sailed farther than from one side of the Tigris to the other—was taken violently ill as the ship was clearing the harbor. He had every hour got more and more ill. Now he was lying in his bunk praying earnestly to Allah to release him from the burden of life.

Everybody had been very kind to Mesroor. Marwan in particular. Marwan had sat for hours at Mesroor's bunkside telling him that the captain believed that the storm would be much worse before it was better. He was very solicitous that Mesroor should keep up his strength, and to encourage him told him what the cook was preparing for dinner. He gave it as his opinion that a nice lamb chop would do Mesroor a world of good. But Mesroor only groaned again, and turned his face to the bulkhead. He requested Marwan as a personal favor to go away and let him die in peace.

It was on the fourth day out, while the storm was still unabated, that Mesroor first made a suggestion which, to all intents and purposes, was *lese majesté*—he suggested that the ship be put about so that he could be set ashore while the breath of life still animated his tortured body.

"But the Calif!" Marwan reminded Mesroor in a shocked voice. "Didn't the Calif command you to accompany us on this expedition? I remember his very words—'You are commanded to do so, Mesroor,' he said."

Mesroor's cry of anguish would have melted any heart but Marwan's, which wasn't soluble just at the moment.

Later in the evening of that same day Marwan and Sinbad put a proposition to Mesroor—before putting it they had had the captain's assurance that the storm was not likely to abate for twenty-four hours at least.

His misery was such that, for a time, Mesroor didn't understand. Then he managed to gasp out: "A pack of lies!"

"I said," said Marwan, "let us assume, for the purpose of the present discussion,

that the fowl in question was a figment of my imagination. . . . As I was saying, what we propose is that, in order to save a valuable life, the ship be turned about. When it reaches El-Basrah, I and my friends will go into hiding, and will remain in hiding until such time as you have prevailed upon Haroun the Upright to accept the fact that he must continue to feed his household on the eggs of the ordinary domestic hen."

"And we on our part promise that no one shall know that you were afraid of the sea, and that you failed to carry out the Calif's command," said Sinbad.

Just then the ship gave a most fearful lurch and groaned in every timber.

Mesroor groaned with it, and said feebly, "I agree."

WHAT, if anything, happened to Talib, is unknown, and it is not recorded which of Marwan's father's prophecies was ultimately fulfilled.

After he was pardoned and had returned to his place in Baghdad society, Sinbad took a delight in telling the stories which Marwan had originated. He added touches of local color and improved upon the stories generally, and when he grew older fell into a habit of telling them as if the things had happened to himself—a habit common throughout the ages.

Sinbad's family, his friends, and even his slaves refused at last to constitute themselves his audience. Sinbad thereupon resorted to the practise of getting some one in from the streets and telling the tales to him.

So now you know how Sinbad the Sailor came to recount those remarkable stories to his namesake Sinbad the Porter.

"She fought him off, and tore his face with her nails."

The Picture of Judas

By FRANCIS HARD

A strange tale of Italy during the Renaissance—a story of the great painter, Leonardo da Vinci

BUZZING like a swarm of bees, the group of choir singers walked rapidly through the narrow streets of Milan to see the restless Leonardo at work on his Cenacolo in the refectory of St. Mary of the Graces. The great Duomo, still uncompleted, towered behind them. The forest of white columns drew closer together as the choristers increased the distance, and the cathedral itself loomed vaster and more majestic as it receded. The chattering stopped as the singers entered the convent, and a twilight hush fell upon their lips. They crossed the portal into the refectory on tiptoe.

On the north wall of the long chamber was "The Last Supper," on which the

159

painter had already spent three years. Two monks stood critically at one side, whispering together. In the back of the refectory, his eyes gazing into the picture from under shaggy eyebrows, sat Leonardo da Vinci.

He made a handsome figure, the young Leonardo, with his long, silky beard and commanding head. His aquiline nose was the embodiment of strength. The sensitive mouth, topped by narrow, long mustaches that tapered off into his beard, was firm and yet tender. Beetling brows overhung gray eyes that restlessly searched the world as if seeking what of truth or beauty lay there. The noble forehead, with its finely chiseled planes and its strength, dominated his splendid figure and gave to his appearance a commanding majesty that instantly challenged attention. His long, wavy locks were covered by a soft, black velvet cap that sat airily on his head, and a loose-fitting doublet of the same rich velvet encased his body. Such was Leonardo da Vinci, the Florentine, already known throughout Italy as poet, philosopher, painter, engineer, anatomist and sculptor.

Among the choristers from the Duomo, who thus invaded the refectory in the hope of seeing the master at work, was one who had not been there before— Galeazzo, sweetest and most boyish of the singers. The great picture came before him in its beauty, despite the scaffolding that partly concealed it. In the foreground was the long table around which were the excited disciples. In the exact center, vaguely suggested, was the unfinished figure of the Christ, his palms extended. He had just uttered the fateful words, "One of you shall betray me." In little groups the agitated disciples were asking, "Is it I?" In the background were green fields of Lombardy and a peaceful, winding river, which the art of the painter had put there to accentuate the turmoil in the hearts of the apostles.

The masterwork was incomplete in its two most important figures—the Christ and his betrayer. Judas sat in the dark, clutching a money bag, his face a black smear; and the Christ-head was represented only by a nimbus.

Galeazzo's eyes roved from end to end of the picture. There seemed something sinister in that dark blotch of pigment that covered the yet unpainted Judas-head. But in that golden nimbus at the center, over the gentle figure of Christ— what glory of feature, what sublime gentleness had the painter in mind to place there? What man so blameless in his thoughts, so pure in his life, that he could dare hope to be the model for the Christ-head?

Meditating thus, Galeazzo realized why the painter had left both figures unfinished. Truly, there was no man on earth worthy of the first honor, nor any living soul so black as to attain the evil distinction of being the Judas-model. Leonardo must perforce delve into the storehouse of his own mind to portray two such faces for the world to gaze upon. The young singer's eyes swept to the black smear. He thought of his lovely young wife, and the happiness of his own life, and was glad that no such sinister figure stalked the streets of Milan, to throw its evil shadow upon his happiness by its mere presence in the same city.

As he gazed, oblivious to his whispering companions, to the quiet figures of the two monks, to everything except the uncompleted masterpiece before him, he had the uncomfortable feeling that he was being watched. The dark unpainted Judas-head seemed exercising a baleful influence upon him. The feeling became so strong that he shivered, and raised his eyes.

O. S.—2

Leonardo's gaze was resting upon his face, seeming to bore into his soul. The painter had been watching him thus for many minutes. Galeazzo let his glance fall, and a troubled presentiment took hold of him. Then Leonardo spoke, in a soft, musical voice. He had found in Galeazzo the model for his Christ-head.

Galeazzo could not believe his good fortune. He, the young cathedral singer of Milan, to be immortalized in this greatest of paintings! For it seemed inconceivable that there ever could be another painting as splendid as this, or another master as great as Leonardo. Gratefully he thanked the painter, and hurried home to break the wonderful news to his young wife. And Leonardo, mounting the scaffold, worked a short while on the gabardine of Judas, then hastened away from the convent to his colossal statue of the horse in the square before the ducal palace.

2

GALEAZZO, in his joyous excitement, omitted the whistle with which he usually announced his approach. His wife gave a little shriek of dismay as he bounded into the room. The sound died away in a hysterical laugh.

"You frightened me, Galeazzo. Why did you not whistle, so that I could run to welcome you?"

Galeazzo became aware of a young man, standing awkwardly in the shadows of the ill-lighted room, clumsily fingering the jewelled hilt of his dagger. He was a handsome blade, rather effeminate in his beauty, with a slender, neatly twisted black mustache and a short beard that came hardly to the point of his chin.

"My cousin, Giovanni Malpierro," said Galeazzo's wife. "Giovanni, this is my Galeazzo, whom you have never seen."

The young man removed his fingers

from the dagger-hilt. His white teeth flashed in a smile. Nervously he lifted one hand to twirl his mustache. His black eyes met the gray ones of Galeazzo, and fell uneasily.

"Giovanni?" asked Galeazzo. "Malpierro?"

"From Brescia," his wife explained. "Surely, Galeazzo, I have told you of my cousin, Giovanni Malpierro, from Brescia. He is the nephew of my Uncle Buoso. Do you remember now?"

"You are welcome, very welcome," said Galeazzo. "But in truth I took you for a southerner, for your skin is almost as dark as our duke's. You will stay and break bread with us, for nobody in Milan can cook like my Gianna."

He tilted her head and kissed her full on the lips, which was not his custom. She exchanged a look with him whom she had called Giovanni Malpierro.

"I must beg off this time," Giovanni hastened to reply. "I have a dear friend, Pietro Corni, who is expecting me, and I can refuse him nothing, even though," he added glibly, "it keeps me from my Cousin Gianna, whom I have not seen for two years, since before she was married."

"Well, I will not interpose," said Galeazzo, "especially since I have pleasant news for Gianna's ear alone. But we count on your company tomorrow."

So saying, he saw Giovanni to the door, and waved him adieu. Then he turned to Gianna and kissed her again, on the forehead, tenderly. She pouted.

"Galeazzo, why will you come like this, without warning me? You know how dearly I love to greet you, and today you bounded up the stairs like a wild beast, and were upon me before I could even smile."

"Gianna, my dearest," he answered, "it is because I was bursting with glad news. The great master Leonardo, the greatest painter since the world began, has chosen me for his Christ-head."

"Is that all?" asked Gianna. "Indeed I thought you were going to tell me that the duke had taken you under his protection, and you were to sing at the palace. But now I can have those blue slippers, and the ruby clasp for my bodice."

"Gianna, dearest, I will get you the slippers, but not the ruby clasp. For I have nothing, as you know, Gianna, except my cathedral pay, and what I have put away from the largess at the duke's ball."

"But will not the painter pay you?"

"Not a single soldo. But I am grateful beyond words that he has chosen me. I pose for him tomorrow."

Gianna's eyes opened wide in incredulity.

"But the duke?" she asked. "He has the painter under his protection. Surely the duke will give you something."

"No, my own, he will not. But no more of this now. Let us eat."

IN THE master's study Galeazzo roamed as in a fairyland. Half-finished heads were on the walls; strange, fabulous monsters fought; hideous faces laughed and leered from all corners of the room. Lying on a table was a pen-and-ink sketch of Bacio Bandini, the assassin, hanging from the gallows. Galeazzo shuddered, from horror of the subject more than of the picture. The criminal's hands were tied behind his back, and his face was in repose, as if he were merely sleeping.

Above the sketch were several lines of strange characters that puzzled Galeazzo. He studied them in mystified curiosity. They seemed to run from right to left. He took up the drawing and carried it to a small, burnished mirror that graced the sideboard Leonardo had carved for himself. A joyous chuckle escaped him as he held the sketch to the mirror, for he had solved the master's secret script. It was looking-glass writing, in which Leonardo had noted the date and circumstances of the hanging to mystify any prying eyes.

A soft voice trolled a snatch of song in the corridor, and the master entered his workshop. Galeazzo shamefacedly carried the sketch back to the table, crestfallen at being caught ferreting among the master's secrets. Leonardo laughed a mirthful, quiet laugh, so full of gentle humor and merriment that Galeazzo forgot his embarrassment and laughed too, but rather nervously.

"You remind me, Galeazzo," said Leonardo, "of a Florentine gamin, who climbed into my window and thought he was in a necromancer's den. So many terrible faces looked at him from the walls that he was quite beside himself with terror when I found him there. I told him funny stories, and sent him away with a picture of himself, as pleased as a peacock and as happy as a lark. But come, let us to work. I am in the working humor today, but I fear I have chased away the mood of revery in which you gazed at my painting yesterday."

He placed in Galeazzo's hand a notebook of sketches.

"Study the book," he said. "I want your eyes somewhat downcast, but not purposely so. Look at the pictures in the book."

As the master worked, he trolled again the song he had been singing when he entered the workshop. The mood seized Galeazzo, and he sang too, involuntarily. Then he remembered where he was, and sat with downcast eyes, gently humming from time to time. Leonardo caught a certain expression of the mouth, and encouraged him to hum some more.

They worked until Galeazzo began to

weary. Then the master sent him home, and he walked rapidly through the streets, for Giovanni Malpierro was to be at dinner. Gianna came running to meet him as he whistled his approach, and they entered the house together.

With the beginning of the next week, Galeazzo went with Leonardo to the convent of St. Mary of the Graces, and there the master began the head of Christ. He had studied the moods of the young singer, until he felt able to draw from them the expression of divine resignation and beatific peace that should shine from the features of Christ in the Cenacolo.

The picture was already the wonder of Italy, unfinished though it was. The sunlight seemed to break through the wall of the convent and flood the place where was to be the face of Christ. The painter's individuality had made even the hands of the disciples eloquent with meaning. Every gaze, every gesture, every line of the great painting carried the eyes of the beholder to that central nimbus.

Galeazzo could no more keep from breaking into song, while the master painted his head in place of the golden nimbus, than could the skylark, lifted up to heaven. He seemed no longer a mere chorister from the Duomo, but felt that he had taken on much of the nobility and tenderness of the Christ himself. The features grew and changed and gained in majesty under the slow, sure hands of the master, and Galeazzo thought of his young wife, Gianna, whom he loved more than life, and in the gratefulness of a full heart, he sang.

He went home, betimes, to find the dark-skinned Giovanni Malpierro with his Gianna. The young man, said Gianna, would stay in Milan longer, for he was trying, through friends, to gain a position in the duke's service, a position of trust that would pay him well. Gio-

vanni gave him to understand that he was in the duke's favor, and that in a short time he would be a prosperous man. His cousin Gianna and her husband would share in his prosperity, he said. Galeazzo did not see the meaning looks they exchanged behind his back. Glad that Gianna had such pleasant comradeship, he was too happy in his love for her and his joy in Leonardo's painting to view their comradeship with eyes of suspicion.

4

THE day came when the Christ-head was completed. Bathed in the soft sunlight of a Lombard springtime, Galeazzo saw himself idealized, the central figure of the master's painting. The Cenacolo was now finished except for the portentous spot of black that topped the Judas-figure. Galeazzo shuddered, as he had shuddered when he saw that smear for the first time, and as he had shuddered when he saw the sketch of the assassin in the master's workshop. In that minute he hoped that Leonardo might never complete the painting, and that the dark Judas might be forever without a counterpart in this world.

Leonardo let him gaze his fill. Then he addressed him cheerily, and invited him to his workshop.

"I have something for you, Galeazzo," said Leonardo, "that I think you will esteem, and keep always with you."

They walked rapidly through the streets, but the young singer fretted at what seemed to him a snail's pace. The master had a gift for him, and he was consumed with eagerness to know what it was. Why, then, did they not hurry? But Leonardo smiled at him, and gently rebuked him, and asked him to come often to see him and he would sketch him again.

They entered the workshop, and there the master gave to Galeazzo a porcelain medallion, hung on a slender silver chain. On it he had painted Galeazzo's head in the attitude of the Christ-head in the Cenacolo, and signed the token in the back-handed script that Galeazzo already knew how to decipher. Leonardo had made the porcelain himself, and baked the colors into it.

Galeazzo cried out, as delighted as a child. He thanked the master profusely, and would fain have kissed his hands, but Leonardo forbade and sent him away to show the miniature to the young wife whom he adored.

A group of jovial companions from the Duomo accosted Galeazzo as he passed through the street, and wanted him to drink with them. Impatiently he would have put them aside. He showed them the medallion, with the Christ-head—his own head—baked into the porcelain. He could not tarry, he told them, for he was burning with eagerness to show this treasure to Gianna, and perchance her cousin Giovanni Malpierro, who was a frequent visitor in his household.

A hoarse laugh greeted mention of Giovanni. The merry fellow who uttered it was plainly intoxicated. His companions tried to silence him with deprecating glances and shaking of heads, but he only laughed more obscenely than before.

Galeazzo seized him by the arm.

"Come now, Gian," he exclaimed. "What is behind all this ribald noise?"

Too much Lombardy wine had made Gian hilarious. He leered, and laughed again.

"You said, eh? Giovanni Malpierro? Ho, ho, ho!"

Galeazzo's face grew dark. He shook the drunken Gian.

"What do you mean? Giovanni Malpierro is my wife's cousin, from Brescia!

Is there anything wrong about that? Speak up! Let me have the truth of this, or I will squeeze it out of your throat!"

He shook the now terrified and helpless Gian again, and let him fall into the street.

"Malpierro?"

Gian weakly strove to clamber to his feet.

"Yes, Malpierro! Giovanni Malpierro! What of him?"

Galeazzo's companions had never seen him aroused. But never before had any whisper involved his young wife Gianna, and a nameless frantic terror drove all other thoughts from his mind. Gianna unchaste? Gianna deceive him? It was unthinkable!

The drunken chorister succeeded in rising from the cobblestones, but Galeazzo seized him by the throat and forced him down into the filth of the gutter.

"Speak, dog!"

Gian's eyes rolled, and his face became purplish. The other choristers intervened, and dragged Galeazzo off.

"Come, Galeazzo, have you never suspected?"

Galeazzo shook himself free.

"Gianna? What of her? What of Giovanni Malpierro?"

"Galeazzo," said the chorister who had just spoken, "this man Giovanni is not Gianna's cousin, neither does he come from Brescia. He is no kin to you or yours, nor is his name Malpierro. Look well to your wife, Galeazzo."

The look of terror deepened in Galeazzo's eyes. His face became livid. He looked like one whose heart has been plucked out. Then suddenly he struck his informant in the mouth, and ran, frantically, wildly, clutching the miniature to his breast. He bounded up the steps of his home and burst into the house, out of breath, pale from fear.

"Gianna!" he called. "Gianna! Gianna! Gianna!"

Gianna did not answer. Galeazzo rushed through the rooms like a maddened bull. In the bedroom he stood for a minute like a stone statue, then knelt beside the bed and sobbed like one in purgatory. For Gianna had gone. She had left only the simple dress in which she had performed her household tasks. The oaken chest was burst open, and she had taken even the coins he had saved from the duke's largess, the night he sang at the palace.

The whirlwind in his thoughts cleared somewhat, and he knelt beside the bed and prayed to the Virgin. He clasped his hands together, and cried out in his pain. Why should he, who had been so happy, be thus thrust into hell?

He turned the medallion tenderly in his hands. It was all that was left to him, now that Gianna was gone. The picture of the Christ-head, tranquil, resigned, full of peace unspeakable! Surely he, Galeazzo, had never looked like that! And yet here was the proof, in the calm, beatific features of the Christ-face in his hand.

He crossed the room, and looked at himself in the metal mirror that Gianna had kept so bright. He hardly recognized himself. What wildness in his eyes! What terror! And yet it was the same face as that on the porcelain medallion. The little oval seemed to promise that he should again be the happy, tranquil man he had been, though his heart was leaden and his hopes were dead. Despairingly he put the silver chain about his neck, and the master's amulet hung below his throat.

5

GIANNA walked along cautiously, somewhat furtively, in the gathering dusk, notwithstanding that she did not see the figure of her husband. Galeazzo followed at a little distance, like a cat stalking a bird, fearful lest she should fly and avoid him. He skulked in doorways, and ran from one to another, silently, always keeping the object of his pursuit in sight.

He slunk into hiding as Gianna stopped. She searched the street on all sides, then suddenly entered one of the doorways. Galeazzo stood for a minute undecided. His blood raced like a millwheel, for he had found Gianna's hiding-place. And with her, doubtless, was Giovanni Malpierro, the dark-skinned betrayer of his hospitality.

Galeazzo leapt across the street, and dashed up the narrow stairway. He broke into the room like a hurricane. Gianna shrieked, once, and backed against the wall. She looked very white and frightened, and shot an imploring glance at her husband. Her chin trembled, and her eyelids fluttered.

Galeazzo stood with one hand on the latch, breathing hard, and looking at Gianna. How lovely she was! So delicate, so beautiful, so affectionate! Could it be she who had shattered his happiness and thus basely plunged him into the fires that were eating his brain and his heart? He would plead with her. He would ask her to go back with him. They would live happily together, and he would forgive. Who could not forgive his Gianna? It was Giovanni who was to blame. On Giovanni alone would his vengeance fall.

"Gianna!"

His voice sounded thin and far away, as if it issued from some other throat than his own. He scarcely recognized it. But its effect on Gianna was magical. Her fear vanished, and her voice rang out defiantly.

"What do you want? Why do you follow me?"

Galeazzo was on his knees in an instant.

"Gianna! Gianna! Come back to me! I love you, Gianna! I will forgive! Only come back to me!"

Gianna frowned, and bit her lip.

"You forgive? I am the one who should forgive, for it is you who have brought this about!"

Galeazzo seized the hem of her skirt, and pressed it to his lips.

"Gianna! Why has this happened? Say you love me, Gianna, as I love you! You must say that you love me, Gianna! Think of the past!"

"Yes, fool, I think of the past!" Gianna burst out, in a rage. "I think of the many months I spent with you, whom I despise, weakling, ninny that you are! I did love you, once, or thought I did; but that is all past, long ago. You and your contemptible goodness! I want a man I can love with all my body and soul, and not a goody-goody weakling who sings in the choir!"

The words cut like a knife. Galeazzo rose to his feet. His tongue had turned to ashes in his mouth. He felt his senses reeling.

"But I love you, Gianna!"

"Love me?" She laughed, hoarsely, mockingly. "Love me? You don't know what love is. Love is passion! Love is fire! Love is the meeting of souls that burn with longing! You in love?"

She laughed a little, mirthless laugh. And then her scorn blazed out with consuming heat, and lashed her husband, as he leaned against the wall, very pale and faint.

"You have dragged me through hell! I have cursed you every day and every night, almost since the day we were married! Oh, how I have hated you, with your woman's face and your silly little affection that you call love!"

She stamped her foot, and her voice rose shrilly.

"Leave me, do you hear? Giovanni will be here, and he will tear you limb from limb! I never truly loved you, and I hate you now! I hate you!"

She shook her fist in his face, and screamed into his ear.

"I hate you, Galeazzo! Do you hear?"

He threw his arms about her, and pressed his lips desperately against her mouth. She fought him off, and tore his face with her nails.

"I hate you!" she shrilled. "Now go, before it is too late."

Too late? Giovanni was coming, had she said? She wanted to get rid of him, then, because Giovanni was coming? These thoughts rushed like evil phantoms across his dazed brain, and wrought in him a fury. Gianna clawed his lips with her nails, and the taste of blood was in his mouth. He struck out madly, blindly. His clenched fist smote her on the breast, over the heart. She struggled for breath, convulsively, and uttered a little, stifled cry, then crumpled and sank to the floor.

Galeazzo bent over her, and shook her by the shoulders. She did not move. He put his ear to her heart. There was no sign of pulse. He chafed her hands, and covered her face with kisses. The whirlwind in his thoughts, the horror in his heart, the unutterable dread that gnawed at the pit of his stomach, were combining into one terrible cry for vengeance on the man that had wrought this ruin in his life. Gianna was dead! And he, Galeazzo, was her murderer!

Whose step was this ascending the stair, with stealthy, cat-like tread? Had not Gianna been expecting Giovanni? In a moment her seducer would stand within the room.

Stung with horror at his deed, mad with anger at him who had caused it, Galeazzo sprang noiselessly behind the door, and brandished a chair over his head. The door opened, and Giovanni entered the room. The chair came down upon his head with crushing force, and stretched him on the floor beside Gianna.

Every tongue of light from the windows of comfortable homes seemed an accusing finger as Galeazzo fled through the dark streets. He crept by in the shadows, to the safe haven of darkness, then ran desperately through the night until halted by another shaft of light. Fear clutched him tightly, choking him. Nameless terrors surrounded him. In each dark corner he fancied he saw her whom he had killed. He longed for light, yet shrank from it like a ghost.

His deed must have been discovered before now. Surely some one had heard Gianna shriek, and recognized his name as she spat out her taunts, before he struck her down! Surely Giovanni's heavy fall had not been unnoticed! It had seemed to shake the house. Even now they must be hunting him. Again he fancied he saw Gianna in the gloom, white-faced and scared as when he confronted her a few short hours before. He stopped short, and a strange trembling came upon him. But approaching footsteps sent him flying past the dreadful spot. The panic dread of capture scourged him forward.

He could not return, and he knew not where to flee. He dared not even confess himself. The thought that even the sanctuary of religion was denied to him made his whirling brain sick, and he fell, striking his head on the sharp cobbles of the street.

He was walking with Gianna, he thought, in the green fields in springtime. His brain was on fire with love. Intoxicated by her alluring beauty, he threw his arms around her, and hotly kissed her eyes, her throat, her brow, her lips. She struggled against him, gently, then yielded to him. Her soft arms crept around his neck. He was living over again the great day of his life. But now she melted from his grasp, and other arms were about his neck, as he lay on the cobblestones. Some one was rolling him over. The hard reality of life laid its soiling hands upon him, and he groaned, and sat up. Fear of the duke's officers was strong within him, but it was only a poor thief that was searching him.

"Hide me!" Galeazzo begged. "Take me away where no one can ever find me!"

"Va!" said the thief, and spurned him with his foot.

Galeazzo sprang up. His many wrongs rushed hotly through his brain. He delivered a sturdy blow and knocked the fellow down.

"Lead me to your den, to your companions, or by all that's holy, I will murder you!"

He spat the words out through clenched teeth. One look at the anger-maddened face, and the thief no longer thought of refusing. Plainly he was in the hands of a madman. He rose from the dust and carefully examined himself. Then he motioned Galeazzo to follow, and slunk silently away.

The young singer overtook him and kept abreast of him, and they wandered off together. Not a word passed between them. But as they turned out of the narrow street, a burst of light from the rising sun flooded the city with silver, and the song of a shoemaker at work floated sweetly up from the neighboring street. The city was resuming its customary habits.

Galeazzo followed his unwilling guide down a dismal labyrinth into a dirty room, and threw himself wearily upon a pallet of straw. For him had begun a new and strange existence, and his old life was irrevocably closed.

6

THE swirl of carnival filled the streets with singing, laughing, shouting throngs. The Duke Lodovico was marrying Beatrice d'Este, and this auspicious union was the occasion of a joyous fête, in which the whole city joined. Happy, joyous, carefree, Milan gave itself up to rejoicing. Showers of confetti filled the air. Huge, multicolored lanterns were carried high upreared, and long streamers shot over the crowds. Groups of youths ran through the streets kissing the girls, and many an unwilling old crab was forced to drink the health of the duke and his bride in the sourest of sour chianti because he objected to being tripped up by the heels. The crowd gathered thickly about the horse of the duke, as he proceeded toward the Duomo, preceded by mounted men-at-arms and followed by the notables of Milan. He spoke a word from time to time to his chamberlain, who thereupon reached into a well-filled purse and scattered small silver coins among the crowd. Then was laughter, indeed, and gay shouts, and a wild scrambling to pick up the trophies.

Thieves worked among the throngs, for there were rich purses to pick that night. As the horses cavorted, and the long line moved slowly past, one of the boldest of the thieves attached himself to the vicinity of a stately, bearded man, dressed for the fête in green silk doublet and parti-colored tights, with slashed trunks that showed green and yellow as he walked. The man wore a strange wallet attached to his girdle, richly wrought in curious little figures and strange monsters and laughing heads, curiously tinted in contrasting tones. The wallet was a find worth having, for it was made by him who wore it, Leonardo da Vinci. The thief watched his opportunity and cut it from its moorings, only to find it fastened by a silver chain. He wrenched this free and shoved his way rapidly through the crowd, darting a glance over his shoulder. His eyes met those of Leonardo in a startled look of recognition, and he fled from the place as if it were accursed.

Leonardo's holiday mood vanished, and a somber musing fell upon him, for the face of the thief had struck some strange chord of memory. He fell to thinking of the Cenacolo in the refectory of St. Mary of the Graces, and a shadow gathered darkly on his brow, accentuating the lines that were already beginning to mark his face with the disillusionments of his life in Milan.

The men-at-arms and the notables of Milan had passed by, and the crowd had thinned. Lost in his musings, Leonardo took no note of the youths that ran shouting on both sides of him, until they caught him about the ankles with a long rope and spilled him into the filth of the street. He darted upon them a look so sour, so fierce, that they hustled him away to a wine-shop to make him buy drinks for them all. But his wallet was gone, and he had not a soldo on his person. They forced him to gulp down a bitter, vinegarish wine, and mocked his grimaces as he drank it. Then he wandered the streets, restless and perturbed from the evil presentiments of his mood, and deeply troubled by thoughts he could not explain.

7

THE Duke Lodovico, visiting the convent of St. Mary of the Graces to see what additional gifts his bounty could provide, stopped before the great mural of Leonardo and gazed with ill-concealed displeasure at the unfinished figure of Judas and the sinister blot that represented the head. The prior took this occasion to voice his complaint against Leonardo.

"Sire," he said, "the great painter sits sometimes a whole morning in contemplation of the Cenacolo without so much as approaching the scaffolding. At other times he makes but two or three strokes with his brush and hurries away. And here is the Cenacolo, my lord, with the Judas incomplete, while Montorfano's painting, begun a scant six months ago, is already finished and perfect. I have complained in vain to Master Leonardo. Can you not use your good offices with this Florentine, my lord?"

Irritation showed for a fleeting instant in Leonardo's face. But immediately he masked his feelings, and gave ear to the prior's complaint with an air of lofty condescension. Lodovico looked grave, for the prior had expressed the thought the duke himself was thinking.

"I have asked for greater speed," said the duke. "You have vouchsafed no explanation. For years the picture has been like this, with no perceptible change. The black splotch where the Judas-head should be remains a reproach to the convent. Select your Judas, Master Leonardo, and bring your picture to completion."

Leonardo bowed low.

"My lord, it is a deep sorrow to me that the picture is as you see it," he said. "But the complaints of the prior are unjust, for I work just as truly in these hours that I spend in contemplation as when I actually have the brushes in my hand. There is the time when one builds his ideas, and there is also the time when one brings them into reality with his paints. I have been unable to find any face so base that I could use it as the model for the Judas. But if my lord insists, I will delay no longer. I can always fall back on the prior for my model; and indeed his head will not go badly in place of that black smear."

The duke smiled paternally, as at the sally of some child.

From that day Leonardo forsook his paintings and his sculpturing until he should find his Judas-head. He wandered into low dens of vice, and haunts of crime. Many evil faces he saw, but not evil enough. He demanded perfection in evil. No ordinary head could represent the betrayer of Christ. In the last extremity he could fall back on his imagination, but he continued the search longer, to find a living model for the face that, next to Christ himself, should be the most important in the whole great picture.

He appealed to Duke Lodovico for permission to seek in the prisons, and he searched the dungeons, and the cells occupied by prisoners awaiting trial. Much of evil he saw, and many faces that were marked with patient resignation. Some were sullen, others stolid. Some had been cleansed by suffering, and others had been hardened. But only in the last cell of all did he find a face so lost to good impulses that it could fittingly represent the face of Judas.

The occupant of the cell was a felon condemned to die. He had treacherously murdered two companions in crime for their share of plunder. He was still a young man, but his face was old in evil. The features were hard, and the furtive, steely eyes were the perfect expression of cruelty and treachery. The face was devoid of all soulful qualities, and evil sat on his countenance like a dark cloud.

Leonardo had found his Judas. Satisfied at last, yet secretly chagrined that he could not now use the head of the prior, he ordered the criminal taken to the convent of St. Mary of the Graces.

Wrathfully the felon glared at the painter who had obtained for him this brief reprieve. He leered at his guards. His tongue was silent, but the sullen fires of his hate blazed out unconcealed as he transfixed the Christ-head and the Judas with his terrible gray eyes.

The man's eyes troubled Leonardo, for they reminded him of something he had seen. He pondered as he painted; then suddenly the picture of that night of carnival came before him, and he remembered the stolen wallet and the startled glance of the thief as their eyes met. The Judas was the thief who had robbed him.

He painted rapidly, for the guile and craftiness of the face disturbed his calm. He felt the felon's eyes fixed upon him, and he wished the man gone. The prior came in as he painted, and rubbed his hands in satisfaction at seeing another head than his own in the place of the betrayer. The felon turned upon him a look so charged with poison that the prior's chuckle died in his throat. He stammered out a few words to Leonardo, and removed himself from the chamber.

The Judas-head was soon finished, and the model was returned to his felon's cell. The prison authorities laid violent hands upon him, and twisted a rope about his neck, in accordance with the sentence of the law. When the law was satisfied, they lowered the body and searched it.

Around the neck of the dead criminal, hanging on a silver chain, was a small porcelain medallion that bore the picture of a handsome young man, with eyes downcast in quiet resignation. Strange characters ran from right to left on the medallion. The prisonmaster recognized these as the secret script of the painter Leonardo, and he carried his find to the master.

Deeply agitated, Leonardo looked long at the face on the medallion. He turned it in his hands and pondered the features, as if he sought from that little oval the answer to some tremendous problem that vexed him. At length he motioned the prisonmaster into the convent, and they turned aside into a small room where was a mirror. With fingers that trembled, he held the porcelain medallion before this mirror, that the prisonmaster might read therein the strange characters that had puzzled him.

Under the youthful face were written these words:

"To Galeazzo, in whose joyous features I have seen the image of the Christ.— Leonardo da Vinci."

And fear not lest Existence closing your
Account, and mine, should know the like no more;
   The Eternal Sákí from that Bowl has pour'd
Millions of Bubbles like us, and will pour.

When You and I behind the Veil are past,
Oh, but the long, long while the World shall last,
   Which of our Coming and Departure heeds
As the Sea's self should heed a pebble cast.

                —*Rubáiyát of Omar Khayyam.*

"Like a poor creature crucified, she stood flat against the barrier."

The Desert Host

By HUGH B. CAVE

A story of Babylon and Semiramis its wanton queen—a vivid tale of the sinister priests of Baal, and an armed host that rode out of the desert

SELARON, riding out of the desert, passed through the great gate swiftly, his good horse panting and heaving under him. Saluting the guards at the walls, he sped on into the deeper darkness, where the houses and parapets of the Great City loomed up before him.

Riding thus, he had covered more than half the distance to his home and entered the loneliest square of those abandoned byways, when the steed beneath him swerved in sudden warning, nearly unseating his rider.

And a girl's scream, rising full and clear in the night, came up from the shadows of the palace wall ahead. Like the terrified cry of a wounded bird it reached Selaron's ears, only to be stifled with uncanny abruptness, leaving tense silence in its wake.

Digging heel to flank, Selaron lashed his horse forward, freeing his long sword as he went. Thus, in a roaring thunder of flying hooves, he smashed forward into as ugly an affray as ever soldier of Ninus had confronted.

There was no time to prepare. In a flash Selaron caught sight of three burly negro slaves crowding about the struggling body of a girl. Then he was upon them, and out of the saddle, forcing them back against the wall as he laid about him with gleaming blade.

In a moment it was four to one and five to one, as other slaves emerged from the darkness. A single sword to offset six weaving, whining tongues of death. Yet Selaron gave no quarter and expected none.

Great Babylon had never before looked upon such a combat. One by one the giant negroes felt the keen point of the youth's weapon, to fall writhing at his feet. Thrice the boy fell back, stumbling, only to regain his poise and impale those who rushed upon him. Thus it became one against one, in a carnage of blood, until the final jackal, throwing down his sword, ran like a lumbering water-bull into the protecting gloom.

Gasping, Selaron reached down to loosen the girl's bonds and lift her upright. His eyes widened as he looked upon that oval face of loveliness, those trembling lips and great eyes filled with terror. Not even the Great Queen herself, he thought, was reputed to be as beautiful as this!

She clung to him, hiding her face on his breast, ashamed that her veil had been torn loose so that he might see her naked-

ness. Not until he lifted her head in his hands did she deign to meet his glance and hold herself erect.

"Who are you," he demanded softly, "that walks alone through the city at this hour?"

"Inar, my lord," she whispered. "It was my mother's name also."

"Inar! A name fit for the queen herself. By Ashtaroth, it is a name fitting for a goddess!"

"Rather for a humble handmaiden of the queen," she smiled wearily. "For that I am, brave lord, and not the goddess you would make me."

Selaron's brows furrowed quickly. He took her arm not ungently and drew her back close to the wall.

"Handmaiden of the queen?" he muttered. "Does that, then, explain why these slave dogs, who obey the command of Kardak, high priest of Baal, made attempt to capture you?"

"That is so," she trembled. "It was because Kardak threatened me, when I scorned him. He vowed that he would have me——"

Selaron's lips curled in a bitter snarl. Driving his sword back into its sheath, he caught her in his arms and lifted her to horse. Thus, with a single bronzed arm about her smooth waist, he escorted her to the palace gate. There, setting her down, he leaned from his saddle and held her hand firmly.

"With fiends like Kardak prowling the night," he advised, "it is safer for one with your loveliness to keep within the palace walls."

"It was on a message of the queen——" she began.

"Ay, the queen should entrust her messages to more sturdy hands," he said firmly. "But go now, and say nothing of this. I have dealings myself with Kardak this night."

"Who are you?"

"Since I am likely to be dead before many hours," he laughed easily, "I would not trouble you with my name. If I live, you shall hear it from my own lips enough times to make you think I am King Ninus himself."

Then he wheeled his horse and spurred into the shadows, without another word. She stood and watched him until the clank of his harness had become still in the distance. Turning, then, she ran into the palace grounds, face flushed and lips quivering.

"Five of them," she whispered to herself, "and he fought them hand to hand. Surely he is no Assyrian, with those smiling features and tanned skin. He is from the far north, where men know the joy of life and love, and sing as they fight!"

2

GREAT Babylon slept, brooding black and mysterious in the night, whispering with suspicion. High above tent and terrace, palace and guarded wall, reared the tower of Baal, ever watchful over the shadowed plain. Far below, muttering its ceaseless complaint, curled the River Euphrates.

How was one to know, while innocents dreamed of Ashtaroth and the Seven Spheres of Heaven, that words of treachery were mumbling forth out of twisted lips high up there in the dark; that a single bare arm, clamped with a gold bracelet, was pointing from the parapet of the pile of Baal down into the lower dusk? Or that Kardak, high priest of Baal, leaned there peering down with smoldering eyes?

"Know you his dwelling-place?" he said sharply to those behind him.

"Surely, O Kardak," answered one. "Who does not?"

"Then go; and when you return here, be sure you bring him back bound. With his arms unfettered, Selaron is mightier than the Great King himself. I have no wish to feel those fingers in my throat."

There was a mumbled assent, and then Kardak was once more alone in his domain, while seven lesser priests of the temple groped silently down the stone staircase in the belly of the black column, on their mission of death.

Kardak, lifting flat hand to forehead, stared long and steadily at the massed shadows beneath him. His glittering eyes contracted with malice; he spoke aloud the name uppermost in his mind.

"Selaron! He knows more than is good for any living man. This night will find him silenced, and I wonder what *she* will say."

EVEN then, in a paneled chamber not half a bow-shot distant, twelve men and Selaron held council. Ay, and they were *men*, not pale-faced priests of the underground. Warriors, all twelve, well armed and mightily prepared for trouble; shield on arm, lance in hand, sword on thigh, despite that they sat quietly at the long table listening to the words of their leader.

And Selaron, but a moment since returned from his first meeting with the fair Inar and his destruction of her slave-abductors, surveyed these men with proud eyes. Himself not of their blood, but a wanderer out of the far north, he had become one of them for love of battle.

"The queen must not know of this," he frowned; and they nodded agreement, though he was the youngest of them all. "It is for us to curb Kardak's passion and lay low his slinking horde. Ninus, our king, is away to the south on the march; it is for us thirteen, left behind to guard over our king's queen, to stand against the pot-bellied curs of Kardak. Ay?"

"Ay!" they responded. "And who better?"

"Then go and guard the walls. It is there the danger lies."

The twelve rose quickly, whispering among themselves and muttering, with one accord, the name of the traitor. So they went out, while Selaron stood with folded arms and wide-spread legs, watching them with unmasked admiration. King Ninus had done well to leave these twelve to defend the Great City. Not one of them knew the name of fear!

Ninus had done wisely, too, in leaving Selaron to captain them, though the thought did not enter the boy's head. Youngest of the king's captains, this youth could hurl quicker spear, draw stronger bow, ride mightier charger than any in the king's host; yet Selaron himself knew it not.

Alone now, he threw off his harness and stepped to the brocaded couch close by the wall. He must needs stay here this night in the event that any of the twelve came hurrying with warning of peril. And danger was imminent, by the serpent of Ashtaroth! Kardak, cunning and unscrupulous, would stop at nothing to bring the Great City under his control now that the king and the king's warriors were away on the march.

Thinking thus, Selaron failed to note the opening of the door behind him. In truth, the barrier swung wide with no sound more than a whisper. Naught but the vibrant scrape of sandaled feet gave warning of his peril. Swinging about with face convulsed and fists knotted, he found himself struggling in the grasp of many hands and surrounded by the scowling faces of Kardak's priests.

He laid about him lustily, levelling those who clung to him. A lesser warrior might have fallen to his knees under the sheer weight of the seven straining bodies; yet Selaron found his balance and crushed three of the leering masks before his legs were torn out beneath him and he flattened to the floor.

A wooden bludgeon descended upon his forehead; and he saw, last of all, before darkness swooped over him, the blood-smeared, frightened face of the man whose throat he gripped.

His fingers stiffened and relaxed. They lifted him then and bore him swiftly out of the chamber, carrying him through the outer halls, down marble steps, into the street. Thus he was escorted, unprotesting, through untravelled byways of the sleeping city to the tower of Baal. And here, filing between two massive stone bulls with eagles' wings and human heads, the white-robed priests carried him into a magnificent room leading from the central corridor of the temple.

Here they laid him upon a silken couch to await the coming of Kardak, where vaulted walls, sculptured with strange deities of cedar and gold and ivory, flaunted above him.

They knew it not, but Selaron's eyes were already open and his fists already folded.

Ay, it would have meant death for Kardak had he opened the door at that smoldering moment. But the high priest of Baal was no fool and had no wish to face Selaron alone. Therefore, when the barrier fell inward and Selaron sprang to his feet like a swift tiger, it was to find two huge negroes confronting him, armed with broad flat shortswords. The blades crossed before his face, thrusting him back again against the couch; and peering beyond, out of bitter eyes, he discerned Kardak standing passively in the doorway, eyeing him with discreet smile.

"Bind his arms," Kardak shrugged.

"Unconscious, is he? By the Host of Heaven, those jackals of mine will one day learn the difference between shamming lion and one who truly sleeps!"

The negroes obeyed him, making fast Selaron's wrists and elbows, twisting the limbs roughly behind the youth's body in the hope of bringing a moan from those set lips. Failing in this, they stepped backward and stood like graven images before the entrance, while Kardak, smiling with supreme cunning, paced nearer.

At that moment Selaron saw untold wisdom and evil in the priest's countenance. Kardak's words, droning through thin lips, were even more sly.

"You know the penalty?" he spat. "You who plot to overthrow the great queen and seize the city?"

Selaron lifted his proud head to stare into those bloated features. Disdaining an answer, he spread his legs wide and stood firm as the wall behind him.

"The queen shall have her will with you," Kardak smiled knowingly, "when I breathe your guilt to her. Ay, the pits will have you."

"The pits," Selaron shrugged, "are a better death than looking upon your ugly mouth."

Angered, Kardak fell away with livid face.

"Seize him!" he rasped to his slaves; whereupon they gripped Selaron's bare arms and dragged him forward.

Thus, with Kardak pacing ahead, the youth was forced through a succession of long and narrow corridors until, descending a flight of marble steps, he found himself once more in the cool darkness of the outer night.

"We shall see," Kardak muttered close to his face, "if the great queen herself can silence that tongue of yours. Or perhaps she would suggest some certain method of so doing."

Frowning then, Kardak moved into the dark, allowing the two negroes to drag their victim after him. And the gloom dissolved into details as the walls of the tower contracted in their narrowest part to permit the light of the stars to shine down. Selaron found himself at once in a wide garden, a labyrinth of tangled verdure which seemed to hang above and below and on all sides, thick as an opaque veil. To the left—or to the right, for no man could be sure of the direction of the cool sound—a brook murmured and whispered pleasantly. Song-birds sent up their silvery cries out of nothingness. And the sky above was blotted out, at broken intervals, by interlaced vines, so that it was like pacing through an irregular tunnel and might have been a delirious dream of sweet sound and scent except for the pointed shortswords that tickled Selaron's flesh.

IN A moment the stars winked again without interruption and the hanging gardens fell apart to reveal a tiny lake of ebony water, reflecting in its smooth surface a thousand pin-points of light. Here rose a conical temple of silver and ivory hue, magnificent in the dusk, mirrored like a dream structure in the waters beneath. And Selaron knew, with leaping heart, that he looked upon the queen's fabulous garden retreat—that which no warrior's eyes had ever before reported. Here was the temple of Dagon the fish-god, where Semiramis herself retired to be alone with her beauty.

It was death to enter here. Selaron's broad shoulders tightened with the thought, then relaxed with indifference. If it were death, there could be no greater honor before passing than to gaze upon the face of her he served.

Presently Kardak stopped and hesitated, only to advance again and mount the alabaster steps with silent tread, motioning the slaves to follow. And so Selaron was taken through the temple entrance, to find himself confronted with ponderous silken hangings embroidered throughout with golden lotus. Perfume reached him, rising to his nostrils with subtle persuasion, blinding him to the great vaulted hall which extended at his feet.

Thus, all at once, he found himself in the central chamber, staring with wide eyes upon a serpentine form which reclined lazily on a low couch before him, at the very rim of a mist of crimson torchlight. And he realized, with a start, that he had been pacing forward scarce conscious of his surroundings, for only Kardak stood beside him gripping his arms; the slaves had vanished.

"He is here," Kardak said humbly. "Would the great queen look upon him and accuse him?"

Semiramis raised her head with mock indifference, bending the full force of her gaze upon Selaron. Without flinching, he returned the stare, meeting those eyes deliberately, seeing nothing of the beautiful body bedecked in golden breastplate and headpiece, resplendent in jeweled tiara and carven anklet. Being a nomad of the north, he had never learned to prostrate himself before a human being, and so remained at his full height, defiant.

"Leave him," Semiramis said evenly. "Wait outside with your foolish gods, Kardak. I would speak with this spirited warrior alone."

Kardak, scarce repressing his frown of disapproval, backed away obediently, touching head to floor in submission to her will. Lifting herself then, Semiramis looked long and steadily upon Selaron, and finally smiled.

"I have been told," she shrugged,

"that there is none so brave in my lord's host as this Selaron. Yet I find you no more than a boy."

"I have seen twenty-two summers of desert heat," Selaron answered stiffly.

"And so you are as old, in wisdom, as Kardak!" she laughed. "Proud youth!"

He had no reply for this. She studied him from head to foot, then became suddenly cold and stiff. Her loveliness faded before the anger which crept into her face.

"Kardak has told me that you would plot to sell the city to an invading host of desert tribesmen, while your king is away to the south," she accused. "Is this truth?"

"If Kardak says it," he shrugged, "it must needs be truth. Would you believe my word against his?"

"There are others plotting with you?"

"Kardak," he said bitterly, "can also tell you that. His tongue is free."

Semiramis allowed her lips to press with anger.

"I am asking questions of you," she said cuttingly. "Answer them!"

"There is but one answer, my queen. My words would but make you smile, since Kardak has already filled your ears with his whispers. My answer is silence."

A hint of admiration crept into the queen's cold eyes, yet they lost their displeasure not one whit. She leaned forward even closer, bending supple to examine this rash youth who stood so straight before her. Then, with a bitter laugh, she fell back and clapped her hands together.

"This," she said cruelly, "is *my* answer."

Selaron moved not a muscle. Presently, in response to her summons, came the queen's handmaidens, filing silently from the silken curtains on either side. None more lovely in all Babylon than

O. S.—3

these girls, though little of their bodies was visible and white webbed veils covered their downcast features. At the queen's bidding they moved forward and took their proper places; six in all and three to a side.

"You," Semiramis said coldly to one of them nearest her, "bring Kardak here. I have looked long enough upon this traitor."

The girl went noiselessly. Selaron, staring all about him with unflinching eyes, scarce heard her steps; he was peering, even then, at the half-raised face of a maiden who stood a little back watching him covertly. And his heart had leaped into his throat at the sight; for this—this creature lovelier a score of times more than the queen—was his girl of the night, his Inar!

Ay, hers was not the cold, haughty, defiant beauty of the Great Queen, but something finer and rarer without name. This girl, though her face was hidden to him, caught and held the throb of his heart until his own face flushed crimson with embarrassment.

From behind him then came footsteps, and he turned to find Kardak reaching to seize his fettered arms. An evil smile curled the priest's mouth; and Semiramis' words, coming at the same instant, matched it in cruelty.

"He has refused to answer my questions," she said without concern. "Take him to the dungeons beneath your tower of gloom, Kardak. If I remember, there is a certain pit which sees not the light of day or ever breathes fresh air. In such a pit, with the cold and blackness and no food, it is likely he will open his mouth more willingly. Take him!"

Selaron turned slowly, fighting to subdue his fear, hardly conscious that Kardak's fingers bit savagely into his bare forearm. Without a backward glance at

O. S.—4

the reclining figure of the Great Queen, he paced from the chamber into the huge hall without. Here waited the two giant negroes, still brandishing their shortswords as if only too eager to strike a fatal blow. And in truth, their chance came before Selaron was aware of it.

OUT of the silence behind him came a sudden pitiful cry and a patter of naked feet. Soft hands clutched at his arms, then slid down all too swiftly, warm and fragrant, along his braced legs as the girl sank to her knees and turned her head to Seriramis.

"No, no!" she pleaded. "Not—not the pits! No!"

Selaron looked down upon her in amazement. Her veil had fallen aside, showing him her oval face, utterly lovely, pale, full of concern for him, with large, terrified eyes that welled with unchecked tears.

But it was only for an instant; then Kardak, with black face and growling lips, stepped against her and thrust her aside. She fell with a sob under the cruel force of his hands—fell, and lay still, trembling pitifully.

Selaron, at that instant, was once more a man of the north. With a single mighty wrench he freed his hands and leaped forward. His clenched fist ground full into Kardak's leering mouth, hurling the priest into the solid wall. Whirling about, Selaron stood for a moment free and untouched. Then, springing to Inar's side, he sought to lift her up.

A seething blade met him with sickening force, crashing flat against his forehead. With a great groan he pitched to his knees against the girl's limp body. Rocking blindly, he groped at the bloody welt in his head; then a second blow caught him on the broad of the shoulders, smashing him to the floor. He felt nothing more after that, but lay still, unconscious, on the white floor.

He did not know that Kardak, limping erect, was barely in time to prevent the negro's sword from impaling him where he lay, and the girl with him. Nor did he know that Semiramis, rising from her couch, stood to her full height and laughed derisively, saying with curled lips:

"Ay, by Ashtaroth, it is well for you, Kardak, that you have slaves to guard you! I should have liked to see this youth in action, if this is a sample of his courage. Such fighting heart one does not find in the skulking priests who attend me!"

3

THE dungeons of Baal, feared intensely by those who were unfortunate enough to sin against the will of the Great Queen or arouse the cunning ire of Kardak, were black as the pits of a nether world.

Sunk deep beneath the level of the hanging gardens, deeper even than the lower level of the tower itself, they were a subterranean maze of labyrinthin tunnels and vaults, where the light of day was blotted out by bricked walls reeking with the stench of dead air.

Selaron, unconscious from the wound in his head, scarce knew that he was carried out of the temple of Dagon, back through the darkened garden to the lofty tower. To be sure, his eyes flickered open intermittently and he was aware, in twitching moments when his senses returned only to vanish again, that darkness lay all about him and heavy hands bore him.

Death seemed already upon him, and he shuddered at the nature of it. More than once he had faced death on the plains of Shinar astride a champing horse or in a war chariot, with lance and javelin

in hand and bow slung over harnessed shoulder. But this death, in the black hole of Baal, was worse a hundredfold than hanging or impalement.

Still, his thoughts returned often to the girl who had cast her life upon the Great Queen's mercy—a risky trust, by the Seven Stars!—in pleading with her for his life. Ay, she was lovely, that Inar. And courageous in spite of her slender heft and smooth features. Could he but look upon her once more and perhaps hold her close to him for an instant of comfort before these ungainly blacks threw him into the dungeons, he might die a braver man.

These thoughts came intermittently, with the consciousness that harbored them. But ere the silent procession reached its destination in the marble halls of the lower tower, Selaron was thoroughly awake and seeking furtively a chance of escape. Blood ran into his eyes and mouth from the gash in his forehead, warm to his lips and sticky; his head throbbed with the incessant hammering of a hundred anvils. Yet he lay still and limp, lest his captors discover him conscious and inflict further wounds to sap this feeble returning strength.

Thus, with Kardak showing the way and holding a sputtering torch high overhead, the two slaves bore their burden deep into the pits, through tunnel after tunnel, until it seemed to Selaron that the very bowels of the earth were about him, and that Shamash, god of light, had in truth no access here. A great stone door was swung aside before him; he was carried into a stinking stale vault of granite and flung upon the floor. And Kardak was bending above him.

"In two days," Kardak scowled, leering triumphantly, "I shall return here to listen to you. Ay, listen! The silence here drives men mad; hunger and darkness stalk hand in hand through these pits. Listen while you are here, and soon you will hear the screaming wails of another prisoner who was brought here but a little while past because he failed to carry out my commands."

Staring up with open eyes, Selaron shrugged his shoulders with forced indifference. He might, in truth, go mad with fear, but this slinking priest would never know!

"While you lie here," Kardak continued, "think of the flower-faced Inar, whose soft fingers caressed your arm but a few moments ago. Ay, she is a queen of beauty. Were it not for you"—the priest's lips curled with the thought, exposing close-set teeth and tongue fiery red in the torchlight—"Inar would even now be mine. And the man whose moans you will soon hear, my meddling warrior, is the slave who escaped your sword this same night. He came running to me with his tail between his legs like a frightened gazelle, to babble his tale—how you fell upon him and his companions and wrested the girl out of their grasp, slaying all but him."

"He is here?" Selaron muttered, unable to repress his amazement at this fiend's cruelty.

"He is here," Kardak leered. "You will know his wail when you hear it. And others have met the same fate, for failing me or"—his sandaled foot prodded Selaron's thigh meaningly—"for pitting their wits against mine. Remember that in your hours of agony. And remember, too, that Inar whom you love will no longer have a protector."

Saying this, Kardak fell back, motioning the two slaves to precede him. The stone door swung close, allowing a heavy bar to thud down into its sockets and blotting out the sputtering glow of the torch.

THE tread of footsteps became less and less distinct, at length dying away altogether and leaving the stillness of the grave. No sound was here except the scrape of his own body as he groped to his knees and drew himself erect on uncertain feet. Thus, standing there facing the unseen door of his dungeon, he heard only the sucking intake and exhalation of his own breath.

At that moment he would have thrown himself against the barrier and screamed aloud, had he not known that Kardak, still within earshot, would hear the cries and laugh in glee. And so, holding himself stiff as an arrow, Selaron fought to control his terror and forced himself to stand motionless.

Standing thus, he pondered over his fate. He thought of Inar and of the Great Queen herself, blinded by Kardak's treacherous mutterings. By Ashtaroth, unless these pit walls held an opening, all Babylon would pay the price! Kardak, with his slinking curs of the temple, would overrun the city and make himself king, removing Semiramis and setting Inar in her place—lovely, unwilling, courageous Inar! And when the king, resplendent and imprudent with well-won victory, returned with his conquering host to the city walls, Great Babylon would turn upon him and slaughter.

With these thoughts for companions, Selaron set about to examine his prison. The vault itself was not large, but high enough for its ceiling to be out of reach. No niche presented itself in those smooth walls of granite; no opening was there except the long perpendicular grooves of the sealed door. Not even the whole of the king's host could batter that barrier down without a ram.

Despite this, Selaron sought feverishly and muttered half-formed anger

through tight lips. Another man might
have implored assistance of Ashur, god
of battle, and Nisroch of the eagle's head.
And presently a sound of human voice
disturbed the silence of the pits, beginning and ending in a high-pitched roar
of confinement.

"Who is there?" Selaron called.

The bellow came again, terminating in
high-flung words which spit forth like
daggers reflecting on stone.

"Selaron! Selaron!"

"Who are you?" Selaron shouted,
pressing his mouth close against the
closed door.

"I am Reb, my lord, the slave who
faced you this night early and fled from
your sword. By Shamash, this darkness
will creep into my eyes in another hour,
and into my soul!"

"You have no pity from me," Selaron
growled in reply. "A cur who obeys Kardak and assaults helpless maidens deserves
madness."

For an instant there was silence, and
Selaron heard the almost inaudible scraping of fingers on stone, as the unfortunate slave clawed at the walls which
confined him.

Then in a broken voice, full of pleading, came again:

"Selaron!"

"Well, what now?"

"I would be your servant and fight for
you. And for her! When Kardak sent me
and the others to drag her before him, I
knew not who she was. Kardak swore
she was a slave-girl."

"Liar," Selaron retorted. "If this be
truth, why did you return to Kardak to
tell of her escape?"

"Lord, I did not."

"I pity you not, nor believe you. Were
I free, I would break you in my own
hands."

Selaron stepped back, scowling. The
muffled voice died away then and became
silent again. With a shrug, Selaron
realized the futility of his rage. Ay, he
might need the sound of this man's voice
before long to keep madness away.

And the voice came again.

"My lord, listen."

"I am listening," Selaron said curtly.

"When I looked into her face, there in
the shadow of the palace wall, I made
ready to fall upon my companions and
free her. It is truth, my lord. But then
you came and we were forced to fight—
even I, lest I wished to die on your blade.
And I ran, not to Kardak but to the temple of Dagon where lay the queen, to tell
her of Kardak's evil."

"You went not to Kardak?" Selaron
demanded, half believing.

"Nay. They caught me in the forbidden gardens—Kardak's priests—only to
drag me back to the tower before Kardak himself. That is why I am here,
Selaron, not——"

Selaron's hands clawed savagely at the
stone. His face contracted with doubt;
yet a sense of pity invaded his anger and
he called out:

"You would have defended her? You
speak truth, slave?"

"What good," came back the reply,
distorted to a whisper, "would it benefit
me to lie, my lord? We both die here
with no hope of escape. I would have
you think well of me before we go."

"Ay, lying would avail you naught.
Well then, Reb, we are comrades. Know
you any way out of here?"

"There is none."

"So I have heard," Selaron said grimly. "Yet we were led here and so can be
led out again."

There was silence then for many moments, only to be broken again by the
slave's voice.

"Selaron, unless we call out to each

other at intervals to break this silence, we both will go mad. Do you hear?"

"I hear you."

Thus Selaron lapsed once again into brooding silence. In a while, realizing the uselessness of his endeavors to find an exit, he flung himself to the floor and rested.

4

GREAT Babylon, slumbering in the longest and darkest hours of that scheming night, knew nothing of the torment enacted in the deep pits of the tower of Baal, which rose, like a pointing sentinel, above the majestic parapets of the city proper.

The Great Queen herself, surrounded by her retinue, slept an untroubled sleep broken only by rare dreams of a young and handsome warrior who came ever to stand before her couch. Ay, that was a weird dream. Beginning in mist, it came clearer and clearer to reveal a solitary white horse in a wide expanse of desert; and the horse, racing nearer with flying mane and thundering hooves, came all at once, for no reason at all, into the temple of Dagon. Here its rider flung down and took form. She saw him in blurred outline; yet he stood boldly erect, defiant, unflinching, in sharp contrast to the sallow-faced priests who attended her.

Through this vision came ever the snarling face of Kardak; and Semiramis saw this young warrior led away, whereupon another vision appeared in which she discerned him lying on a cruel stone floor in utter darkness, with a rivulet of blood running down his fixed face, blinding him.

And the blood woke her with a start.

Thus, peering about her in bewilderment, Semiramis lay for the better part of an hour thinking strange thoughts for the queen of a mighty king. Yet those thoughts were not of King Ninus but of a bronzed, broad-shouldered youth who lay even then within bow-shot of the temple wherein she pondered.

Finally, clapping her hands sharply, Semiramis called one of her ever alert handmaidens to her side and said, in a queer modulated voice:

"Go and bring Kardak to me."

The girl turned and would have obeyed without protest. Yet not more than three steps she took when Semiramis summoned her back with curtly spoken command.

"Nay, I have thought better," she said. "Go to the palace and summon the palace slave-guards—six of them. Bring only the bravest and sturdiest. I want no creeping cowards for this task! And here——"

Plucking a silver amulet from her arm, the queen dropped it into the girl's outstretched hand.

"This will take you past the sentries in the garden," she smiled casually. "Otherwise you would be seized and impaled for being discovered there. Now go, and hurry."

The maiden clutched the amulet and turned quickly. With expressionless face concealing her astonishment at this unusual mission, she paced from the chamber and so proceeded through the paneled hall to the outer door of the temple. Descending the marble steps with timid tread, she faced away into the darkness and followed the unlighted path toward the distant bulk of the palace, passing beneath an endless canopy of hanging verdure sickly sweet with scent and menacing in its touch.

She knew it not, but she was not alone in the forbidden gardens of the king. Barely before she had passed out of sight in the gloom, a second figure crept from the sheltered wall of the temple and moved furtively forward. Despite the veil tight-clasped about her face and throat, and the silken cloak wrapped about her slender form, none but a blind man could have failed to discern the loveliness of this slight figure. She was in truth a goddess, as Selaron had so named her!

Ay, but Inar held no amulet to give her safe passage through the garden, and so must proceed with fearful caution. The darkness itself held no terrors for her, but the thought of other things made her timid feet heavy. The penalty for discovery here in the queen's gardens was impalement on the lance—no small horror for a mere girl to face. Yet she found her way desperately and deliberately from shadow to shadow, shape to shape, tree to tree, keeping the tower of Baal ever before her as her objective.

So, even before the first servant of Semiramis had delivered her message in the palace, the second maiden, unknown and unsummoned and a thousand times more beautiful, drew aside the door of Baal's mighty pile and, keeping flat against the grim wall, sought her way into the pits. Queen of courage!

SELARON, lying prone on the floor, head on arm, heard the approach of footsteps and stood erect with fist clenched. It would be Kardak, he reasoned, come to gloat. Ay, Kardak might well gloat from the far side of the stone barrier; but let him once draw that door aside and the gloating would die on dead lips! With wide legs and uplifted hands, Selaron set himself.

The steps drew nearer, unsteady and hesitant. Thinking to lure them close, Selaron pressed his lips and moaned softly, as if in anguish. In answer came a voice. Her voice!

"Selaron!"

Soft—barely a whisper, yet enough to unclench his fists and cause his lithe body to tremble violently.

"Inar!" he called softly. "Here, Inar!"

"Shh!" she warned.

Then her fingers struggled with the massive bar of iron; he could hear them straining and slipping with its dead weight. God, how she must have labored to lift him to freedom! Such a bar would have taxed the strength of a husky warrior, yet this frail girl gave her very soul to bring it out of its sockets and swing the big door aside.

And so she stood before him, framed in the opening. He felt her there, though he could see but a shadow. Groping forward, he clasped her arm and drew her close to him for a single instant, though he made no attempt to draw her veil.

"Come," she whispered. "If—if we are found here———"

Selaron thrust his arm about her shoulders and stepped into the corridor. She gripped his hand and would have led him into the gloom, but he hung back abruptly.

"Wait," he said. "There is another."

She did not protest. Turning, he strode over the stone flagging, calling as he went:

"Reb! Speak, man; we are free."

A muffled voice answered him. Inar, waiting fearfully against the wall, heard a second bar scrape on stone, a second barrier groan open, and then there were two men beside her where one had been before.

She asked no questions. Leading back the way she had come, she showed them the way out of the labyrinth and mounted ramp after ramp until the darkness lessened. Thus they reached the upper level; and in a moment the outer door of the tower closed behind them. Before them, extending on all sides, lay the forbidden gardens through which they must pass.

Here, in the light of the stars overhead, Selaron hesitated long enough to peer into the face of the slave, Reb, who had sworn him allegiance. And of a sudden Selaron's face expanded with astonishment and his eyes widened.

"You—you are no negro!" he exclaimed.

"Nay, my lord," Reb said softly. "Those with me were negroes, but I am an Israelite from the far south, captured on the desert by Assyrian warriors as I journeyed with my brothers and father seeking a new home."

Selaron's fingers closed firmly over that strong arm, signifying pleasure and approval. Then, obeying the soft command of the girl, he moved into the darkened tree-maze with Reb trailing.

A hundred paces they proceeded. Selaron saw then that the girl was leading them to the palace gates, whence they might escape beyond the walls into the streets, and so be free. None would know the manner of their going. There would be no peril to Inar. Free of Kardak's clutches then, Selaron might join his twelve comrades and so wage silent, quick war on the high priest of Baal who sought to capture the Great City. Ay, the gods were smiling this night!

Thinking thus, he moved close to Inar and took her hand, to show his appreciation and perhaps inform her of his love. It was darker here, almost, than in the pits from which he had come. The matted foliage overhead cut every light from the stars and——

Of a sudden the girl shrank back with muffled outcry, falling against him. His arms went about her defensively as he sought to choke the sound on his own lips. And on all sides of them, like grotesque forms rising out of the turf, sprang slaves in harness—guards of the palace!

Selaron had only time to whirl about, shouting a warning to the slave, Reb, who paced twenty strides behind him.

"Escape!" he cried. "Go to my dwelling. Warn my warriors——"

Then he was fighting as no warrior in the king's host could have fought against such odds. Unarmed, weakened by confinement and the ugly gash in his forehead, he flung himself upon the guards who would have seized him. And he heard a woman cry out in the thick of it:

"Take him unharmed. It is her order!"

His legs were wrenched out beneath him. Stumbling, he found his balance by sheer dexterity and returned blow for blow. But his naked fists were no match for iron-clad knuckles and flailing steel-shod arms. Again and again he went down, once at the very feet of the girl who had given him liberty. And so he was seized, and Inar with him.

Standing rigid, with four pairs of hands gripping his arms and shoulders, he struggled like a trapped lion to break loose, but without avail. Inar, too, struggled bravely, until another woman stepped close to her out of the darkness and said sibilantly:

"It will be impalement for this, my pretty! The queen herself has eyes for this fighting buck."

Gathering himself, Selaron strained forward, dragging his captors with him.

"The queen looks for me?" he demanded.

"Ay, and for this rival of hers, more than likely. Know you the feel of a lance through the breast? Then whisper the agony to her, to prepare her. That is the queen's way."

"Is this," Selaron gritted, glancing at the slaves who held him, "the queen's reception of me? Is this too her way?"

"Nay, my game-cock. Semiramis sent me, but now, to fetch these palace guards to her, so that she might send them to release you secretly, without the knowledge of Kardak. Ay, I am no fool blinded by her beauty. She is a woman, with a woman's desires. And I was leading these slaves to her, at her command. She will not be pleased to learn that her handmaiden has already released you. Come, we have tarried long enough."

Harsh hands dragged Selaron forward. He strove to reach Inar's side, to speak words of encouragement to her, but her captors and his would not allow it. ·

Peering about him, he saw that Reb, the Israelite, had escaped.

And so, with this faint hope to keep his heart whole, Selaron was escorted once again, like a captured lion, to the temple where Semiramis, the Great Queen, would receive him.

5

SEMIRAMIS, Great Queen of the Great City, leaned supple elbows on her knees and stared long, penetratingly, into the faces of her captives.

There was nothing of admiration in that frowning face of beauty; rather it was hate, unadulterated and intense. And the presence of the palace guards did not tend to make those cruel features relax as perhaps they might have done if Selaron had ventured here alone.

The queen's anger was directed most upon the girl who stood close before her, locked in the embrace of masculine arms. For the moment, at least, Selaron was ignored if not forgotten.

"Lift her veil!" Semiramis said coldly. "I would look upon the features of her who dared to disobey me."

One of the soldiers tore aside Inar's silken veil, revealing her frightened pale face and eyes wide with anticipation.

"Think you," Semiramis said icily, "that a mere handmaiden of mine can take that which the queen desires for herself? Speak, girl!"

Inar murmured something scarce audi-

ble. Turning her head fearfully, she caught Selaron's fixed, fearless glare; and drawing courage from him she straightened to her slender height and choked off the words of apology on her lips.

"A woman's heart," she said quietly, deliberately, "knows no queen."

"What are you saying?" Semiramis replied curtly.

"I love him."

"By Ashtaroth!" Semiramis cried, her lips colorless with sudden rage, "the woman is more presumptuous than Selaron himself. Girl, I have impaled slaves for less——"

She caught herself and leaned back, frowning with displeasure at her own outburst. Then, lifting her shoulders in a slight shrug of indifference, she faced the palace guards.

"Take her," she said evenly, "and give her the death. Nay, better than that, lock her in the dungeon from whence she liberated this bold warrior-fool. Ay, it would be a pity for Kardak to find the cell empty when he goes there to hear the moans of his victim. He shall not be disappointed, though in truth he may be somewhat surprised to find the sex of his victim suddenly altered. Take her!"

Shifting her gaze, she smiled upon Selaron.

"And now—what say you?" she said with mock pleasantry.

Selaron's hands clenched and unclenched. Stiffening, he stepped closer, pulling his retainers with him, for they refused to release those twisted arms.

"I say," he growled savagely, "were you a man with sword in hand, by God——"

Then, knowing the futility of this, he let pleading words come from his lips.

"You know not what you do," he entreated. "Kardak himself desires her——"

"I care nothing for Kardak's passions!"

"But he will take her——"

"And better if he does," Semiramis shrugged. "It will save much discomfort, and should be truly entertaining to her. Take her away, I say! And I command you to silence. If Kardak learns what has occurred this night there will be more prisoners in the dungeons than ever the pits can hold. You hear?"

Saying this, she leaned back and closed her eyes in satisfaction, until the receding footsteps informed her that Inar, uncrowned queen of beauty, had been carried from the chamber. Had she opened her eyelids at that instant, her hatred might have increased a thousandfold; for Selaron, standing straight as a javelin, held in his tracks by uneasy hands, extended both arms in a gesture of comfort and love to the girl who was being led from him. In mute agony he stood his ground, helpless to intervene, while Inar, fighting her captors every step of the way, looked back at him with eyes full of silent supplication. Unveiled as she was, there could be no doubt of the meaning of her glance.

But when Semiramis stretched herself, cat-like, a moment later, only Selaron and Selaron's guards stood within the chamber, and the sound of departing footsteps had died to emptiness. Only Selaron, black-faced, rigid, scowling with unmasked and terrible hate, confronted her; and she shuddered involuntarily at the smoldering fire in his eyes.

"I would talk with you alone," she murmured uneasily. "No!"—as the guards would have released him and retired—"Hold him! Would you leave me unguarded with a wounded lion of the northern deserts? Take him to the Well of Rest, beyond the city walls, and bind him securely there in my hunting-tent, leaving two to guard over him. Later I

will go there to speak with him. Now he would not listen."

The captain of the guards repeated the order forthwith.

"When that is done," she commanded, "return to your quarters at once, and keep your lips sealed of this night's doings."

"They are sealed already, O Queen."

"Then take him away. In the morning I will go myself to the Well of Rest. You hear that, Selaron?"

"I hear," Selaron answered grimly.

"And you will look to my coming with —eagerness?"

"With hatred," he said simply, "as you well know."

"Ay, but when we are alone, there in the palms, I shall make you forget this unlovely girl who has captured your foolish heart. We shall see, my Selaron!"

"You will see," Selaron shrugged, "that I am a trusted captain of your lord's host, and faithful to Ninus my king."

She laughed derisively at that, and he was pulled away ungently, leaving her there to follow him with her stare. Thus, with guards on all sides of him, he was led into the outer hall, where they bound his arms behind him and took him into the night.

INQUISITIVE eyes, peering down upon the streets of the silent city at that hour, might scarce have seen the six horses moving through abandoned streets to the southern gate of the mighty wall. In truth, Selaron's captors kept discreetly to the shadows where they might not be seen; for Kardak, high priest of Baal, was reputed to have eyes in many heads.

Sitting astride his horse, a good steed with rippling muscles and quivering nostrils, Selaron rode without a word. Escape was impossible, since the guards pressed him close on all sides.

In this manner, keeping tight rein on horse, the party of six rode through black streets to the Brazen Gate. Selaron, searching the gloomy portals with the despairing hope that some of the twelve warriors of Ninus might here be on guard, hung his head again in defeat. The gate was unguarded. He had expected nothing better, since the twelve, being too few to watch every gate of the city, would be undoubtedly placed high on the parapets to command a view of the flat desert below.

Thus steeds and riders passed through the gate into the outer night and so into the broad starlit expanse of shimmering sand.

6

REB, the Israelite, escaping from the forbidden gardens, went immediately to Selaron's house at the remote end of the city. Knowing not what he would find there, yet wishing to obey his new master's command to the utmost, he crept through the marble entrance, down a paneled hall, and into chamber after chamber with noiseless steps.

Yet for all his care he found nothing but desertion. The warriors of Selaron's defending band, standing secret guard at the city walls, had not returned from their posts. There was nothing here in Selaron's abode but the usual retinue of servants who, at this hour, were asleep in their private quarters at the rear.

Pondering this, Reb hesitated many minutes, undecided what next to do.

"My lord and Inar," he thought, "will be returned at once to the dungeons of Baal. Without them I can do nothing. True, there are warriors in the city under Selaron's command, but I know them not; and were I to question every warrior I met, I should likely be stuck with a spear and carried before the Great Queen under suspicion. What then?"

Thinking thus, Reb armed himself with longsword and dagger from a cast-off harness which he found in one of the rooms. In truth, though he knew it not, this harness had lately adorned the frame of Selaron himself and had been thrown aside earlier in the night, before the first assault by Kardak's slinking priests. So armed, Reb went forth again into the darkened city, with a full-formed plan in mind and lips drawn tight over set teeth.

It would take courage, this plan of his. Ay, but the Israelite possessed no small share. With sword gripped in hand, he was a match for any of the palace guards or creeping curs of Kardak!

Straight to the palace he went, in search of others of his own breed who recognized him as a leader. Slaves they were, yet even slaves, beaten and lashed by masters of the city, could know the feel of a strong blade. And smoldering hate had long burned in the eyes of these Israelites from the south.

It was no easy task to reach the palace slave-quarters unobserved. Once again the task entailed a passage of the forbidden gardens, and more than once Reb was forced to flatten himself against a massive tree-bole or smooth wall as idle footsteps and scattered bits of conversation moved past him. Thus he heard words which set his nerves aflame.

"Ay, she has been taken to the pits, for Kardak to play with. I envy her not. It is dark as the nether world down there——"

"The queen will have her impaled, mark my words. Semiramis was ever jealous of a beauty greater than hers; and when a brave warrior enters into the tri-angle——"

Hearing this, Reb spurred his feet to swifter flight, and so reached the palace gates. Slinking through familiar darkness, he passed by sleeping negro guards and reached the inner corridors of the great structure; and thus, like a wraith in those vaulted halls and passages, he reached the slave-quarters.

Here, in a single sleeping-chamber, he found the men of his own blood. Nay, they were not negroes, but Israelites, captured far to the south as he himself had been. Six of them in all, and though branded by the marks of long slavery, they were still bronzed and hardened and filled with the burning hate of the south for the conquerors of the north who had bonded them. Never did Israelite bear much love for Assyrian.

Reb talked to them long. They listened, and nodded silently, and finally followed him. Creeping through the palace, they stopped long enough to arm themselves as he was armed, stealing their weapons from the racks standing before the quarters of the guards. Thus, in less than an hour's time, Reb and his six moved through the gardens and found access to the tower of Baal.

They knew it not, but a bent figure watched them from the high parapet. Beady eyes followed their approach until they reached the very shadow of the grim wall; then the eyes receded and vanished altogether.

REB and the Israelites found nothing to impede their progress. Passing noiselessly through the lower halls, they descended forthwith the great ramps to the pits and began the tortuous route through the subterranean labyrinth.

So, having completed half the distance, they found themselves suddenly surrounded, hemmed in on all sides, and fighting for their very lives.

Ay, it occurred quickly as that! And it was a cunning trap, executed by a cun-ning devil. Kardak, aware of their coming, had prepared for them mightily.

Torches blazed out with uncanny quickness, baring smooth walls and black floor, revealing the priests of Baal like scurrying rats rushing upon hapless intruders. And the rats were many—as many as leaves in the hanging gardens of Semiramis. Here, in the pits, they were in their element, knowing every turn and wind of the maze, while Reb and the invaders could only stand ground and fight at elusive shapes.

Flat against the barrier behind them, the six hewed an open circle in front. Blades sank into blood, spilling it at their feet. Man to man, the low-bellied denizens of this deep dark were no match for the thick-shouldered, strong-hearted men of the southern deserts. But they were many—too many—for six brave men to combat.

"Forward!" Reb cried shrilly. "Square about me. Close up. Form a wedge!"

They followed his orders; all but one, who was dragged down from behind by innumerable hacking hands and slaughtered upon the stone floor as he writhed to defend himself. The others, snarling like trapped cats, beat their way past body and blade, hewing a path down the passage; until Reb, leading the pack, raised his head suddenly and began to shout a name.

"Selaron! Selaron!"

And above the grunting of human throats, above the moans of tortured flesh, came an answering sound—not Selaron's voice, but a thin, anguished, feminine cry muffled by walls of impenetrable granite.

"He is not here, Reb! They have taken him to the Well of Rest beyond the ramparts! Go there. You can not help me here."

A great sweep of Reb's arm lopped the

head from a body as a figure rushed forward, spilling a well of blood over his legs.

"Where are you?" he rasped. "Inar——"

Then, again: "You can not help me. Save—him. Save Selaron!"

Reb hesitated. Being the servant of Selaron and knowing much of Selaron's mind, he fought to find a decision. Save Selaron? Ay, he could do that. With his men, now only four in number, and one wounded horribly from a slashed breast, he could retreat out of this pit of hell and go to the Well of Rest, but Selaron would wish otherwise. Selaron, were he here, would lift the mightiest blade in all Assyria and shout: "Fight to the end, Reb. Fight for *her.*"

And so Reb, shouting encouragement to his fellows, waged the assault anew. Metal clashed on metal. Faces came out of the gloom, shimmered in red torchlight for an instant, and then became a blur of blood, falling before him.

"Fight!" Reb grunted. "Show these curs how Israelites seek vengeance!"

And they showed. Ay, they rallied to him with a fire that could not be quenched.

The priests of Kardak scuttled back, clawing over one another to get out of the way. Turning, they fought to escape. Torches were flung to the floor. Scurrying feet made a continuous noise like the scraping of papyrus over stone. And all at once the passage was empty.

Leaning on his lance, Reb turned with a grim smile. But one man remained at his side—a huge fellow with scarred face and a livid slash running from elbow to wrist of one arm. The others had fallen in that last mad slaughter. Ten times their number lay about them, piled up like the dead debris of a blackened battlefield.

Striding into the gloom, Reb sought the door of the girl's cell.

"Inar!" he called. "Where are you? Inar!"

Getting no answer, he continued in the direction whence he had last heard her voice, certain that she had fainted with the horror of the conflict.

Thus he found her vault. The massive stone door hung open on its heavy hinges. The cell was empty.

7

SELARON, lying on his low-slung cot, was aware that daylight, pale and gray, marred the tent wall above his head. He paid little attention to it, except to clench his fists in frustrated anger. Daylight would bring the sun above the burning sands of the desert waste, baking the roof of the tent with relentless tongue. Daylight, too, would bring Semiramis, the Great Queen, on her mission.

All night long Selaron had not closed his eyes in sleep. His head throbbed; his bound arms, lying half beneath him in a contorted position that brought no surcease, were stiff and semi-paralyzed with the incessant pain of their cords.

His guards—two of them, left here at the Well of Rest to watch over him according to the queen's orders—had not bothered to slake his thirst or to converse with him. Even now, he knew, they would be lying in the cool shade beneath the knot of feathery trees which surrounded the watering-place some hundred yards distant. Here, at the Well of Rest, coolness was more precious than gold. None lived here. The scattering of black tents marked but a hunting-station for the queen, wherein she might rest after a day's forage in the desert before returning to the near-by city.

Thus Selaron lay listless, awaiting the

arrival of his royal visitor, which would also be the arrival of death, since he could not and would not accede to her demands.

Pondering on his plight, he lay motionless while the tent grew to broiling heat with the rising of the sun. Testing his bonds then in desperation, he found them unbreakable; moreover, his wrists and arms had perspired profusely during the hours of their strained contortions, and the ropes, made tighter by swelling flesh, seared his skin. Nothing but a keen edge would free those hempen cords.

Presently he lifted his head to listen, and heard the scuffing thud of hoof-beats. Familiar with such sounds, Selaron recognized more than one note and knew that more than one steed was approaching, and that not slowly. They came at a canter, drawing nearer with swift stride; and soon he heard a movement even closer at hand, as his guards stirred from their position near the fringe of palms.

Voices came then, not a little excited, but unrecognizable. Passing close beside the tent wall, the advancing steeds pulled up snorting; and then came sounds that brought Selaron up with a jerk.

The movement caused his mouth to twitch with torment. This intense heat, added to the natural reaction from the efforts of the past hours, had overwhelmed him with weakness. He strove to roll from his cot, and so succeeded in precipitating himself headlong on the ground, striking his wounded forehead roughly and breaking the sealed gash anew.

Fresh blood coursed into his eyes, blinding him and bringing semi-unconsciousness. He strove to crawl to the tent flap, but his body refused to stir beneath him. Thus, sprawled inertly on the sand, he fought for consciousness enough to hear what went on without.

Ay, it was a sound to stir any warrior's blood. Snorting horses were prancing with swirling forefeet. A man cursed, then screamed. Blade struck blade in ringing clash. There came the sound of a warrior running, of a horse following in swift pursuit—then a screech of terror and gurgling silence.

Presently there was no other sound but footsteps drawing closer to the tent. The flap was thrust open, revealing the figure of one of the guards, swathed in sweat and grinning widely, with sunlight gleaming on his metal accouterments. Selaron saw it but dimly, through a bloody haze.

"Selaron——"

The figure stepped closer. Then, of a sudden, a second voice cried aloud from the outside.

"Back! She is coming!"

The guard withdrew hurriedly, leaving Selaron alone and bewildered. But not so for long, for a second series of hoof-beats drew nearer over the sand in a very little while, and the flap of the prison tent was once more drawn aside. Selaron, lifting his weary head, stared through a mask of crimson into the frowning features of Semiramis.

She surveyed him coldly for an instant, then laughed mockingly.

"Is this," she asked with a disdainful lift of her shoulder, "the customary position for a brave warrior of my lord the king?"

Selaron struggled to move; whereupon, seeing his anguish, she bent to his side and assisted him back upon the cot, then stood over him without pity.

"You expected me, my lord?" she said quietly.

"Ay, I expected you."

"And were happy in the thought?"

"You know better."

With another shrug, Semiramis glanced outside the tent where the two guards lounged beneath the palms close to the tethered horses. Seeing that they were out of earshot, she paid no further attention to them, but drew the flaps close and came again to stand directly above Selaron's prostrate form.

"I came to speak with you," she said evenly, and into her voice crept a touch of admiration for his courage in thus facing her without cringing. "Will you listen?"

"Can I do anything else?" he said.

"Then hear me. You think, my lord, that Kardak himself is plotting against me. Is it not so?"

"Ay, I know it."

"You are mistaken, Selaron. Kardak plots with me—not against."

Selaron lifted himself suddenly up and remained propped on one elbow, staring into her face with open amazement.

"You are saying——" he faltered.

"I am saying, Selaron, that I am queen of Great Babylon. Long have I awaited this opportunity, when King Ninus should be safely away to the land of the Egyptians. I am young, Selaron. None more beautiful in Assyria. And he is ancient."

"None more beautiful?" he repeated. "Ay—but one."

"But one, say you? But you see with the eyes of a youth, not as a man. One day you will thank me for taking her away and keeping you for—myself, my lord."

"I tell you," Selaron lifted his head to rasp the words, "if aught harms her——"

"Be still!" she answered coldly. "I do not permit warriors to address me in that tone, Selaron. Would you test the metal of my anger?"

He was quiet, waiting for her to press her bargain.

"Ninus will not return for many days," she smiled at length. "Meanwhile through Kardak, I have sent messengers to the nomad tribes of the desert, to north and

to south, bidding them come to Babylon and fight for me. Thus, when Ninus and the host return, they will find Babylon turned against them. They will find the priests of Baal and the priests of Belus, led by Kardak, opposed to them; and they will find also a nomad host of desert tribesmen, armed to repel them and led by—Selaron!"

"You"—the words choked on his lips —"you ask this of me?"

"I command it. And the reward is fitting, my lord."

"There could be no fitting reward for such treachery. I serve my king."

"Your king," she said sullenly, "is an aged warrior with flowing beard and parched skin. Such a man can no longer rule the greatest nation in the world. The people would have another king, a young warrior like yourself. And I—ay, I would have a king also, like you."

"I love another," Selaron said bitterly.

The queen's eyes fixed in his face. For an instant she held control of her anger; then her bosom, beneath its breastplates of carven gold, heaved violently.

"You refuse?" she cried blackly. "I offer you rule of Assyria! I offer you command of the Great City! I offer you myself! And you refuse because of——"

"Because of honor," Selaron said quietly, drawing courage and self-reserve from her flushed heat. "What you ask is not for a warrior to accept. I am a captain of the king's host, not a flesh-mad priest of the temples."

Semiramis stood stiff for a moment only. Then she rushed upon him, clutching at his arms and chest, staining her hands with the blood of his wound.

"You—you dare to refuse the highest honor?" she snarled. "By Ashtaroth, you——"

Then, with superb control, she fell back. Once more her features hardened in that characteristic cold smile which was so much more dangerous than uncontrolled temper. Folding her arms, she stared down at him.

"Either you accept my terms," she said evenly, "or you die by impalement. And she who is in your thoughts so much that you can not reason without her, she dies likewise. Now, your answer?"

"You would—kill Inar?" he gasped.

"Knowing me, you know it."

"And—and if I do as you say?"

"I send her away alive, into the desert."

SELARON'S fingers dug into his palms, bringing blood. He lowered his head in torment, afraid of the chill smile that burned into his soul. Her life—Inar—by impalement—*God!*

Thus, for many minutes he did not move, but lay there with averted head, fighting to find the answer. And she, misunderstanding his silence, said very quietly, with ominous tranquillity:

"You are slow in speaking, my lord. Methinks I am able to hurry your response."

Turning, she stepped to the aperture of the tent and called to the guards. They came quickly, both of them; and she, without deigning to cast more than a glance upon them, said sharply to the bolder of them:

"Draw your lance."

The fellow did so. His companion remained by the tent wall, watching hungrily.

"Now, place the pointed tip where a single thrust——'

Smiling grimly, the guard stepped to Selaron's cot and obeyed. The head of the shaft pressed significantly into Selaron's bare chest below the breast bones. A single silent thrust would carry it through, transfixing the prisoner in agony.

Without raising his head high enough

to see the fellow's leering face, Selaron glanced at the lance and shuddered.

"Your answer?" Semiramis smiled.

"And if I — refuse?" he muttered through dry lips.

"If he refuses," she commanded, speaking to the guard, "it is a signal for you to drive the lance home. I have spoken."

The fellow nodded, turning his black face half toward her.

Cold sweat glistened on Selaron's brow. Ay, he was brave enough; but no man, lest he be a god, can face death by impalement without flinching. And she would fulfill her threat, he well knew. No man ever doubted the Great Queen's cruelty and anger when frustrated in her desires.

"You would give me time to decide?" he asked.

"What time would you have, my lord?"

"But a moment," he begged. "Leave me alone. Withdraw your guards and take this infernal point from my flesh. Go yourself. And in a moment—perhaps two —after being alone with my God, I will answer."

"Your gods are not mine, Selaron."

"Nay. I know only one, and He the God of truth and love. Alone with him for an instant, I will know my decision."

And it was truth, for no thought of escape entered his mind. Such thoughts were but madness. But he would be alone for a final moment, to think of *her* and whisper *her* name aloud, for in truth she was his God. Already he knew his answer.

Semiramis smiled cunningly. Retreating to the tent entrance, she said easily:

"The lance will not disturb your prayers, my lord. I will go and drink of the cool water of the well. When I return, I shall expect your word. Fair dreams, Selaron!"

Thus she went, stooping gracefully to pass beneath the tent rim. Her steps sounded in the sand, pacing away to the distant gathering of palms. And then, with a twinge of muscles, Selaron turned over, buried his face in the cot beneath him, and lay silent.

He lay thus only for an instant, until the queen's steps were no longer audible. Then a sudden hand on his bound arms brought him about again. He opened his eyes, blinking, to gaze into the face of the guard who was bending close above him.

A knife gleamed in the fellow's hands. The bonds had already fallen away, slashed cleverly. The lance was thrust into Selaron's fist.

And the face grinning down at him, under its covering of black, disguising grime, was the face of Reb, the Israelite!

8

SELARON, choking his astonishment, groped up to grip the hands of his savior.

"You!" he muttered. "By Ashtaroth, Reb——"

"Shh!" the Israelite warned. "Can you stand?"

"Ay, I think. But——" Selaron's glance fell meaningly on the second guard who stood quietly by the entrance, peering out to keep watch on the queen's movements.

"He is one of us," Reb smiled, "an Israelite slave like myself, and there is none more trustworthy, my lord."

"Then, help me up."

"The horses are waiting," Reb said quickly.

"Ay, and she is between us and them!"

"She is but a woman, my lord. With one hand I could hold her——"

"Nay, she would fight. I have no wish to lay hand upon a woman."

"What then?"

Selaron, strengthened by this new courage, exerted himself and managed to stagger to his feet, where he stood trembling, leaning upon the Israelite's shoulder. For a moment he stood thus, then turned toward the rear wall.

"You and I," he said evenly, "creep beneath the tent and stand without where she can not see us. This other one, our companion, cries out to her to bring her running. Thus, while she searches for me, we are free to reach the horses without encountering her. And this fellow can easily join us while she looks in amazement upon the empty cot where I lay."

Reb, smiling at these words, dropped to his hands and knees and raised the tent wall, allowing Selaron to crawl through. Turning then, he gave soft instructions to the guard at the entrance.

The scheme worked. Aroused by the guard's shout, Semiramis came quickly. Finding the tent empty and her hapless victim flown, she stood nonplussed for a moment, glaring about her; and the guard at her side sped quickly away, reaching the tethered horses just as Selaron, stumbling through the sand with Reb's assistance, gained the stirrups.

Thus, when Semiramis realized her blunder and turned with snarling lips, three steeds dashed past her into the expanse of the desert, leaving her alone to stand there.

And she, knowing the hopelessness of pursuit, remained rigid with fists clenched and mouth twisted so that every semblance of loveliness was ebbed out of her face.

THE sun was high in the heavens, burning down upon the sands, when the three flying horsemen reached the outer wall of the Great City.

During that race across the desert, there had been little conversation; yet Selaron, strengthened by his seat in the saddle, had learned the magic truth of his escape.

"After finding the girl gone," Reb explained, "we came straight to the walls where, stealing horses from the sleeping gate guards, we disguised ourselves as negroes and sped into the desert. Arriving at the Well of Rest——"

"Ay, I heard you come," Selaron said grimly. "I heard the queen's guards die!"

"There was no fight, my lord. Blackened to seem like negroes, we rode upon them before they recognized us for enemies. Then, when we had dragged them to a place of hiding, I would have come to you, to release you. But Kandeb, my companion here, shouted a warning that the queen's horse was approaching. She would have suspected, had she seen one of us within your tent. Then, too, I knew that you would wish to hear her speech; and so I withdrew, knowing that she could offer no opposition when the time came to free you."

"And now," Selaron said, reining his steed close to the high wall, "we must separate."

"Separate, my lord?"

"A desert horde is coming to the city," Selaron said bitterly, "at her command. Ninus must hear of it. In truth, the king's host must be already returning from the south. You, Kandeb, would you risk your life for the king?"

"Ay, if you command it."

"Then ride, man. Speed across the desert to the south, bearing this message: Tell the king to select those of his warriors who are swiftest in the saddle, and come to the city with all speed. Ay, they will need it!"

"And a token, my lord, so that I be not taken prisoner and disbelieved when I reach the king's camp?"

"A token? By Ashtaroth," Selaron frowned, pawing at his garments, "I have nothing——"

"Here." The word came from Reb as

O. S.—**5**

he nudged his horse closer and extended his hand. "Here is your own dagger, my lord, which I took from the harness in your own house. See, it bears your seal."

Eagerly Selaron snatched it, to pass it as quickly into Kandeb's fist.

"Now ride," he cried. "Ride like the winds of heaven!"

With grim smile the Israelite put spurs to his horse and wheeled about. The beast reared with forelegs flashing and bit champing, then shot forward like a missile out of a sling, sending a great cloud of dust up behind.

Then Selaron gripped his companion's arm.

"Go you," he ordered crisply, "along the walls, with my name on your lips. Seek out those warriors who bear harness like mine. You will find them not at the gates, but perched high on the parapets where they can overlook the desert. Ay, you will make no mistake; they are the finest of the king's host, and look it. Tell them what has happened. Bring them together in my house an hour hence. I will be there."

"And you, my lord?"

"I go," Selaron snarled, "to discover if all Kardak's gods can protect him from the point of my sword. And by God, he will need many such!"

Muttering thus, Selaron drove straight for the Brazen Gate where, high above the roof-tops of the city within, rose the frowning tower of Baal.

THE Great City, as Selaron rode through it, was alive with industry of early morning. The huge walls, ramparts forty cubits in height frowning down on the ant-like figures beneath, hemmed in a scene of life and activity far remote from the shadowed streets of the past night.

Close to the ramparts clung huddled tents of merchants and despised lodges of

sun-dried brick. Watch-towers, set at regular intervals, leaned over the streets; and
between them hung huge brass gates,
open with the coming of day. Streams
of hurrying people swarmed in and out
of the city. Long caravans wound their
way between the frowning columns,
heedless of the ornamental designs depict-
ing gods and men and animals—the sacred bull predominant—which scowled
down at them from the gates' surfaces.

Bright-garbed Assyrian women, soft-
footed priests of the temples, shuffling
merchants, chattering children—all went
to make up the wave of faces that pressed
upon Selaron as he rode through. To the
left, boats of every shape and hue curled
upon the surface of the Euphrates; and
above all, formidable as night, lifted the
tower of Baal.

Toward this Selaron directed the good
horse beneath him, scarce turning aside
to avoid those who stumbled into his way.
Thus, dismounting before the base of the
column, he climbed the steps and, with
fingers locked over the hilt of his sword,
penetrated the sanctum of the under-
world.

None interrupted him here. Hurrying
white-robed figures, passing by him,
glanced upon him in sudden amazement
and then, noting the glare in his set eyes,
scurried past muttering under close lips.
In truth, they knew that this warrior had
been left in the queen's care. If he came
here on some mission of the queen, it was
the concern of Kardak, not of them.

Nor did they wish to make it their concern. A less imposing figure they
might have accosted and questioned; but
this grim-faced, forehead-scarred youth,
swinging ready sword and striding
through their vaulted halls? No!

Unmolested, Selaron came at length to
the chamber of the high priest, where it
was the custom to beg audience before entering. Hesitating not one whit, he drove
the barrier aside and crossed the threshold,
slinging the door shut behind him.

And Kardak, high priest of the temple,
rose from the carven table in the center of
the floor, with twisted face and eyes full
of sudden terror, to face him.

For a moment neither man moved.
Then without more ado Selaron bared his
blade and strode forward. Seizing the
priest's shoulder in his naked hand, he
thrust the man flat against the wall.

"Where is she?" he demanded.

Kardak licked his mouth stupidly, his
flecked eyes fixed in fascination upon the
point of the sword. At length, turning
his cunning gaze upon his aggressor, he
spoke.

"Where you will not find her!"

"By God," Selaron rasped, "either you
bring her here to me unharmed or I wash
the temple floor in your blood. Decide,
man. I have had enough of this!"

"Kill me," Kardak countered cunningly, "and she pays the price. She is hidden.
Only I know the secret of her dungeon.
Kill me and she dies in agony, from star-
vation and darkness——"

"You——" Selaron curbed his biting
epithet with an effort. "You have sealed
her in your infernal pits?"

"Nay, in a better place."

"Bring her, or——" the sword-point
pressed meaningly against Kardak's groin.
Wincing, the priest shrank even closer
into the wall; yet the gleam did not leave
his eyes.

"You will not slay me," he faltered.
"Ay, you know better."

"She is here in the tower?" Selaron
snapped.

"Nay——"

"Where then?"

"Learn for yourself!"

Selaron's fingers closed uncontrolled
over the thick throat. Dropping his weap-

on, he jerked Kardak away from the wall and flung him against the table, bending him far back and throttling him.

"Where is she?" he roared again.

A moan came from those thin lips, but no reply.

"By God above, I will kill you!"

"If you do," the words came chokingly from Kardak's twisted tongue, "she will die harder."

Savagely Selaron wrenched the struggling form erect and flung it from him. Groaning, Kardak crashed into the wall again, flattened there with arms upflung like a distorted bat.

Then, lifting his head, the priest screamed aloud, yelling a torrent of words. Like a tocsin the sound seared through the temple, ringing from wall to wall and corridor to corridor like the screech of a vulture.

"We will see," the priest muttered, "whether you are as strong against a room full of armed men!"

Selaron stood rigid. Not until this moment did he realize the peril of his invasion here. Here, one against hundreds of clawing denizens of this place, he could expect no assistance. Facing them, he would go down to certain death, leaving Inar in the power of the leering Kardak. To stay meant the end, and would avail him nothing.

Seizing his sword again he swung about and plunged to the door. He raced into the corridor in time to meet headlong the first of the priests who came in answer to their master's summons.

Slashing the man aside, Selaron plunged the length of the wide passage, racing back the way he had come. A shout, thrown up from many throats, rang behind him; and the temple echoed to the patter of pursuing sandaled feet.

Swifter than any of them, Selaron reached the entrance unscathed. Clearing the marble steps at a bound, he vaulted to the saddle and bent low over his horse's arched neck.

So, with a thunder of thumping hooves beating an exit for him, he escaped into the streets.

Still the Great City bustled its busy existence, unaware of the tormented rider who passed through it. Never before had Selaron felt so helpless. Never before had he felt futility and incompetence pressing so heavily upon him. Never before had he been confronted with a problem which had neither beginning nor end nor any alternative in between.

Thus, sick at heart and cursing himself for his errors, he drew rein before his own house in the remote part of the brooding city.

"I am a puppet," he thought, "controlled by strings in the evil hands of Kardak. He can do with me as he wills, since his own death, at my hands or any other, would mean her death as well. Yet I must fight him or allow the city to fall into invading hands. And I am a captain of the king's host—loyal to Ninus——"

WITH dragging steps he entered his abode, to find waiting for him, assembled there by the brave Israelite slave, the twelve fighting-men of Ninus' defending band.

They came forward and crowded about him, besieging him with questions. Yet he had no answer for them except to shake his head dully; until finally, realizing that a problem weighed upon him, they fell back and allowed him to speak quietly to them, which he did.

Standing irresolutely at the head of the long table, with folded arms and hunched shoulders, he stared from one face to another and said at length:

"What would you do if, by fighting

for the city of your king, you destroyed the girl of your heart?"

They stared at him in bewilderment. Of them all, only Reb the Israelite understood the full import of his question—only Reb knew how much their answers would crush his tortured soul.

"Let me say it more clearly," Selaron said bitterly, lifting his head with an effort. "Kardak, high priest of Baal, plots with Semiramis, our queen, to bring an invading horde of desert tribes into the city. Already the horde has been gathered by Kardak's messengers, and is doubtless on its way here."

"Slay Kardak!" answered one, interrupting him with furious outcry.

"Ay, but when Kardak dies, I die also —of a broken soul. For Kardak has taken the girl I love and hidden her in a secret dungeon somewhere in the city; and only he knows her whereabouts. If he dies, she too dies in darkness, in agony of hunger and thirst and loneliness."

The rash one was silent. Peering into Selaron's tortured face, he wished fervently that he might recall his words; yet they were spoken, and Selaron knew they were sincere. These warriors of Ninus were loyal to their king. At any cost they would expect him to remain likewise.

Yet he was but human. And what man, given such a choice, would have chosen loyalty above love? No man in all Assyria had heart strong enough to make such a sacrifice!

"I can not do it," Selaron groaned, moving forward like a dead man to slump down into the chair before him. "She is life to me, and breath. The city might rot in ashes if I could but clasp her close to me again and ride out with her into the desert, to the north whence I came."

He looked up heavily, expecting rebuke and protest from the lips of the twelve. But they spoke not, merely re-

turning his stare and respecting his anguish. Had they not seen this same youth in the thick of blood on the battlefield? Did they not know his heart?

Silence was unbroken then. To Selaron it seemed accusing. At length one of the warriors leaned over to say, with quiet voice:

"Those are brave words, my lord. A lesser man would have veiled such honest thoughts. It needs courage to spill them out!"

"Had I the courage of a jackal," Selaron said roughly, "there would be no question in my mind. I would fight. Ay, and I *would* fight!"

"You say the girl is hidden?"

"Where I know not."

"And the desert tribes, they are due to arrive at the gates at any moment?"

"Ay."

"Then we shall die a glorious death, my lord, no matter what your decision. If we fight at the gates, to keep the invaders out, the priests of Kardak will creep upon us from behind. If we destroy the temple and clean the rats out of Babylon first, such a task will give the raiders time to swarm into the city and destroy us as we fight."

"You speak truth."

"What then?"

"I know not," Selaron said wearily, bending his head in his hands. "We thirteen—we fourteen," he corrected, taking account of Reb, "hold the fate of Assyria in our hands. Yet I am mad enough to feel the fate of a single maiden more dear. Do you stand ready to obey my commands, no matter what they be?"

"Ay, my lord," they shouted with one accord.

"Then," Selaron pushed back his chair and straightened to all his height, expecting accusations of disloyalty and cowardice from them, "go each of you into the city. Seek out every hiding-place, every pit and dungeon. Find her!"

There was no answer, no movement. The twelve stared at one another grimly, seeking the reply in each man's face; and there was no reply, for these men were warriors of the king and faithful to their trust.

What thoughts passed through their minds, Selaron could not know. For an interminable interlude he stood straight, confronting them and waiting stolidly for their decision. These men were his men, he thought savagely. They would follow him to hell itself if he commanded. But never before had he ordered them to forsake their king in a time of need, for the cause of a mere girl. Never before had he asked them to weigh a solitary maiden against the mighty Assyrian kingdom.

Thus one of the men rose slowly, with thin lips and fixed, staring eyes.

"To go on such an errand," he spoke, and the words came obviously with an effort, like sword drawn out of cringing flesh, "would mean the end of the Great City. There is no time for it, my lord."

Selaron's lithe body trembled violently. He reached out, gripping the table with both hands to steady himself. His gaze met the gaze of the warrior, unwavering.

"That is your answer?" he said almost in a whisper.

"That *must* be our answer, my lord. We are warriors of the king, to death. Were the king here, he would say: 'Go to the walls. Bar every gate but one. Leave that gate open as a trap, otherwise the invaders will scale the walls at every point and twelve men, even twelve times twelve, could not repel them. Ay, leave one gate open, luring them in, and then fall upon them!' Thus King Ninus would speak, my lord. We are warriors of Ninus."

Only for a moment did Selaron stand motionless. Then, whirling about with grim smile twisting his lips, he strode to the door.

"My lord"—the voice followed him, pleading—"where would you go——"

"I go to find her!" Selaron growled. "The great Ninus himself would never desert the woman of his heart—not for the whole of his empire. I am a warrior of Ninus!"

Thus he left the chamber and paced with firm steps down the long corridor to the outer entrance, never once glancing behind him.

But before he had flung open the door to the streets, a solitary figure came running after him, to grip his arm in firm fingers.

Selaron turned stolidly, to stare into the face of Reb, the Israelite.

"Well?" he demanded.

"I go with you, my lord," Reb shrugged. "The others are servants of Ninus. I am the servant of Selaron."

A smile of gratitude touched Selaron's lips. Hand touched hand for an instant—Northerner and Israelite. Then, shoulder to shoulder, Selaron and Reb descended to the street.

10

SELARON, pacing morosely through the crowded streets, elbowing and pushing his way through the merchants and trades-people who passed by him, spoke not at all and hardly glanced at the man beside him. But one thing filled the youth's mind: to search out every shadowed corner of the Great City, if necessary, to find the one he sought. Ay, and it would be a task! None knew where Kardak's secret holes extended. The entire city possessed underground passages and subterranean byways built by former priests of the temple and known only to the denizens of the darkness. The search might well run into days; yet it must be completed quickly before the invading tribesmen attacked the walls, for then, of a surety, Kardak would meet death at the hands of the twelve.

Thinking thus, Selaron was scarce aware of the touch of a hand on his arm, until Reb's voice spoke close to his ear.

"My lord, is it safe to walk the city undisguised? Semiramis will have long ago returned from the Well of Rest. All the slave-guards of the palace will be seeking you to drag you before her for revenge. You know not her anger, my lord!"

Selaron pondered over this to some extent, while not slacking his pace one whit.

"Right," he shrugged. "It were better to hide our faces. And I have knowledge of a merchant in these parts who can be trusted."

"No merchants can be trusted, my lord. They are under the secret rule of Kardak himself."

"This one," Selaron grunted, "owes his life to me for a service rendered in the past. Also he is a faithful servant of the king. Come."

Thus, following Selaron through tortuous streets and narrow tunnel-ways, Reb found himself led to an unobtrusive mart in the forgotten end of the city, where an aged merchant with flowing beard and keen eyes sat on an ancient stool and listened to Selaron's words.

And in a little while, where two fighting-men had entered, two priests of Baal emerged, garbed in flowing white robes embroidered entirely with lotus flowers. They wore sandals and ear-rings and silver bracelets; and tasseled cords, hanging from the waist-belt, dangled to the ground.

Selaron, glancing down at his garb, scowled with displeasure. On bracelet, ear-rings, sandal-buckles, even on the metal fillet that bound each man's hair, were engraved the significant and irrefutable mystic winged circle, symbol of holy omnipotence. These were not fit markings for a warrior!

"I like it not," Selaron grumbled.

"Ay, but it is for her sake, my lord."

Selaron's hand touched his thigh. Prying eyes searching beneath those flowing robes might have found something far more potent than the mystic circle! In each man's belt, concealed beneath the linen garment, hung a ready longsword, where a single thrust of hand could swing it clear.

And in this manner, throughout the remainder of that tedious day, Selaron and the Israelite carried on their hopeless search. No black hole of Babylon escaped their groping hands. Palace, tower, terrace, wall, even the market-place gave up their secrets, disclosing more than one unfortunate agonized slave of Kardak's passion—but not her.

Darkness came, thinning the streets and bringing heavy stillness upon the city. Still the two false priests continued their prowl. On occasions, groups of the palace slaves passed close to them, seeking Selaron himself. Once, too, a temple priest scurried along a blackened sideway on some uncertain mission of evil. Still, unmolested, Selaron and his companion patrolled the city.

INCREASING anguish marred Selaron's set face as the precious hours ebbed out. He had seen enough torment and pathos this day to suffice for many a year. Broken slaves had been rotting in the dungeons because of Kardak's will. Things that had once been men, but were now only grim reminders of a grim penalty, were gibbering and wailing in their chains under the city's unsuspecting streets. And these sights had not served to lighten Selaron's heart.

If Kardak wrought this vengeance upon one, he would do so upon others. Inar—Selaron's Inar—was even now somewhere in those fiendish clutches.

As the hour grew later and later, approaching midnight, Selaron's steps turned involuntarily back to the forbidding column of stone that marked the tower of Baal. It was not hope that led him here; rather an inert sense that informed him that thus, in Kardak's proximity, he would be closer to her he sought.

Silent as a ghost, Reb plodded at his side. Neither spoke. Conversation between them had long since become an undesired burden; both men favored the solace, if such it were, of their own thoughts.

Plodding thus along the way which led to the grim pile, neither was aware of the contracted eyes which followed them from the entrance to the tower. Not until the possessor of the eyes—a ferret-faced priest of the cult—shuffled quickly toward them did Selaron stop his aimless stride.

The cowled figure halted before him, lifting indignant head to peer into the youth's half-hidden face.

"Know you not," the priest said in a warning tone, "that Kardak has ordered all priests of the temple to be within the walls this night, in readiness? Would you rot in the pits for disobedience to his sublime will?"

"Nay, friend," Selaron replied, masking his voice to a low guttural, though his face contracted with sudden eagerness which was invisible in the shadows. "We were but walking for a breath of air. But we heed your warning, and even now return to the tower."

The priest scuffed away, mumbling his opinion of vagrants in general. Seiz-

ing Reb's arm, Selaron continued to pace forward without checking his gait. But no sooner had the cowled figure vanished once more than Selaron jerked his companion close to the wall, in the shelter of surrounding darkness, and swung him about.

"You heard?" he said tersely.

"Ay, I heard. But what meaning——"

"Kardak expects the desert horde. He would have his men in readiness to join them this very night and overpower the city. They mean to waste no time, these traitors, in preparing a death welcome for Ninus and the returning host!"

"Ay, but——"

"It means," Selaron muttered with parted lips, "that we can turn the trick on Kardak this very night, by Ashtaroth! Ay, we'll give him the very choice he gave me. His life or hers!"

Reb, bewildered by this reasonless outburst, would have remonstrated further and demanded explanations; but his arm was seized in a hand of iron and Selaron's commands were hurled at him.

"We must keep Semiramis and the palace slave-guards from joining Kardak. You hear? Go to the palace. Find some way to keep them there. I care not how you do it, but *find a way!*"

Then, turning with such vehemence that his robes lashed about him, Selaron ran back into the darkness. The white raiment appeared and vanished like a fluttering patch of ghost-light farther and farther down the black way, then became lost altogether.

Reb, with a shrug of bewilderment, clenched his huge fists and swung into the gloom.

11

THE guards at the Brazen Gate, standing alert at loopholes in the southern wall of the city, were bewildered presently to perceive a white-robed figure hurrying toward them out of the empty darkness.

Babylon slumbered. The footpaths of market-place and palace, temple and terrace, had long ago forgotten the impact of passing feet. And the twelve warriors of Ninus, under the leadership of a newly appointed captain, had long ago finished their preliminary preparations for defense.

All gates of the Great City but one had been sealed and barred with the coming of darkness. Now, on watch for the solitary means of ingress to the sleeping city, the twelve were astounded to find a priest of Kardak running toward them with uplifted hands.

Thus, before Selaron reached the Brazen Gate, rough hands were laid upon him and a sword-point pressed into his breast.

"No man passes here this night," the guard scowled. "Least of all a priest of the temple. What would you?"

"To speak with your captain," Selaron rasped, knowing that the darkness concealed his features.

"On what mission?"

"The mission of Selaron!"

The warrior started back. This time Selaron's voice was not disguised, and the fellow peered in amazement at this swaddling figure. With a low laugh Selaron swept aside the linen covering which half hid his face.

"Take me to your captain," he said fiercely.

The warrior found his voice then.

"By the serpent of Ashtaroth," he muttered amazed, "your mask is better than my eyes, my lord!" Then, with unconcealed admiration and affection, he said humbly: "You are my captain."

"Nay, I have another mission. Who is in charge?"

"Kessalan, my lord."

"Then take me to him."

Forthwith the warrior led him to the captain of the twelve, where, for many minutes, Selaron spoke swiftly, curtly, in a voice full of tension. In response, Kessalan vanished for a moment, to reappear leading a restive horse by the bridle.

"Remember," Selaron warned, "I want the gate unguarded. You will find Reb somewhere near the palace. All of you will be needed to keep the queen's slave-guards secure in their hole. If they succeed in joining the priests of Baal, Babylon pays the price of your blunder!"

Then, swinging into the saddle, he thundered out through the already open portals, leaving the twelve defenders to stare after him in utter astonishment.

But no sooner had the flying horseman vanished into enveloping darkness, than Kessalan strode among the warriors, delivering Selaron's command to each man.

And hearing these orders, the warriors of Ninus were more than ever bewildered. But obediently they withdrew from their station, leaving the gate open.

Fully armed, the twelve took to horse and rode back into the city, to join Reb in his mission at the palace of the Great Queen.

Only Kessalan, of them all, found courage enough to force a meager smile to his mouth. Even he, drawing his sword from its sheath and testing the keen edge with his thumb, muttered to himself:

"It is a rash plan. By the gods, none but Selaron would have attempted it! None but Selaron could have conceived it!"

12

KARDAK, high priest of Baal, stood on crooked legs before the altar of worship in the topmost chamber of the great tower. It was a strange room, this. Here, rising in the semi-gloom cast by niched torches above and beside him, stood the gods of the temple in all their grotesque forms.

Here stood Shamash, god of light, holding in one clenched fist a burnished circlet of gold representing the sun itself. Here, in stone shapes, stood Nebo and Bar and Istar, and Merodach, lord of battle, astride a lion's back. Here crouched Dagon, god of waters, more than human above the girdle; below that foul and unsightly with fins and ugly scales. Here stood Ashur, god of the gods, and Baal the infamous, and Nisroch of the eagle's head.

To them all, without distinction, Kardak directed his moaning plea, chanting in a singsong voice that was less human even than these misshapen creatures of granite, marble, and gold.

"Tonight, O great ones," he wailed, "the conquering horde comes to Babylon. Tonight, if so the Seven Spheres of Heaven will it, Kardak becomes mightiest of the mighty; and Semiramis, unsuspecting her fate, goes down to death. Ay, tonight is the night of the ages!"

Prostrating himself with these supplications, Kardak touched his head to the floor, wriggling abjectly backward while the weird shapes seemed to mock him.

Then, rising again, the priest turned about and left the chamber, descending the complicated ramps to the lower levels of his domain.

Ay, it was a great plan, and would bear mighty fruit! Even now, in the security of her palace gardens, or perhaps in the palace proper, the Great Queen was awaiting word of the coming of the desert horde. Her plan, which she thought was his also, was a cunning one. She would secrete these desert devils, with Kardak's assistance, in the many chambers of the palace. Then, in a few days when Ninus and the victorious host returned in triumph from the land of Egypt, these hidden raiders would be ready to fall upon them for the slaughter. So the queen anticipated.

But Kardak had plotted otherwise. Semiramis? What was she but a hindrance to his own surging ambitions? Unknown to her, he had sent messengers to the invaders; and tonight they would creep silently into the city, coming forty strong to the tower itself. And then, augmented by the priests of Baal, they would attack the palace and the palace slave-guards. Semiramis would die. Kardak would become king of Babylon. And Ninus, returning in a few days, would find the city at his throat.

Ay, one scheming fiend had turned upon the other; and the other knew it not!

Meanwhile, another lust occupied Kardak's mind. Here in the tower of his gods, unknown to any but himself, lay the beloved of that fool Selaron. None but Kardak could have uncovered her hiding-place. The very walls themselves knew not the secret.

Pacing through the lower corridor of the temple, among fetish and idol, Kardak proceeded to the great entrance. Obedient to his commands, the massive door had been closed in its stone frame, blocking the aperture. No other way gave admittance to the blackened pile.

The tower was silent now as a buried tomb. Long ago the priests of Baal, who were even more the priests of Kardak, and numbered more than a hundred strong, had returned by command to their chambers. None but Kardak paced these marble floors.

The wide entrance, blocked now by a barred door of heavy cedar, opened to the central corridor of the lower level. Kardak, turning from it with satisfied smile, descended into the dungeons, taking a torch from its niche and lighting it as he went.

Thus, after traversing many of those snake-like tunnels and passages, he came at length to one of the more remote vaults far beneath the hanging gardens of the queen. Swinging aside the door, oblivious to the moaning supplications which came to him from the stinking darkness as famished prisoners heard his steps and caught the feeble glow of his torch, he entered the empty chamber.

Here, pressing upon a certain slab of flat stone, which worked as a cleverly concealed counter-balance, he opened to himself a second smaller chamber behind the first. Holding the torch at arm's length, he entered.

And here, prone upon the stone floor, lay Inar. She rose fearfully and shrank away from him, holding a hand to her mouth.

But she need not have feared—not then. He had come merely to assure himself that she still breathed and pulsed with life. He made no move even to remove her veil which she clutched close to her.

"It is night up there," he smiled, nodding toward the upper levels. "Before dawn I will lead you forth, and we will rule Babylon together, you and I."

"It is always night down here," she said without emotion. "And as for the other, there can be no dawn such as you offer me."

"We shall see," he shrugged.

He would have touched her, but she cringed back from him. Knowing the futility of forcing her into submission, he turned immediately and left the vault, making the door secure after him.

Thus, with methodical step and lips twisted in anticipation of the coming hours, Kardak returned to his own chamber in the belly of the tower, where, throwing himself upon a brocaded couch, he prepared to await the coming of the desert horde.

13

GREATER darkness, say the ancient legends, comes before the dawn. Yet the moonlight, reflecting the spirit of Ishtar its goddess, flooded the desert plain with subdued light, turning the sand to a shimmering sea of glowing yellow.

And Great Babylon, sleeping the sleep of security in these lean hours before daylight, knowing that no danger threatened since Ninus the Mighty had conquered all lands to the north and south and established here his kingdom, might have risen with perplexed eyes to look upon the desert this night.

Scarce a mile from the ramparts rode a column of swift, silent invaders. Only Ishtar looked down upon them—upon champing horses and grim-visaged men such as seldom rode together out of the wastes. These were the fighting, fearless nomads of the wide sands; stalwart warriors of the homeless plains, strong in stature, uncompromising of heart, quick to anger and slow to die, and loving nothing better than pillage or murder. And these were the finest steeds in all Assyria; true blooded horses of the Asiatic plains, afire with restiveness. Yet a strange figure rode at their fore, beside their scowling captain. This figure, all in white, rode as easy a seat as the best of them, despite the flowing robes which fitted him with ill grace. This priest of Baal, commanding a column of forty bedouins of the desert, was surely not a low-bellied, skulking tool of Kardak?

Nearing the Brazen Gate, the raiders found no eyes to note their movements, no shout of warning to greet them. With this strange priest at their head they rode through the ramparts unmolested, unharmed, unseen.

And as the silent horde swung into the dead streets of the brooding city, the priest turned in his saddle to shout in a loud voice:

"Now forward, ye desert devils! Leave no rat alive in the tower!"

Plodding hoof-beats became sudden thunder as those turbaned raiders put spurs to flanks and bent low over their horses. Lifting their voices to the heavens in a wild, mad shout of eagerness, they stormed through the paved street-ways like a plundering pack gone amuck.

The Great City echoed to their din. Starlight reflected the glare of their weaving lances and lashing swords. Bronzed faces spat out vindictiveness of a sort unknown to the sleeping inhabitants of this peaceful place. And rising ahead, the tower of Baal hurled the thunder of voice and hoof and clanking harness back in a thousand wild reverberations.

There was no halting these marauders, now that the goal lay before them. In frenzy they strove, each man above his companion, to reach the entrance of the pile first. And so, with forelegs braced and nostrils snorting defiance, a score of horses ground to a quivering halt before the portal, to disgorge an equal number of madmen who scrambled up the smooth steps and hacked with sword and knife-blade at the irresistible barrier.

The strange priest himself led them. First to reach the door, first to fling down off sweating stallion, he was first also to lift his ringing voice in a demand for admission. Behind him the ranks of horsemen split asunder, whirling steeds and riders in a wide circle which surrounded the tower and clamored mightily for blood.

And the roar was taken up, from within, with an equal intensity, though of a different note. Screeching wails of fear and uncertainty and bewilderment penetrated those black walls, searing out into the night. No single sound in all that bedlam was intelligible.

BEFORE the door, the lone priest and those behind him slashed and pounded to no avail. Ay, that barrier of massive cedar had been well erected to withstand and repel assault. Naught but a battering-ram would serve to crack it.

"The rats are scurrying," the priest muttered to the desert chief beside him. "Listen—you can hear!"

"Ay," the fellow growled, grinning his evil humor. "I thought the warriors of Ninus boasted better mettle. Are you sure, O cowled one, of the story you told me?"

"Sure as I stand here," the priest muttered. "Had you come alone, as Kardak arranged, this would have been a trap for you. Ay, the priests of the temple are even now locked in the pits and Kardak with them. These scared curs inside are the twelve warriors of Ninus, with their leader."

"Say you," the chief frowned, "that twelve men were strong enough to overpower the hundred priests of Kardak and seize the tower here? *Twelve* men?"

"Ay, the twelve best in Babylon."

"And who is their captain?"

"He is called Selaron," the priest mumbled.

"Selaron! I have heard of him. Ay, I would meet him and test the feel of his sword. If he is in there now——"

The raider swung about with upflung hand. His shout, ringing to those close behind and to those yet farther behind, was a shrilling crescendo above all else.

"Bring a battering-ram! These dogs inside can not hold us for ever at bay with their barriers! Bring a ram!"

The intonation of his command carried like a tocsin through the night. Ay, and it reached inside the walls, through loophole and crevice and spy-niche, to bring further scurrying sounds and more intense screams of disorder.

"They sound not so brave," the desert chief grinned evilly.

Beside him, the priest nodded in silence. He knew better. He knew that these grim walls harbored not the twelve warriors of Selaron, but the horde of Kardak. And the priests of Baal, facing this unexpected attack, might well seek aid in their numberless gods now. Puny in themselves, and unversed in the art of wielding weapons, they must rely on barrier and prayer to protect them.

Knowing this, and being strangely affected by the knowledge, this lone priest bent double to his efforts, wilder even than the raiders beside him in his futile struggle to hack that wooden block to shreds.

"Is there no other entrance?" one man shouted savagely.

"Nay. None but this," the priest grunted. "Is this not enough?"

An echoing roar answered him from the darkness behind. Torches had been lighted in uplifted hands, throwing the scene of turmoil into blotches of vivid detail. Out of the streets came a running knot of desert stalwarts, carrying among them a pile of solid cedar, pointed at one end. They had wrenched it, perforce, from some blurred, unresisting structure back there in the dark.

Into the torchlight they stumbled, faltering under the heft of their burden, yet filling the temple walls with their victorious yells.

"By Ashtaroth," the priest growled. "This will do it."

And, in sudden answer, a voice came from high above him, out of the face of the tower itself.

"Stop!"

The priest's head snapped back. That voice he recognized, and knew it to his hatred. But he could see nothing, for this side of the tower was in the shadow of the moon and the upper darkness was intense as a hanging veil.

Seizing a torch, the priest lifted the flame high above his white robes. Still he could see nothing distinct; but high over him, leaning from a niche in the parapet a score of spear-lengths beyond reach, hung a vague head and shoulders. No face was visible in that well of gloom; yet this priest knew the features of that shape without seeing them. That gargoyle thing up there was Kardak.

The priest's spear arm flew back on this instant, poised and lithe for the cast. But before the shaft was released, Kardak's shrill voice lashed downward again, screaming its message.

"Wait! Otherwise she dies!"

The strange priest's arm stiffened and hung still, gripping his lifeless spear. Turning, he commanded those behind him to be still and listen. And Kardak, seizing this opportunity, delivered his message in a cunning voice that came like the cry of a wounded bird from the narrow opening in the black tower above.

"Ye can not enter," the high priest railed. "Shatter the barrier and she dies with the first impact of the ram. She is bound to it with chains. Your ram will pass through her body."

A great muttering rose behind the unnamed priest's rigid frame. His courage sank within him and became cold as the night air. Swinging heavily, he glanced into those troubled, bearded faces. Ay, these desert killers knew nothing of a *she*. He had led them here to plunder, to kill, to sink their blades into blood.

Knowing this, he strode quickly to their chief, holding the raider's shoulder in a powerful grasp. They would not hear him, he knew. They would attack, no matter what he said. Gone thus far, they

were uncontrollable. They were devils of
the sanded wastes, gathered from the re-
gions of hell, untempered and unruled by
mercy.

"Wait!" he gasped, and his voice
reached every man of them. "Wait. Hear
what he says. Then——"

"There is naught to wait for," Kardak
screeched triumphantly from his hidden
perch. "Enter here and you enter through
the flesh of her body. I give you the space
of a long breath to take these plunderers
beyond the city walls, else she dies by my
own hand, by impalement. And it will
be no sharp, keen weapon that pierces
her; but a blunt one and jagged! By *my*
hand!"

The words beat into the strange priest's
brain, even as the leering visage vanished
from the aperture above him. He had no
time for choice. Cursing himself, he
raised both arms stiff above him as if
tortured already by the death wound in
her body.

"God!" he moaned. "My God, what
can I do?"

And the reply, though silent, was all
the more sure. What could he do? Nothing, for the men of the desert would do
it regardless of his command. They would
finish their holocaust in spite of him. Already the murmuring dissent had become
a wave of thundering voices, and their
chief was staring at him angrily.

"Wait——" the cowled figure moaned
again, frantic with the torment upon him.
He could see her already, lashed against
the inside of the great barrier, chained
flat against the paneled wood. The huge
ram with its pointed terminal would splin-
ter through the door, break her lovely
body. . . .

"We wait no longer," the raider
snarled. "We came here for no woman's
pleasure."

Turning away in scorn, he rasped his
own command.

"Bring up the ram. Hurl a way
through. I would taste of blood, not listen to this fool's chatter."

The priest's lips writhed, flecked with
foam. Staring about him blindly, he
groped forward, only to be thrust aside
at every turn and growled upon. Once
again the thick pile of timber was lifted
in eager hands, ten men on either side of
it, to begin its forward movement.

Then, with a voice gone mad, the priest
hurled himself upon it, beating it down.
Lunging, he ground a clenched fist into
the chief's throat, bearing him backward.

"Wait!" he thundered. "Give me one
minute. Watch me, and I will show you
who this *Selaron* is!"

WHEELING in his tracks, he raced up
the marble steps. Here on either
side of him, flanking his approach, squat-
ted two immense shapes of stone, representing human bodies with heads of vul-
tures, ugly, glowering, black. With clawing hands he climbed one of these, groping from one foothold to the next,
mounting higher and higher until only
the niched wall of the tower frowned
above him.

And here, turning to look down upon
the desert tribesmen, the strange priest
tore off his robes and flung them at his
feet. A wild shout went up from those
bronzed throats as they saw his harness.
Their amazement changed to frustrated
rage. This man was no priest of the temple. That harness, glittering down at
them in the torchlight, was the harness
of a warrior! And they knew, even before the name spewed out of their chief's
lips, that the man was Selaron!

But Selaron's hands were already
clutching for a hold. Seizing feeble juts
of stone, he climbed higher and higher.

A flung spear struck the wall beneath him and clattered back. His swinging legs sought a single sickening instant for a footing. A second spear found a mark under his armpit. If he fell, those grinning stone things beneath would break his body.

"God," he muttered, without realizing that he implored the help of his own god and not the many grotesque deities of Assyria. "God help me."

Up and up he went, climbing out of the torchlight where the spears of the raiders could not find him with any certainty. His fingers gripped the ledge of the narrow, slit-like opening through which Kardak's head and shoulders had been visible. And, swinging himself through the aperture, he sprawled gasping to the floor beneath.

He lay but an instant, sucking breath in great gulps. There was no time to rest, he well knew. The men below would go mad with defeated rage in another moment. Already he had deceived them blindly. Riding into their camp, he had told a cunning story and they had believed him—how the twelve warriors of Ninus had stormed the temple of Baal and overpowered Kardak and the priests; and how these same warriors, holding the temple, were prepared to lure the raiders into the pile and slay them.

And his scheme had worked. Believing him, the raiders had sprung to horse and followed him to the city, to enter the temple and spill blood.

A good plan, by Ashtaroth! He had warned them, too, that the warriors were disguised as priests, garbed in robe and cowl. If the plan had worked, these desert dogs would have stormed the temple and slaughtered Kardak's curs to a man. It was but turning one pack of wolves against the other.

But the ruse had failed, thanks to Kardak. The roar of those below roused Selaron once more to action. Stumbling erect, he turned toward the black, unlighted ramps that led to the lower levels.

14

THE priests of Baal had no defense against the silent demon who descended into their midst. Racing down the long central corridor, Selaron was among them with a flailing blade in either hand before they were fully aware of his presence.

They fell shrieking away from him, those who were not trampled beneath his sandals. Unhampered now by clinging robes, his body was a lithe slashing thing of bronze suppleness.

Not one of those subterranean curs stood up to him. They fled in all directions, screaming their bewilderment and fear; yet their very flight plunged him into the midst of them, and his twin blades wrought a living, moaning hell before he was clear again.

Thus, only one man stood at length before Selaron's rush. For this one there was no escape, since he had been crouching flat against the barrier listening for sounds of attack from without, and straightened too late. Now he turned with ashen face, and the wail that came from Kardak's lips was like the wail of a man impaled.

But Selaron's eyes, in that moment of ultimate achievement, were upon something else, wide with horror. Plunging forward to reach it, he met Kardak's escaping rush, folding the high priest back with knotted fist rather than stain his sword with such evil blood.

Then, leaving Kardak a limp thing to fall where it might, he stepped to the shape on the door.

It was Inar who hung there, staring

into his face with half-conscious, pleading, terrified eyes, wide as gaping spearholes of horror and supplication. Like a poor creature crucified, she stood flat against the barrier, her arms outflung and secured at the wrists with immense chains.

Selaron scarcely looked into her face. Already a thunder had arisen from without. The desert horde, knowing him to be here inside, had forgotten reason and thought and all understanding in their desire to reach his throat.

Seizing the chains which encircled one of her wrists, Selaron braced both legs against the door and exerted his strength, weeping from the agony of his effort. Inch by inch the iron staple pulled from its bed of solid wood, until, coming free with a jerk, it snapped into his hands, hurling him backward.

The bellow of rage and impending triumph on the outside had tripled in intensity. He could see them out there, in his mind—blades uplifted hungrily, lips twisted over yellow teeth; and the bearers of the ram rushing with their pointed weapon up the steps. . . .

The second staple came free in his fist. Limp as a wilted flower, Inar slumped down at his feet. He stooped to lift her, bearing her backward. And then something sprang upon him from behind.

The blade seared into his thigh, burning a path of pain. Whirling, he swung savagely upon the man behind him. His fingers closed upon that skulking figure who was even then struggling feebly, madly, in an attempt to scuttle away.

Jerking the man up, Selaron pressed him back against the barrier. With deft movement he lashed the chains about Kardak's wrists. The staples, rammed back into place by a single blow each from the metal haft of Selaron's girdle-knife, held that gibbering, pleading thing in position.

Thus, with a splintering crash which drove a thousand wild echoes through the temple, the huge barrier cracked asunder. The sharpened head of the great ram sank deep into Kardak's writhing body, wringing a yell of agony from his dying lips. The big door fell in.

Selaron, falling back, had scarce time to pull the girl to a niche of safety. Whirling with sword clenched in either fist, he found himself suddenly fighting.

Back to the wall, with Inar at his feet, he wove a circle of death about him, hardly realizing that his breath was choking in his throat and his legs were ready to buckle beneath him.

He fought blindly, mechanically. He hardly heard the yells of the tribesmen who surged upon him. He knew only that Inar, prone beneath him, had not moved. . . .

And then he knew that another figure fought at his side, smashing through the desert raiders to reach him. And other voices—the voices of his own twelve warriors—rose above the uproar.

The man beside him—holding those devils away — was Reb — the Israelite slave.

After that he stumbled. Above his agony he heard only the shouts of the twelve—the twelve finest warriors in Ninus' host. Those shouts were sweet music to his soul. And even as they burst upon him, his sword slipped; a burning stab of pain went through his body; he sank across the girl he loved.

15

DAWN, in vivid splendor, burst over the Great City, reaching the warrior who lay limp upon the brocaded couch in the private sanctum of Semiramis, the Great Queen.

Selaron, opening his eyes in bewilderment, raised himself on one elbow and peered about him. He was alone here, except for a handmaiden who stood close to him; yet at his first movement this girl vanished swiftly through the silken hangings.

Presently came another woman, this one the greatest of them all. Semiramis, kneeling at the couch, lifted Selaron's hand to her soft lips.

"I am a prisoner?" Selaron asked wearily.

"Nay, my lord," she answered. "You are no prisoner here."

"Then why do I lie——"

"You were wounded, my lord. At my command you were brought here to rest. Reb the Israelite waits in the antechamber to pay homage to your courage, with seven of your twelve followers. The others—are——"

"Dead?" he demanded huskily.

"Ay, some of them are, but they died valiantly, my lord. It was the greatest battle Babylon has ever known. Those desert devils fought to the last breath, and died fighting. Had not a score of the king's host come riding into the city in the thick of the battle, led by the Israelite slave Kandeb, the tale might have had a different ending."

"Ninus—is here?" Selaron said eagerly, raising himself higher.

"Nay, but is even now on his way here with the rest of the host. These twenty who came were the swiftest riders and bravest warriors of the camp. Your Kandeb led them here in time to turn the tide of battle."

Selaron smiled heavily. Still he did not understand his presence here in the palace.

"Why—why am I brought here——"

"Because, my lord, there is no more fitting place for a brave warrior. And also because"—Semiramis looked straight into his face and bowed her head a little in humble respect—"you have shown me the meaning of truth, Selaron. The Great King returns today from the south; his advance guards have already been sighted on the distant plains. When he comes, I shall tell him of my sin."

" 'Twas no great sin," Selaron said gallantly. "He will forgive, my Queen."

"It was for love of you, Selaron, that I schemed. But during the past hours of darkness, while your twelve sturdy warriors held the palace under guard, keeping my slaves from joining the conflict, I was alone here on this couch with my God. Ay, with *your* God, my lord, for I know now that your God of the north is more true than all my strange deities. I loved you, Selaron; I love you yet and always will; but you are worthy of a better love."

Semiramis rose slowly, letting go his hand reluctantly. Turning, she moved away quietly. And presently, to take her place at his side, came Selaron's followers—all that were left of the twelve, grouped together in strange formation with Reb the Israelite leading them.

"My men!" Selaron said eagerly. "Ay, there are none finer in all Assyria!"

Smiling at his words, the warriors fell apart, allowing another figure to approach his couch and kneel beside him.

Thus Selaron, reaching out with both hands, drew Inar's lovely head to his breast; while Reb and the others, standing stiff as lance-shafts, lifted their bloody spears in silent salute.

The Gardens of the Nawwab

By GRACE KEON

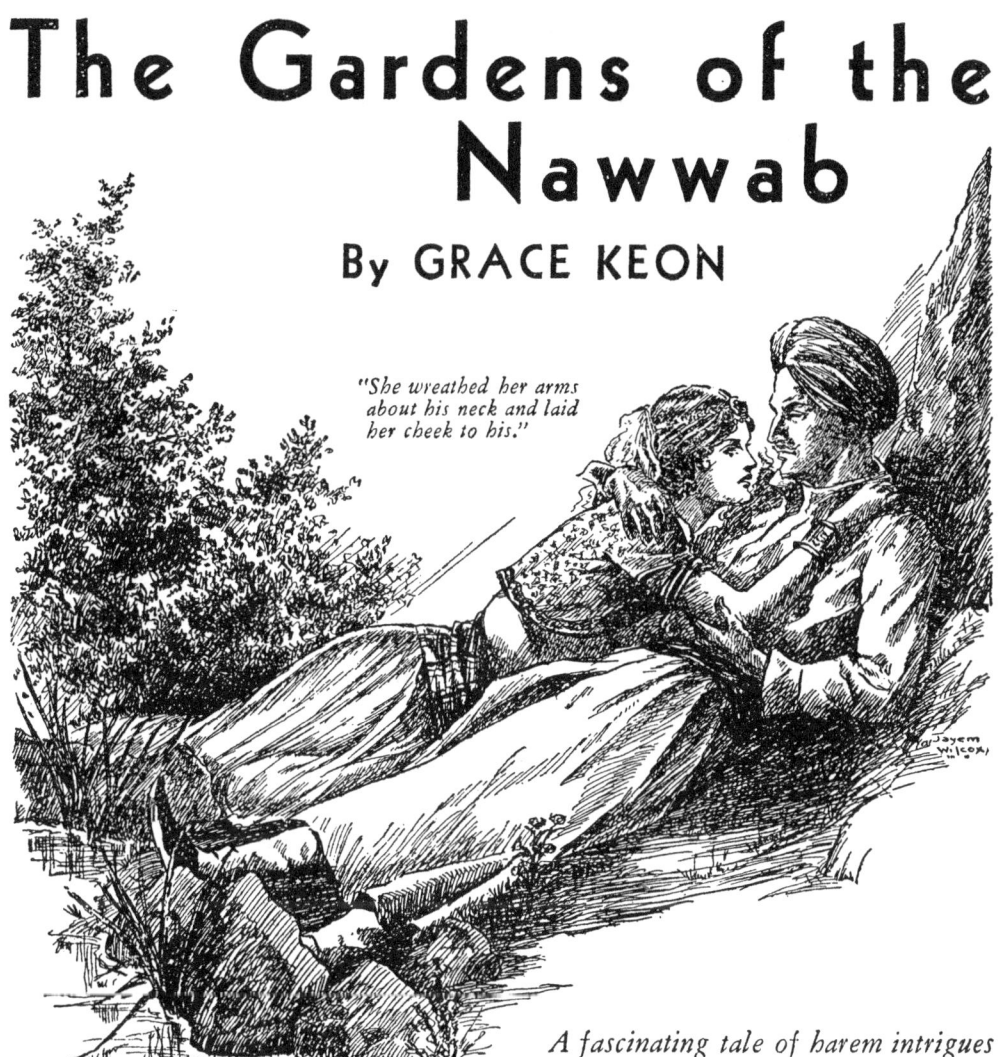

"She wreathed her arms about his neck and laid her cheek to his."

A fascinating tale of harem intrigues at the court of an Indian potentate— a story of stolen love

YUSUF crouched low on his stool, beating his breast, his face distorted with anguish.

"Thou fool, Ramdass! Thou fool, Ramdass!" he moaned. "Oh, why have the gods thus afflicted me? The finger of scorn will be pointed at me, and men will smile and whisper, 'That is he! That is Yusuf, father of Ramdass, the senseless one!'"

The young man looked at him, and his look was evil.

"Why went I from Tazhur?" he demanded. "Why went I with the Sahib Morton four months—four months!—from my home, and my beloved? To earn this!" He threw a small leather bag upon the floor at his father's feet and the coins in it jingled as it fell. "That I might return and buy the wedding-gifts and win Lalri, my beloved! And now!" His voise rose. "Thou darest to sit there and tell me that Lalri hath been given in marriage!" The last word was a shriek so ear-piercing that Yusuf shuddered.

"Thou art indeed a madman, Ramdass!

'Twas the Nawwab of Dahra Dun who took her. The Nawwab! Pallur, the father of Lalri, has become a rich man. The entire household is clothed in costly garments. Six sleek bullocks rest under a new shed! When was a maid ever worth so much? Save to please the fancy of a Nawwab!"

A paroxysm of rage seemed to convulse the lithe figure before him.

"To please the fancy of a Nawwab! Didst thou not know that I would wed with Pallur's daughter?"

"But——"

"Answer! Didst thou not know it? Had I not asked thee—dutifully—as a son should——"

"Yes, yes, yes."

"And I went with the Sahib Morton to be his clerk to earn sufficient to satisfy Pallur. Pallur, too, knew I desired Lalri! Thou wert aware that I would have Lalri!" He laughed shrilly. "The maid is mine. She will never willingly give herself to another!"

A curious sound from the opening that served as door caught Yusuf's attention. A half-dozen heads were thrust inside. There were open mouths, and wide eyes. . . . They were his neighbors, attracted by the din. . . .

"Lower thy voice," he said. "Thou art crazed. How couldst thou discover whether or not Lalri ever thought of thee? How——"

"She knew I meant to wed her. I told her so——"

Yusuf sprang to the door, then, and closed it.

"What evil spirit prompts thee to say such words?"

"I saw Lalri at the river bank. There I used to wait for her—and when the others had gone we talked. Only thrice. But 'twas enough."

"Enough?" His father tore at his hair.

"Lalri and thee alone, and she unveiled? Enough? I am disgraced for ever."

"I care naught for thy disgrace," shouted the young man. "Thou hast cheated me. Pallur, also. Lalri is mine. The Nawwab shall never keep her——"

"Ramdass, Ramdass, cease! Hold thy tongue! People are listening—they will talk——"

"I care nothing for people. Between Pallur and thee has been done an evil thing. For I am in the heart of the maid. She will be true wife to none but me."

This was terrible. It frightened Yusuf thoroughly. Striving to regain his composure he approached his son and put a hand on the young man's shoulder.

"The maid is gone. Her old servant, Kala—the one who has had care of her since her birth—went with her. There was a great wedding and a feast for the poor, the temples were adorned, and there were processions, and the name of the Nawwab of Dahra Dun was blessed and praised. Canst thou not realize what harm this wild talk of thine will do? If any could say with truth that thou hadst seen Lalri or talked with her—wawaila! —the Nawwab would send her back disgraced for ever, would make Pallur return the wedding gifts—there would be no end to the scandal! Have sense! What is a woman? Is not one like the other?"

His son started up with menacing eyes.

"Dahra Dun! Dahra Dun! That is many miles away——"

"Three hundred at the least."

"I go to Dahra Dun."

Yusuf screamed again and tried to hold him, but Ramdass broke away and pulling in the frail door, strode past the dozen odd figures grouped about it. They fell back at sight of his face, with its raging eyes, its blood-flecked lips, fearing a blow from his clenched fists. On he went, his father's wails following him.

"My son! My only son! He hath been afflicted! The evil spirits have gone into him! Have pity on me, have pity on me! *Wawaila!* My son hath left me, to wander as an outcast for ever! His brain hath melted into water within his temples. *Ah-ha-e!* His eyes look upon visions, his tongue uttereth false words. My son, my son!"

Thus moaned Yusuf, loud enough for all to hear, striving to counteract the danger that Ramdass had brought upon him. If those words went to Pallur—he would have to bear it, he alone!

FINALLY an old man ventured into Yusuf's house and sat beside him on the floor.

"Take comfort. Make a sacrifice in the temple and all evil will be averted. Ramdass hath been puffed up by the *Inglesi.* He will recover. Once the Sahiba Morton called him a prince. A prince! The son of Yusuf a prince!" He cackled, swaying back and forth with laughter.

Yusuf straightened, ceased his cries.

"And why not? Who smarter than Ramdass, son of Yusuf, in the Government school? Who handsomer, straighter, more pleasing to the eye? Didst not thou, Iran, seek him for thy daughter?"

Iran had not forgotten. His lip curled venomously.

"Luckily, I thought better of it——"

"Thou? My son Ramdass would have naught to do with her."

Mortally offended, Iran rose.

"Thy son, Ramdass, hath been evilly guided. Praised by the English Sahiba! Praised by the teachers! Clerk to the Sahib Morton himself! Ah-h-h! Thou wert a proud man, Yusuf. And now thou hast a son . . . Ramdass—wanderer and fool!"

Better that, thought Yusuf, complacently when Iran had left him. Better

that, than word to Pallur—or a repeating of the things Ramdass had said in his rage. And he raised his voice once more, shrilly.

"It is Yusuf, weeping for his son," said the village mothers, compassionately. "Ramdass, who hath been taken by a sickness of the wits and wandered off. Poor Yusuf! Poor Ramdass! Would that he might return and comfort his father!"

But the feet of Ramdass, fleet and strong, had already carried him away from the village of Tazhur. He was intensely angry. Lalri! Lalri! Let Yusuf excuse himself as best he might—let Pallur profess ignorance of his desires—they lied! Lalri was his, and they had given her to the Nawwab of Dahra Dun. Her little face, with its luminous eyes, her little teeth like gleaming pearls, her shy smile, her soft hands, her hair so dark and lustrous. And they had given her in marriage. . . .

RAMDASS slept that night under the shade of an oak ten miles from Tazhur. When he roused in the morning his senses came back to him. He had no money. In his excitement he had forgotten the canvas sack that held his savings and his earnings. It was lost indeed, by this time being in his father's possession. But he had one fixed notion in his mind. He was going to Dahra Dun.

Now this was the sheerest sort of lunacy. There was not the slightest chance of making the journey safely. He might beg a few grains of rice on the road and at night find a place to sleep free from the claws of wild beasts. But how to cross the stretch of sandy dry desert that lay between? No caravan would let him join it without payment.

With the rash courage of youth he would not think of that. He must reach

Dahra Dun. He went through village after village. People were carelessly kind, and he did not starve, nor was he ever refused a night's shelter. Curious, they asked him whither he was bound, and when he told them they looked at him, open-mouthed. How could he cross to Dahra Dun? He was alone, on foot. One could not enter the desert so.

"Foolish youth!" cried out the old men. "The desert has no pity. It can not give thee food or water. Why dost thou go to Dahra Dun? From all we hear the Nawwab is a harsh master. Turn back once more to thine own village, and make glad the eyes of thy father."

Ramdass laughed. In the morning he was gone. So far the road had been easy —but the desert! Only a fool indeed would attempt to cross it as he was do-ing—with a few dry cakes and a tiny flask of water. He was indeed the stub-born-headed. But never, never should it be said that Ramdass of Tazhur set out for Dahra Dun and failed to accomplish his end! He plodded on, a bleak, scrawny figure. Not even the romantic Sahiba would have detected the slightest resem-blance to a prince in his thin features. The thing that bothered him most, how-ever, was his head. At times it left his shoulders and went soaring up into the air—ten—twe ty—fifty feet above him. That was nothing for a head to do, he thought, complainingly. He needed it nearer. At the end of the third day all water and food were gone and his head was farther away than ever. So he lay down in the sand, and made a pillow of his arms. In the morning, he told him-self he would lie there until his head returned. . . .

He fell asleep. He was roused after a little while. Men were talking. Laugh-ing. Cursing. There was a wailing sound, too—some one in pain or fear.

Ramdass shook himself impatiently. He had had a dream—and now he was back in Tazhur. But no! The wailing grew more shrill. Rising from his hollowed couch of sand he saw what had hap-pened. A camel-driver—one—an old man, was crouched beside his beast and two sturdy vagabonds stood over him, beating him. With a shriek, Ramdass rose, tottered forward, waving his arms —and when the two heard that dreadful sound and saw that fearful apparition, evolved as it were from the very air, they shouted with terror. Taking to their heels with loud cries of *"Shaitan! Al Shaitan!"* they threw their clubs away. The old man lifting his head was equally horror-stricken.

"Who art thou? Harm me not! I am but a poor trader. Never have I done evil to any one——"

"Hush," said Ramdass. "Do not fear —I am a creature like thyself. I would drink. Hast thou water?"

"Water thou shalt have, my deliverer, and food if thou art in need. Thou hast saved my life. May Allah reward thee."

Ramdass drank thirstily, ate sparingly. In the blinding light of the desert moon the old man watched him without speak-ing.

"What art thou called and whither art thou bound?" asked the youth at length.

"I am called Abdul the merchant and I am going to Dahra Dun," he answered.

"It is fate," murmured Ramdass. "I, too, am going to Dahra Dun."

"And thy party?" faltered Abdul. "Where is thy beast, thy——"

"None have I," replied Ramdass. "I am alone. Thou wilt take pity on me, and I, in turn, shall protect thee. Why did the robbers attack?"

"They sought gold—I have no gold. Naught but a few poor yards of silk and some worthless trinkets——"

"I see," mused Ramdass. He looked at Abdul scrutinizingly. "Yet thy turban seemeth over-large—nay, fear me not, my friend! I am no thief such as those who have left us. I am going to Dahra Dun—and will share the road with thee."

"For which I am grateful," murmured old Abdul a little sardonically. Gratitude was a good thing—though to be saddled with this scarecrow for four long days and five longer nights—surely gratitude need not reach so far? While Ramdass composed himself to sleep in the shadow of the camel's hump—this time knowing that he would rise on the morrow and that he would surely reach Dahra Dun.

IT HAPPENED SO. For two days the youth spoke little, but gathered strength from the food that was portioned out to him, the grain and dried cheese and figs and frequent cups of water. Once more his head had fastened itself securely to his shoulders and no longer soared a hundred feet above him. On the third day the camel sickened— and would have died but for his ministrations. A camel had sickened so when he was with the Sahib Morton and he watched a wise man cure it.

Withal Abdul had no friendship for him. He begrudged him his food. Though there had been plenty for one man, there was a lack when two were fed. Yet he dared not refuse, and it was with joy that he hailed the end of the journey. With the camel in health they would have made the city before the gates closed. Unfortunately they were too late and had to camp outside. Ramdass seated himself coolly, his gaze fastened on the blue sky above them, his arms thrown upward, back of him, his head resting against them.

"Tomorrow we part, Abdul. I thank thee for thy kindness to me."

"Thou hast rendered me equal kindness," said Abdul, grudgingly.

"Ay. I saved thee from the robbers, and I healed thy camel."

"I am in thy debt."

"No debt thou canst not pay."

Instantly Abdul was on the defensive, cautious, suspicious.

"In what manner, son of strength?" he demanded.

"One gold piece from thy hidden store. Just one, Abdul."

"One gold piece?" groaned Abdul. "Knowest thou not the robbers took the little coin I owned? Would that they had not! Gladly should I bestow one upon thee, noble friend."

"Spare thy words, Abdul. My sight is keen. When I have saved thee so much canst thou not spare a portion willingly?"

"This is idle speech," whined Abdul. "Why dost thou talk so foolishly?"

Ramdass was silent then—and Abdul feared his silence. Shivering and weary he dared not close his eyes, and Ramdass, evidently, needed no sleep. It was a bitter hour for the miserly camel-driver. He knew that the request of the young man had not been casually made, and he was apprehensive of danger. Then Ramdass, still with glance turned upward, began to sing, under his breath.

"She is so fair, my gazelle . . .
  Her eyes are like the rays of the moon, searching out the secret places of my heart,
Filling them with silver ecstasy.
Hold me close, sweet rays,
Lest I perish and die of joy."

No sound from Abdul—but his gaze was open and watchful.

"Her loveliness is that of the morning,
Red her lips as the day-dawn—
Her little feet, like small white clouds,
Drift lightly above me . . ."

Abdul growled.

"Save thy songs," he said. "Save thy songs for those who would listen."

"Thou wouldst not, Abdul?"

"Nay."

"Then I shall leave thee. For I am happy, and I must sing. Beyond the gates is Dahra Dun, and the beloved of my heart. Tomorrow I shall breathe the same air that she breathes———"

"A woman! Faugh!"

"Thou hast never loved a woman?"

"I have loved many women."

"Not as much as I love one."

Abdul broke into cackling laughter. "Let me tell thee something. Thou art denied this woman———"

Ramdass started abruptly, and Abdul pointed a derisive finger. "Eh? I have hit it! Thou canst not have this woman, else the flame should not burn so high. And mark me—'twill burn low and blow out the more quickly once she is in thine arms."

"That is very sad, Abdul."

"Life is sad. But the love of man for woman is the saddest thing of all."

"And why?"

"Because it doth promise much and come to nothing, young fool."

"A young fool hath time to mend, an old one remaineth ever in his folly."

"Thou wilt not find me foolish."

"No? But the guards—alas!—when they come out tomorrow morning will discover a poor camel-driver beside his lean beast. And the camel-driver will have found the end of his journey. Here will lie the husk that once covered a noble soul, and that soul will be at rest for ever in the royal courts of paradise."

"Thou wouldst murder me?" shrilled Abdul.

"Like that." Ramdass snapped his fingers. "A click—one—'twill not hurt thee. I am skilful. No one has ever yet complained of the way I do my work."

"Thou———"

"For the sake of one small coin? If I crack thy neck I will take all."

Abdul shivered. There was menace in that light tone.

"How can I believe thee? How can I know thou wilt go in peace if I meet thy demand?"

"On the word of a lover who hath need of that coin to appear in seemly garments before his beloved. Hast no sympathy with a man in love, Abdul?"

"I have no sympathy with a thief in love."

"Poor old one! Every lover is a thief, and so am I. Once the warm blood flowed within thy veins—are there no sweet memories of stolen hours?"

"Will one piece of gold suffice?" asked Abdul, sourly.

"One piece of gold, and my wits," smiled the young man, gayly. "Tell me. Knowest thou aught of this Nawwab who rules Dahra Dun?"

The camel-driver spat.

"I have no love for thee, Ramdass— but I cherish thee like a brother when I consider this Nawwab."

"Is it so? Why dost thou hate him?"

"He is cruel, he is a taskmaster, a usurer, a———"

"He hath a beautiful ruby in his possession and I go to steal it."

Abdul laughed.

"Now I know thee for a worse than fool. Thou couldst no more reach the Nawwab's jewels than thou couldst touch the moon."

"To do it I need thy gold piece," said Ramdass, calmly, and Abdul groaned.

"I shall give it thee, I promise. Wait. Wait until the dawn."

"Oh, he!" ridiculed Ramdass. "Until the dawn, thou sayest? With the guards awake and people everywhere and thou shouting thief, thief! at the top of thy

lungs? Now. Into my hand, now—or
else———"

Abdul moaned and wept and moaned
again, as if in agony. The tears flowed
down his cheeks, but Ramdass was im-
perturbable. So, carefully, slowly, grudgingly, he abstracted a coin from his well-
lined turban.

"Here it is for thee, thou robber of the
ancient," he groaned.

"I take it neither as a gift nor as an
alms," said Ramdass, with emphasis, "but
as my just due for saving thee and thy
goods from a band of thieves, and for
saving thy camel when it lay at the point
of death. Look to it, Abdul. Let naught
tempt thee to place complaint against me
before a magistrate or I shall call upon
thee in the presence of all men to prove
thine ingratitude."

Abdul growled under his breath.

" 'Tis thine. I do not grudge it thee."

"For thy benefaction I render thee my
homage," returned Ramdass, politely.

THE coin was his, his business done.
He was finished with Abdul. Toward
morning the old man fell into a troubled
sleep and when he awoke Ramdass was
gone; for which Abdul thanked his gods
most fervently and went in, when the
gates opened, to the bazar of his cousin.
There he unloaded his wares, telling
meanwhile a wondrous story of adventure, of being beset by thieves, of how
he captured one—a stripling—and made
him act as his servant and his slave, even
to the gates of Dahra Dun, where, heed-
ing his piteous cries and plaints, he released him! 'Twas too bad Ramdass
never heard that tale!

But by this time Ramdass had forgotten Abdul. He changed the gold piece,
haggled with it, bought himself some de-
cent garments and once more appeared
as the "princely youth" of the Sahiba's

praising. Then, boldly, he approached
the steward of the Nawwab's household.
He could keep accounts, he said, being
educated at a school of the *Inglesi*, and
he added, meaningly, that his way of
keeping these accounts would please the
most exacting steward. Fortunately, a
post was vacant—but Thakur, the steward, regretted that he had promised it to
another. Whereupon Ramdass drew forth
the coins that were left to him and placed
them in a little heap on the steward's
table. So how could Thakur deny the
post to the better man?

Though Ramdass thus praised his own
ability he had really obtained a better education than most during his years at the
Government school of Tazhur. To keep
the accounts in order, so that Thakur
made good profit, to go to market occa-
sionally, to run errands—to be observant,
polite, attentive—could one expect more?
But more was given, for Ramdass was im-
maculate, and his fine features, his splendid head, his erect bearing won comment
here as they had done in his native village. Ere long the Nawwab himself noticed him.

Now, though the other servants were
filled with envy, Thakur gave him encouragement. Yes, Thakur was more
than kind to Ramdass—Ramdass knew
not why, Ramdass cared less. For he had
met old Kala. He made himself known
to her, and through her sent messages to
his beloved, his beautiful ruby—Lalri,
who was for ever veiled from him unless
the fates were kind. He knew that her
eyes were often fastened upon him, and
that from behind the screen that looked
down from the women's quarters on the
Nawwab's court she watched him lov-
ingly.

Old Kala brought his tender words to
Meri Lal—and they lost nothing of their
sweetness thus conveyed. She brought

back, too, her shy questions and small endearments. Old Kala was in a heaven of delight. This intrigue was breath of life to her. It made her important. She was aglow with terror and pride. Existence had been so dull, and like all her type she gloried in this subtle feeding of a flame, too stupid to realize whither it was leading her and her young mistress.

But Lalri knew.

"Ramdass must go away," she said, fearfully. "We are surrounded by spies —at any moment we may be discovered, and then what will be our fate? The Lady Shereen, the Nawwab's consort, hates me, is jealous of me. I live in terror of her. She would gladly see thee beaten to death and me thrown into the river. Tell Ramdass if he loves me truly as he says he will go away."

Ramdass laughed at Kala.

"I came three hundred miles to get one glimpse of Meri Lal," he said. "I incurred my father's anger. I crossed the desert, I starved, I thirsted. My heart is on fire with love. Shall it burn unquenched for ever?"

"Lalri fears. Shereen is powerful and the mother of the Nawwab's sons. Should she learn aught——"

"How can she learn? Who can tell her?" questioned Ramdass. "Look, Kala. Tell Meri Lal that we shall meet and have our hour of love together. It is written. Only then shall I leave this house."

"Thou art crazed," said Kala. "An hour with Lalri? How may that ever be? How may that be done?"

"Wise Kala, I leave it all to thee. Thou art a woman," flattered Ramdass. "Thou hast loved and been loved. Think back upon those days and help us now."

"No, no, no," protested Kala, and went away. Ramdass, later, found the eyes of Thakur fixed upon him benevolently.

"Why art thou so kind to that old witch, Kala?" he asked. "I have seen her near thee of late, Ramdass. She is from a far-off village, Tazhur, by name, and not of Dahra Dun."

"Kala?" asked Ramdass, blankly, and Thakur put a gentle hand on his shoulder.

"To me it matters not. I am thy friend. But talk not to her more than thou canst help when others are near. She is a maker of mischief," he said. He paused; then, thoughtfully: Ramdass, hast thou a father living? I should like to take up matters of importance with him. There is a certain man who hath made note of thee—and is pleased with all that thou dost. This man hath a daughter——"

"I see," said Ramdass, slowly. "Ay, Thakur, I have a father—but he and my nearest kin are hundreds of miles away. As for marriage—I am not ready yet. Presently, when I have money enough for the wedding gifts——"

"Ah, but thou art as wise as thou art thrifty," declared Thakur. "I shall come to the matter again. She is beautiful, this girl of whom I speak, a young virgin, fairer than Lady Shereen herself, or perhaps . . . the little ruby . . . that the Nawwab brought with him so recently. . . ."

Was there menace or warning in that hesitating sentence? Ramdass could not tell.

"I am the lowest in my master's house," he said, "and I know naught of the value of his possessions, nor whence their origin. I agree with thee, however, that I should wed. Give me time to lay by enough to do all things decently and honorably and we shall talk of this again."

Thakur's face beamed upon him.

"Agreed!" he said.

WHEN Kala came the young man was impatient.

"Soon, soon," he urged. "I tell thee, Kala, I shall die of longing. Is there no way?"

Kala could do naught but shake her head. To Lalri she brought his message.

"He loves thee, Meri Lal," she mumbled, "but he asks the impossible. One hour with thee! Ah, weep not, little one, weep not! Let Kala think, let Kala think——"

All Kala's thinking could not accomplish this, but Fate stooped down, the moving finger wrote. Messengers came to the Nawwab. There was to be a great religious ceremony at Krishnalur. Many nobles were to be present, but unless the Nawwab of Dahra Dun attended all would be flat, stale and worthless! So the great man prepared to make the journey. The powerful Shereen, the Nawwab's principal wife, would have little leisure now for the pettier details of the women's quarters, for she, too, was to accompany her lord.

"We shall see, we shall see," exulted Kala, when she heard this news.

"We dare not," breathed Lalri.

"It will be something to remember all thy life."

"That life will be over-short if we are discovered."

"What is death?" asked Kala. "Not dying. It is to live to be like me—old and toothless and wrinkled and undesired. That is death."

"Oh!" said Lalri, looking at her strangely. "Old and toothless and wrinkled and undesired. That is death. Kala, I hate the Nawwab and all that is his—this house—this place—these people. And I love Ramdass."

"That I know."

"My happiness depends not on the prince but on Shereen, upon her whim, who is the mother of sons, and is far more beautiful than I. Should I have no sons and grow old, then that will be death"—her voice shook—"while far away in our little village of Tazhur, Ramdass will wed another and be happy and forget Lalri."

"'Tis true," agreed Kala. "'Tis true. What else? What is a woman but the creature of a man and the slave of his impulses? Hast not learned the lesson?"

Tears surged hotly to those young and glowing eyes.

"I am thrice thy age," went on the relentless old voice. "I was given in marriage to the headman of our village. I bore two children—daughters—and he cursed me, and my mother-in-law cursed me. I was a slave. The headman died, and I was thrice accursed in that my sins had deprived me of a husband and his mother of her son! I went then with mine own kin, into my father's household. I have had no man travel three hundred miles to look upon my face or beg an hour of my friendship. Would that I had! 'Twould be sweet to enshrine in my memory now."

Lalri shivered. Her eyes were tragic, her lips drooped.

"I should be glad, but oh, I fear! I fear! I love him and I fear."

"When Shereen hath departed," exulted Kala.

SHEREEN went, and the Nawwab went, and silence fell on the Nawwab's household. Vigilance relaxed and Thakur was indulgent with Ramdass. Thus it chanced that paradise encompassed the gardens of the Nawwab. Birds sang more brilliantly than birds had ever sung, flowers bloomed more richly and gave forth sweeter perfume. The moon trailed her glory across the radiant sky and the stars laughed over the happiness of lovers.

Hours of delight, followed by brief partings. Days of dreaming, nights of fulfilled desire. . . . And then the shadow on the sun, the muting of the note that throbbed with ecstasy.

In two days the Nawwab would return—but worse, far worse, was the knowledge that had penetrated into the consciousness of Ramdass. He said naught of it to Lalri until they met for the last time—and then he told her.

"I think," he said, "that Thakur knows."

Lalri struggled from his arms.

"What sayest thou?"

"I think, Meri Lal, that Thakur suspects us both—and even now the Nawwab is on his homeward way."

Lalri's eyes were wide and luminous.

"This is our last hour, Ramdass. I shall not see thee again."

"Nor I thee, beloved."

"I knew it had to end, dear one." She wreathed her arms about his neck and laid her cheek to his. "But I shall have my dreams for ever."

"Meri Lal!" his lips sought hers.

"If Thakur knows—he will tell."

"Perhaps."

"What wilt thou do?"

"I have not thought."

"But I have. Here is one parting gift for thee." She fumbled at her silken belt and drew out a filigree box. Opening it, she displayed two tiny vials filled with golden liquid.

"One for thee and one for me, Ramdass," she said gayly. "I have had them since I came to Dahra Dun—and now I share my happiness."

"What is it?" he asked, as she pressed the vial into his hand.

"Our armor against the vengeance of the Nawwab," she whispered. "Oh, Ramdass, to live and to remember these past days! To wake and know I shall

never see thee again! To lie in another's arms, and feel another's lips on mine! Ramdass, soon I can not bear it—and when I can not——"

"Meri Lal, if I could take thee far from here——"

"Hush!" She put her hand across his mouth. "The lash for thee! The thong with iron tips! Or prison for all thy life —these may yet be thy portion. Thou art going from me—but I shall come to thee again, some day——"

"It is time," whispered Kala, at the door.

Ramdass arose. His face was troubled.

"Go, lover," urged Kala.

"Not yet, not yet," implored Lalri.

"I must, Meri Lal, I must." He kissed her and vanished. Love had gone, and Lalri was alone. Alone with her memories of stolen hours. . . . Kala lifted her in her strong arms and placing her on a couch began to chafe her hands and feet. Presently the girl struggled up.

"Kala," she said, "men never die of love."

"Nay, my sweet."

"But a woman could."

"And does—often."

"Ramdass leaves me. He will not return. He has possessed me, yet he will go back to our Tazhur and wed another and she will be the mother of his sons——"

"My pigeon, my little one, my dove with the gleaming eyes," soothed Kala. "Ramdass will not return to our village, ever, nor wed a maid there."

"Thou sayest that as if—as if . . . dost mean it truly, Kala?"

"Truly, little dove. Thakur is giving him his daughter. For years hath the steward been trying to find her a husband, but all men balked at her ugly features and crooked form. Thakur, at last, hath overcome his disgrace and is wedding his miserable one to the handsomest lad in Dahra Dun."

Lalri's face was frightening.

"Kala, Thakur knows—Thakur knows, and Ramdass . . . oh, my beloved is paying the price to save me and thee! Thakur *knows*."

She sank back then, and covered her eyes from the fear-stricken old woman.

ON THE morrow Ramdass was to wed Raina, the daughter of Thakur. It was indeed the price of Thakur's silence and he would pay it with equanimity. He was a lover, a poet, but he was also a philosopher—and if Thakur's daughter meant that he kept his honorable place in the Nawwab's household, then Thakur's daughter it must be. He had never seen the maiden, but descriptions were not wanting. Thakur had shown him favors and would show him more. He had seen to it that Ramdass was given many ways of earning money. If he continued thus, Raina's ugliness need not bother him. He might even be able to buy a camel—or open a bazar—he would spend weeks away, and any woman—any woman—could be the mother of sons. What mattered how she looked?

He thought of Lalri. Lalri, his little love, whom he must forget. The hour of madness was over . . . Lalri . . . who belonged to the Nawwab of Dahra Dun . . .

He slipped his hand into his sleeve and took, from its inner hem, a tiny vial. She had given him—this. He held it in the palm of his hand. The liquid within it gleamed like gold. He fingered it, smiling sadly. Lalri . . . Lalri . . . her little feet, like soft white clouds . . .

And then the room changed subtly. He was in the gardens of the Nawwab. A bird cheeped sleepily. The scent of the roses smote upon his nostrils . . . and she was in his arms, her head upon his breast, and one cool soft hand upon his wrist.

"Drink, my beloved," whispered the sweet voice, so faint, so gentle, so alluring. " 'Tis a sweet potion. Drink."

Nay, nay! He was Ramdass, who the Sahiba had said was handsome as a prince! Ramdass, who on the morrow was to wed Thakur's daughter—and buy camels—and grow rich trading. . . .

"No," he muttered. "It shall not be. I am to wed——"

" 'Tis Lalri, thy beloved. I have taken the draft of death and come to thee. Beyond us is the Scented Dusk, the road of the Great Stars, the Path of the Moon. 'Tis Lalri calling—thy beloved——"

"No, no!" He thought he shouted the word, though it was the merest whisper. There was fear in his heart, drops of perspiration on his forehead. But he had no strength against the strength of that little hand. The vial reached his lips and the gold within it ate into his vitals.

NO ONE dreamed of associating the death of Lalri, the Nawwab's lovely plaything, with that of Ramdass, the steward's assistant, soon to be his son-in-law. Thakur knew. And Kala knew. But both kept the secret for ever.

Furlough

By EDGAR DANIEL KRAMER

Though I walk with Nan or Nelly
  Out of Chelsea to the Strand,
With 'em cuddlin' close an' smilin',
  While they're clingin' to my 'and;
Though the streets are jammed with people
  'Urryin' to work an' play,
Blind to all the 'elterskelter,
  Lord, I'm miles an' miles away,
For I'm ridin' through the desert
  With the red sun sizzlin' down,
With the shiftin' sands like jewels
  In the Queen of Sheba's crown,
With the mirages recedin'
  Back into the blindin' glare,
Till I'm sightin' palm trees liftin'
  Through the palpitatin' air,
Beckonin' like tremblin' fingers
  To the wells, whose waters wait,
An' the camels, mincin' forward,
  Put some speed into their gait.

Though I'm takin' Sue an' Sarah
  To the pictures an' the 'alls,
With 'em whisperin' the Bow Bells
  Always echo old St. Paul's;
Though the rumble of the traffic
  Flings itself against the stars,
Shoutin', curses, sobbin', laughter
  Mingled with the clang of cars,
Lord, I'm deaf to all the clatter,
  For I'm sprawlin' at my ease
By the sunken wells of Obak,
  While the night wind in the trees
Brings the callin' of a jackal,
  An' wide-eyed the camels stir,
Till I pacify their feelin's
  An' they go back as they were,
While I'm laughin' at the cities,
  'Uddled 'eaps of cruel stones,
For you can't be 'appy elsewhere,
  When the desert's in your bones.

Kaldar, World of Antares

By EDMOND HAMILTON

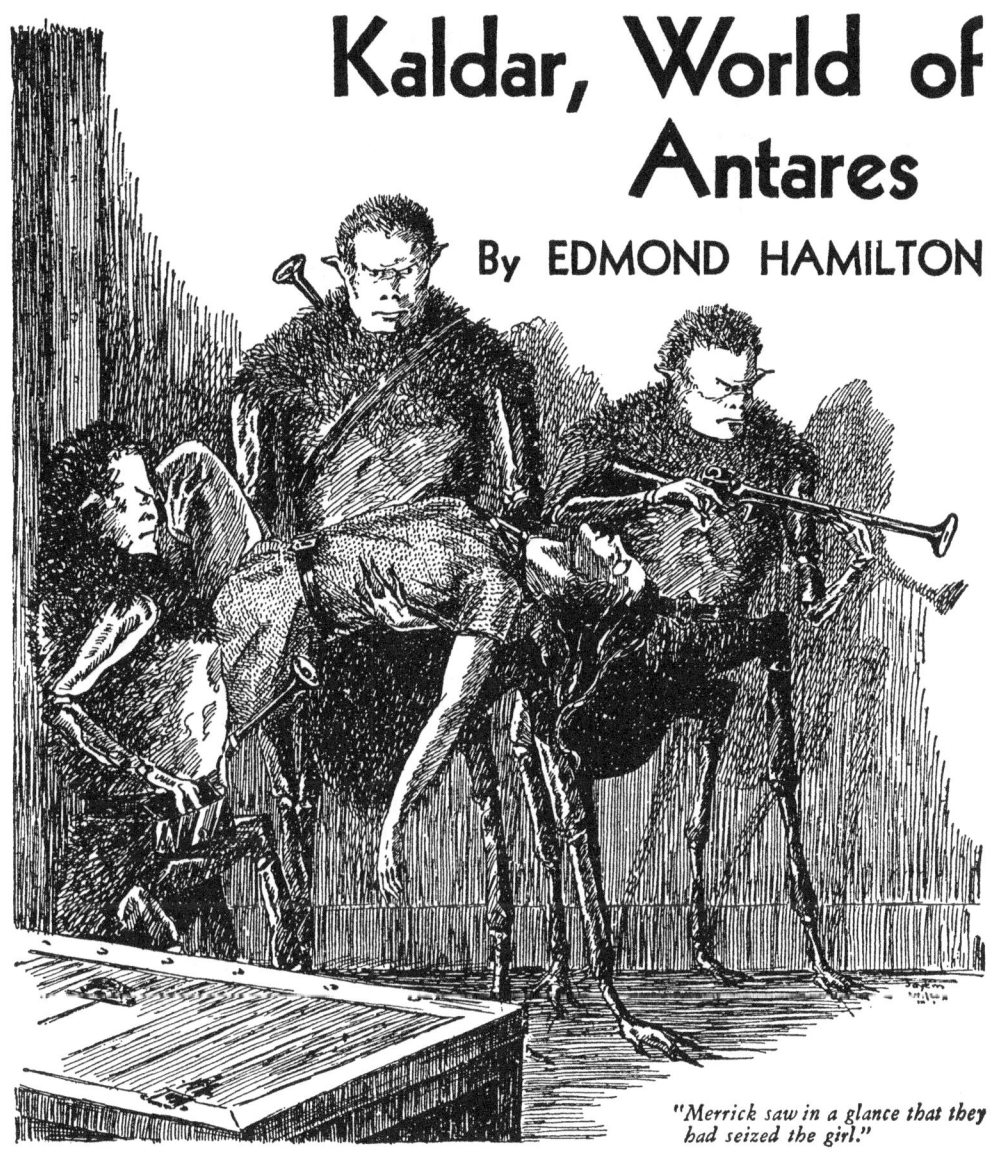

"Merrick saw in a glance that they had seized the girl."

A stupendous novelette of a world far removed from Earth, of the Chan of Kaldar, and the spider-people from beyond the metal mountains

1. The Start

"YOU will find yourself, if you accept, on another world!"

Stuart Merrick half rose from his chair in amazement at the statement, but the nine men who faced him across the long table did not move. He searched their faces as though to discover some sign that they were joking, but found none. All were men of middle age or over, of serious, scholastic type, and the one who had spoken was an elderly man with iron-gray hair and eyes like swordpoints.

They were all watching Merrick intently. He was perhaps half their average

age, a rather shabbily dressed dark-haired young man whose deceptively lean figure held muscles that only the broad shoulders hinted. His dark eyes were the eyes of a dreamer, but in the tanned face and set of the cleft chin strength was evident.

"On another world," the speaker repeated. "If that statement frightens you, say so now and save our time."

"It doesn't," Merrick answered evenly, "but it interests me a great deal."

"Very well," the other said crisply. "You possess the qualifications which our advertisement mentioned?"

"I think I do," Merrick answered. "Adventurous disposition, education, lack of family connections, indigence — yes, you have them all in me, especially the indigence."

"So much the better," the other calmly told him. "It is unnecessary that you learn our names, but I may say that we nine are probably the nine greatest astronomers and astro-physicists now living. Our advertisement was inserted because we need the help of some younger and more adventurous person to aid us in an investigation we have planned for some years. That is nothing less than the personal exploration of a world of one of the fixed stars!

"That may possibly seem to you an insane statement. It is not. Five years ago we nine determined upon it. Astronomers know almost all there is to know about the planets of our own sun, our own solar system. We know their temperatures, have mapped their surfaces, have charted their orbits. But what of the other suns, the unthinkably distant fixed stars? Around them too revolve great worlds, more calculated to be the abode of life than our own neighbor-planets.

"The telescope and spectroscope can show us but little of those worlds of the distant stars, save that they exist. The only way in which we will ever gain knowledge concerning any of these worlds is for a man to visit it. Of course no rocket or projectile that we could devise could ever cross the gulf to the nearest of the stars. But we have worked for five years on the problem and have found a way of bridging that gulf, of sending a living man across the void to one of the stars and of bringing him back.

"Briefly, our way is to split up the body of the chosen man into the electrons that compose it, and of using a terrific vibratory beam to drive those electrons together out toward the star or world decided on. An electron, a mere tiny particle of electricity, can travel faster than anything in the universe, with sufficient force behind it. Our projector's force-beam drives the dissembled electrons of that man out to the world of any star in moments only. On reaching that world, the projector's force halting, the electrons will combine instantly again into the living man.

"In the same way, if the projector's force were reversed, and if the man were to stay in the same spot on that distant world, the beam would reach across the gulf and in an instant decompose his body into electrons, draw those electrons back through the void to earth in a moment, and there recompose them instantly into the man again. Thus our projector can send a man without harm out to the farthest star and can reach out to bring him back again.

"We have chosen a world of the great red star Antares to investigate first. Antares is technically a red giant among stars, a huge sun of great age. Around it revolves at least one great world our telescopes and spectroscopes have glimpsed, and it is of that world that we want first to learn, whether it is habitable and whether it holds intelligent life.

"We are all too old and unfitted for

such a venture as this, however, and the death of any of us would be, all modesty aside, a loss to science. You, however, are young and adventurous and seem to answer all requirements. We will project you out to this world of Antares in the way that I have described, and when we draw you back to earth if you can give any information on conditions there we will pay you one hundred thousand dollars. The risks of it are self-evident. Do you accept?"

Merrick drew a long breath. "Another world—another star! But where on that world would I find myself when your projector sent me there?"

"There is no way of knowing," was the calm answer. "You might find yourself in the center of an ocean or in the pit of a volcano or even on an airless world where you would be instantly asphyxiated. It is a great gamble, for we know nothing more about that world than that it exists. It is to know more that we want to send someone to it."

"And when would I return?"

"In three days. If you survived on reaching this world you would note the exact spot where you found yourself and in three days at the same hour would take that position. Our projector, stabbing its beam across the gulf to that spot with reversed force, would draw you back as dissembled electrons to the earth."

Merrick considered silently. The room was still, the ticking of a clock unnaturally loud. A faint murmur of noise came from the night activities of the city outside.

Suddenly Merrick rose to his feet. "I accept," he said quickly. "But with one condition."

"And that is?" asked the other anxiously.

"That I start tonight—now!"

The nine scientists showed their astonishment. "Now?"

There was a grin on Merrick's tanned face. "Now or never. If I sit around thinking this thing over it's a thousand to one I'll back out on it. You can send me out tonight?"

"We can, yes," the spokesman of the nine answered, "though we hadn't expected to do so. The condensers have been charging for weeks and all is ready. But you'll want to take equipment with you—that will take time to gather."

Merrick shook his head. "Nothing but an automatic, enough food for the week, and different clothes than these. Other equipment would be useless; for if I couldn't live on that world three days without it, it's ten to one I couldn't live there with it either."

"He is right," one of the scientists interjected.

"Then we can have the things you mention ready at once," the spokesman of the nine said.

He turned, gave quick orders, and in a moment the nine had snapped into activity, disappearing into the rear and lower parts of the building, hurrying excitedly.

MERRICK heard the clash and rumble of great objects being moved, caught the whine of dynamos or motors from somewhere beneath. The building that had been so silent was suddenly alive, a buzz of excited voices and rush of hurrying steps echoing through it.

Merrick heard other heavy objects being shifted, voices calling directions. A moment later the elderly spokesman of the scientists brought in to him a suit of rough khaki clothing, a heavy automatic, and a small knapsack that held concentrated foods. Merrick donned these quickly. He felt his spirits rising as he did so, the feel of the weapon and rough clothing familiar to him. A synchronized watch completed the outfit.

When he had them on, Merrick stepped with a sudden whim to one of the room's windows and raised a blind. Outside and beneath in the darkness lay a city street, its curb-lights a double lane of white luminescence through which rolled a golden stream of auto headlamps. Crowds of evening pleasure-seekers jammed the walks. Merrick stared thoughtfully.

The hand of the scientists' leader on his shoulder brought him around.

"All is ready," the other said. "You start at two exactly."

Merrick nodded and followed him through a door into the rear portion of the building. It was a long white-lit laboratory whose roof had been slid aside in some way; only the black night sky was overhead. Masses of unfamiliar apparatus were in the room, but most prominent was the object at its center, a low square platform of metal resting on squat concrete piers. From its sides led heavy, black-cased cables.

These wound through bewildering tangles of wiring to the massed apparatus. One whole wall was occupied by huge condensers resting in a metal rack. There was other apparatus beyond Merrick's recognition, coils and enigmatic cases. Guarding rails of black insulation circled the apparatus everywhere, protecting from its terrific electrical force. On one wall was a large switch-panel.

His guide touched a switch and the lights in the room died. As darkness engulfed them, Merrick saw for the first time that the black sky overhead was gemmed with countless burning stars. Some were calm green and others golden-yellow, others still with the blue of living sapphires. But southwestward from the zenith swung one that was fiery red, a great crimson eye winking and twinkling across the void.

"Antares," said the other quietly. "In moments, if all goes well, you will be upon its world."

Merrick gazed. "What's waiting up there for me—I wonder——"

The other motioned to the platform. "The projector," he said simply. "It is almost two."

"I just stand on the platform?" Merrick inquired, and the other nodded.

"Yes, and at exactly two the force-beam will project you outward. You ought to find yourself almost instantly on that world of Antares. Three days from now at two exactly you must be again at the same spot there, so that the projector's beam can draw you back across the void. Good-bye, and good luck."

Merrick shook the hand extended, then turned and stepped onto the low platform. Through the room's darkness he could see the other's dark figure at the switch-panel, could hear him calling directions to the others as they changed connections quickly. The throb of the dynamos had become terrific and Merrick, his thoughts kaleidoscopic, wondered if they were not audible in the street outside.

His eyes were on the dark figure at the switch-panel. Merrick saw him jerk over three switches in quick succession, then shift a rheostat arm. He was just turning to look upward when another switch clicked at the panel. As it did so Merrick felt incredible forces flooding through him, shaking him in every atom, and with a thunder in his ears the dark laboratory passed from around him and he was hurled into blackness.

2. Kaldar, World of Antares

THROUGH that black unconsciousness Merrick seemed to flash but for instants before out of the blackness there sprang again light. There was a sharp shock that jarred him through, the thunder in his ears receded, and then, staggering, he was looking about him in stupefaction.

From above a blaze of light and heat beat upon him and as he raised his eyes he could have cried out. For in the sky above there burned such a sun as Merrick never had imagined, not the familiar golden sun of earth but a colossal crimson sun whose arc filled a third of the heavens and whose dazzling brilliance half blinded him! Antares, that mighty sun, and he was upon its world!

He lowered his eyes, looked about him. His brain reeled.

Around him there stretched the looming buildings of a mighty city. Giant pyramids of black metal they were, sky-storming structures with terraced sides. Far around him lay the mighty city's mass, broken by wide black streets and a single great circular plaza. At the plaza's center rose a small round dais of black metal and on it Merrick was standing. And crowded in the plaza around the dais were thousands on thousands of awe-struck, silent people!

They were people such as Merrick had never seen before. They were tall and dark of hair and white of skin, though with a ruddy tint that the red sunlight explained. Each of them, men and women alike, wore a short flexible garment of black metal woven like chainmail, reaching from shoulders to knees. Each of the men wore in a belt around this a sheathed sword of long, rapier-like design and a short metal tube with a bulging handle or stock.

Merrick stared stupefiedly at them from the central dais on which he alone stood, and for a moment utter silence held the vast throng. Then from them there burst suddenly a tremendous shout.

O. S.—**7**

They were pointing up to him in the wildest excitement and crying to each other. Merrick, half stunned by his transition to this strange world and strange city, caught of their cries the one word "Chan! Chan!" repeated over and over. The place was a wild bedlam of maddest excitement. Merrick, dazed by the wild uproar his sudden appearance on this world had created, was hardly aware of more than that he had reached his goal.

Out of the madly shouting throng there sprang toward the dais a single man, great and black-bearded, fury on his face. He jerked from his sheath a long, slender sword of metal as he leaped, and the sword shone with white light all along its blade the moment after he drew it. With the shining sword in hand he was charging toward the dais when others caught him and held him back. Merrick's automatic was in his hand by then and he remained on the dais despite the incomprehensible uproar.

Suddenly out of the throng another figure pushed close to the dais, a single one that he saw was a girl. Tall almost as himself she was, her slim figure sheathed from shoulders to knees by the black metal garment. Her piled hair was as black as the metal, and beneath it her dark eyes were wide with amazement as she stared up at Merrick. She turned from him then, flung up a hand, and the huge throng quickly quieted.

She spoke quickly to the throng. The black-bearded man interrupted, pointing to Merrick and seeming to urge something, but the girl shook her head decisively and haughtily. Merrick saw her pointing up to him on the dais and repeating the word "Chan." When she ended he was stunned, for there flashed up into the air thousands of shining swords and these rolled toward him a shattering shout of "Chan!"

Merrick waited tensely for developments. He saw by now that he had been
flung into some strange situation among
these people of Antares' world. A double
file of sword-armed men approached the
dais and he stiffened.

The girl seemed to comprehend his
doubt. She came forward, extended a
hand as though motioning him down
beside her. Merrick met her eyes, then
stepped unhesitatingly down to her side.
She said something to him in her low,
musical voice, but seeing that he still did
not understand, pointed simply toward
one of the great pyramids at the plaza's
edge, one that seemed greatest of all in
the city.

They started toward it, the double file
of armed men on either side. Merrick's
eyes clashed with those of the black-
bearded man for a moment as they
passed. The guards pushed a way through
the wildly shouting throng that surged
on all sides about them. The whole thing
seemed still an unconnected sequence of
unreal events to the astounded Merrick.

As they neared the high portal of the
great black pyramid, Merrick looked in
awe about him. Far along the city's
streets he could glimpse hastening
throngs, and overhead flying-craft of some
kind came and went. It was all incredible,
unreal—this city of looming, terraced
black pyramids beneath the huge red
sun. But they were passing into the great
structure that was their goal.

They were entering a huge square hall,
ranks of armed guards drawn up about it.
The girl gave an order and the guards
dropped back. She and Merrick entered
a small metal chamber in which was one
man. This one touched a plate on the
wall, and the door clicked shut behind
them. Another touch and they seemed
crushed to the floor by infinite forces for
an instant; then the door opened again.

As they stepped out Merrick saw that the
small chamber was a super-elevator of
some sort, for they were no longer in the
lower hall of the pyramid.

They were in a big room that was at
the tip of the same building, he saw.
Great windows let in the crimson sunlight and gave a glimpse of the far-reach-
ing city outside. The girl came toward
Merrick, and now with her were two men
bearing a complicated apparatus. Its main
feature was a small generator of some
kind with intricate controls, from which
led leads ending in tiny electrodes. The
two scientists, for such they obviously
were, motioned for Merrick to lie down
on the metal bench beside him.

Merrick went cold. Until then the
sheer strangeness of events had carried
him forward, but now he halted. What
was the apparatus? Was he to be used
as some strange animal for vivisection?

The girl seemed again to comprehend
his doubt, laid a hand on his arm and
spoke reassuringly. The words meant
nothing but the tone of them was reas-
suring, and Merrick found himself thrilling to the touch of the girl's soft hand.
He mustered a grin, nodded amicably to
the two scientists, and lay face down upon
the bench. The two made quick incisions
in the back of his neck, painlessly, and
inserted the tiny electrodes.

Then they turned and Merrick heard
the soft humming of the apparatus. At
the same moment he experienced a strange
whirling of his thoughts. It seemed to
him that all his knowledge and memories
and speculations, everything in his mind,
was being changed and turned over and
crowded in chaotic fashion. The mechanism hummed on while the two fingered
its controls. When at last they turned it
off and undid the connections and withdrew, Merrick's brain ceased its chaotic
whirl.

The girl came forward eagerly as he rose. "You understand our tongue now, O Chan?" she asked. The fact stunned Merrick. The girl was speaking in her own tongue still, yet he understood her perfectly!

"But how—how is it that I can understand now?" he asked, and was aware that the strange tongue rose to his lips as easily as his own.

"It is that apparatus, the brain-changer," the girl told him. "It implants knowledge artificially into the brain. All knowledge, you know, is received by the brain as impulses through the sense-nerves, and that apparatus duplicates those impulses and sends them through the nerves into the brain artificially, received there as knowledge, giving you knowledge of our language as though you had studied it for years. On all Kaldar there are no teachers, only brain-changers."

"Convenient," muttered Merrick. "Kaldar—that is this world?"

The girl was wide-eyed. "Of course. Kaldar is the only one of our sun's worlds that is habitable, as far as we know. Surely you know that, O Chan!"

"Chan?" Merrick repeated. "They were calling me that before—what does it mean? And what is your own name?"

"I am Narna," she answered. "But surely you understand that you are Chan —Chan of Corla?"

"Corla—what's that?" Merrick asked, bewildered.

"Is it possible that you do not know?" said Narna, astonished. "Come——"

She led the way to one of the high windows. Merrick followed, looked forth upon a breath-taking scene.

From the tip of this great pyramid, a thousand feet in the air, they could look out far across the mighty city of black pyramids. Far away in all directions it stretched. Men and women thronged the streets below and jammed the great plaza, the one clear spot upon it being the round little dais at its center. Over the excited throngs and the city black, projectile-like flying-craft were rushing and dipping.

Here and there the city's black mass was laced with crimson where were parks and gardens, all filled with blood-red vegetation. Out beyond the city's edge Merrick glimpsed in the distance crimson fields, and forests or jungles. Beyond these, walling the horizon on all sides, there rose a titanic circular range of black mountains that was like a colossal, awful wall around the city and surrounding crimson country. Overhead flamed the huge crimson sun, casting its weird red light down on the whole strange scene.

"The city of Corla," said Narna. "All within the ring of the mountains we hold, against our enemies."

Merrick's dazed eyes took in the amazing scene. "Corla," he whispered. "But what then does Chan mean?"

The girl's eyes held amazement. "Do not you know, you who came out of the unknown to be Chan? It means king, lord, master! You are the Chan of Corla —the supreme ruler of this land!"

3. Chan of Corla

MERRICK, stunned, could not speak for a moment. "I—ruler?" he managed to cry at last.

"Of course," said Narna. "One month ago the last Chan of Corla, who was my father, died. After waiting until the established month had passed, the nobles and people of Corla assembled today in the great plaza to choose a new Chan as is the custom. The dais at the plaza's center is the dais of the Chan, upon which none other than he may ever step under pain of death.

"All were sure that Jhalan would be chosen as the new Chan today, for though many think him cruel and ruthless, he is a great fighter and our land is so sore pressed by its enemies that it needs such a ruler. In moments more he would have been selected, indeed, and would have ascended the dais as Chan. But there came a sudden thunder and you appeared suddenly on the dais. By your strange appearance and unfamiliar garb it was evident that you had come out of the unknown, and since it was on the dais of the Chan that you appeared it was evident that destiny had sent you to us as a new ruler. Hence you were acclaimed as Chan of Corla, and are now its ruler."

Merrick was stunned. He sought to grasp the reality of it. A day—an hour— before, he had been Stuart Merrick, penniless adventurer on earth. And now he had been hurled to another world at the one spot where his appearance had made him automatically Chan of Corla, supreme king of a great land!

His mind began to work. "Then that black-bearded man who tried to rush me on the dais——"

"That was Jhalan. He was mad with rage when you appeared, for if you had not done so he would have been chosen Chan in moments. He is furious, therefore, to lose the rulership of Corla and also to lose me."

"To lose you?" Merrick asked, and Narna smiled.

"Yes, for only the new Chan may wed the daughter of the last one. Jhalan has long desired me and that was one reason why he wanted to be Chan."

Merrick's eyes searched her face. "But it seemed to me you were espousing my cause down there rather than his?"

Narna colored. "I do not like bearded men," she said irrelevantly, then sobered. "But Jhalan will be here tonight with the rest of the Council of Twelve, the great nobles of Corla, to pledge allegiance to you as new Chan. I would try to placate him as much as possible if I were you— he is very angry and would make a very bad enemy."

Something in Merrick hardened. "If I am Chan I will rule as Chan," he answered, a strange new sense of power flooding him like wine.

Narna's eyes were steady on his. "I think that you will, and Corla needs a strong Chan now if ever it has needed one," she said. Then, as she turned toward the lift-chamber: "The Council of Twelve will be here an hour after night falls."

"And you'll come too?" Merrick pursued.

"As daughter of the last Chan I too must pledge allegiance," she rejoined, laughing, and disappeared into the lift-chamber.

THE next few hours passed in a whirl of strangeness for Merrick. Servants came, respectful and low-voiced, apparently regarding their new Chan as something of a divinity, almost. He was led through the great chambers that were his as Chan, at the pyramid's tip, to a huge bath with walls of varicolored metals. When he emerged from its steamy perfumes Corlan clothing was awaiting him, a soft undersuit of some silken material, black metal sandals, and one of the black metal tunics.

It was like all the others he had seen save that on its breast was a brilliant small red sun-disk. The red sun-disk was repeated on the walls around him, and was evidently the insignia of the Chan.

With the tunic went a belt in which were a sword and tube such as he had noticed. Merrick examined these weapons of the Corlans carefully. The sword seemed at first glance a simple long rapier of metal. But he found that when his grip tightened on the hilt it pressed a catch which released a terrific force stored in the hilt into the blade, making it shine with light. When anything was touched by this shining blade, he found, the force of the blade annihilated it instantly. He learned that the weapon was called a light-sword, due to the shining of the blade when charged, and saw that it was truly a deadly weapon, its touch alone meaning annihilation to any living thing.

The tube proved a stubby gun that shot small charges of shining force, called for a similar reason the light-gun. Its accurate range was no more than a few thousand feet, though extremely accurate within that distance. Merrick was later to learn that light-guns of cannon-size had been developed, however, with far greater range and destructive power. As it was, he reflected, any one armed with light-sword and light-gun would make a tough foe, able to fight at a distance or at close quarters with equally deadly effects.

Merrick ate the meal the servants brought, of simple cooked herbs and strong yellow wine, at a metal table beside one of the great windows. As he ate he could look out and see the huge crimson circle of Antares sinking westward, as on earth, behind the black rampart of the distant mountains, and could see the stars twinkling forth in the violet sky. They were brilliant but in strange groups and constellations, and though he recognized some of the greater stars at once, it was only after some search of the changed groups that he located the tiny yellow star that he knew to be the sun of his own solar system. With something of awe he looked at it as the darkness deepened.

Soft lights were shining out by then

over the clustered pyramids of Corla around and beneath. Merrick saw lit flying-craft coming and going, saw that they and the great crowds still beneath were drawn by his own building, thousands gazing up toward his window. He realized anew the strangeness of the destiny that had cast him into this position of power. Could he sustain his part as Chan, as ruler, into which he had been so strangely hurled?

He turned to find the great rooms softly illuminated and a servant bowing. "The Council of Twelve is here, O Chan," he announced.

Merrick summoned his resolution and stepped back into the great central room. A group of a dozen or more black-garbed figures were coming toward him from the lift-chamber. They were led by a fine-faced, white-bearded oldster, and behind him among the others, Merrick glimpsed the ironical dark eyes of Jhalan and the figure of the girl Narna. The group halted and the oldster stepped forward.

"We bring our allegiance, O Chan," he said, bowing. "We know not how or from what world you have come to us but we know that only destiny could have placed you on the dais of the Chan."

The unfamiliar new sense of power flared again in Merrick. "Since you have so chosen me Chan I accept your allegiance as such," he said. "It is from another world — another star — that I come, yes, one far different from this. In that world my name was Merrick."

"Merrick," repeated the other with an odd twist. "It is well, Chan Merrick. I am Murnal, and these the others of our Council of Twelve——"

They came forward, bowing and naming themselves, while Merrick inclined his head to each. Most of the twelve were over middle age, like Murnal. Exceptions were Holk, a great grizzled warrior topping the others by a head, and Jurul, a quiet, slender figure whom Merrick was to know later as one of the most deadly fighters of the Corlan race. Last of the twelve councillors was Jhalan. All watched closely as he stepped forward.

But the great black-bearded Corlan bowed gravely enough. Merrick saw in his black eyes as he straightened, though, a sardonic amusement, as though at some secret joke. He found his hand tight on the hilt of his light-sword as Jhalan stepped back. He relaxed as Narna followed the twelve, her clear eyes on his own as she too gravely bowed.

MERRICK motioned the twelve to a long table beside one of the great windows. When he had taken his place at its head they too sat, the white-bearded Murnal at his right. Far away outside their window stretched the black, light-gemmed mass of Corla, illumined now by the weird light of two crimson moons that had swung up eastward.

"Since it is from another world that you have come to us, O Chan Merrick," Murnal began, "would you know more of this world or is it known to you?"

"It may be that I know, but I will hear you," said Merrick diplomatically.

"Then hear," said Murnal. "Kaldar, this world of ours, is of great size, how great indeed we do not really know. It revolves around our mighty sun at a medium distance, and around Kaldar in turn revolve our five moons. Of these four are crimson like our sun, but the fifth, as you will see, is green, the five moving in a chain around our world at different speeds.

"Of this world of Kaldar, we humans hold only the land within the circle of the great black mountains. This land and city of ours, Corla, lies almost across the equator of Kaldar. We are, so far as our recorded knowledge teaches, the only humans upon this world. And we know little more of Kaldar than what lies within our mountain circle, since outside it there are great and unhuman races as ancient and intelligent and powerful as our own, who have been our enemies always.

"Of all Kaldar's strange races and lands we have but rumors, indeed, for our airboats seldom venture across the mountains. But nearest to us of the other races are the Cosps, the great spider-men. Their great city lies far south from ours, beyond the mountains and strange forests, and from the beginning of time they have been the worst enemies of us of Corla.

"These Cosps, who are much like huge spiders in shape but with intelligence and science, have airboats as good as our own. They do not use light-swords or light-guns for weapons, but have poison-sprays that are as deadly. They have also mechanisms that project darkness wherever they wish, and these have always given them the advantage over us. For ever and again great Cosp raiding parties attack our city, and though we defend ourselves with the great light-guns on the city's pyramids, their darkness mechanisms give them always an unchangeable advantage.

"By them the Cosps are enabled to carry away great numbers of captives and loot for their distant city. Lately their attacks have become more and more frequent and Corla has come to be in terror of them. It is because of that that you have been welcomed so wildly by our people as the new Chan from the unknown, since all hope that as Chan you will be able to halt these terrible Cosp attacks."

Merrick considered. "Your own airboats make no attempt to meet the Cosp raiders in midair?" he asked.

Murnal spread his hands. "It would be useless, O Chan. With the darkness-projectors our boats would be at the mercy of the Cosps and none could escape."

"Then some way of overcoming the darkness-projectors must be found, if Cosp and Corlan are to fight on equal terms," Merrick stated.

Jhalan spoke from the table's end. "Surely it will be nothing for you to find such a way, O Chan from the unknown?" he asked cynically.

Merrick gave him a level glance. "Whether inside it or outside, Corla's enemies are my own," he said evenly. He hardly knew what prompted the answer, but saw Jhalan looking at him with knitted brows when he had made it.

"Spoken like a Chan!" exclaimed the great Holk. "If I had my way we'd load all our light-guns on the airboats and sail south to give the Cosps some of their own medicine!"

As the talk went on, veering from the Cosps to other problems of Corla, Merrick learned much concerning the race into whose kingship he had been so strangely projected. He was beginning to realize that the Corlans, though they had attained super-science in some few things, were essentially a feudal, mediæval-like race. He caught Jhalan's eyes sardonically on him, Narna's with approval in them.

Through the great window beside them he could see the moons swinging up from behind the mountains. Three of crimson hung like seals of blood across the sky and a fourth one of brilliant green was rising over Corla. Merrick, watching them, saw suddenly a long dark mass that moved across one of the crimson moons, high above the city. He was turning back to Murnal and the others when a wild, screaming signal sounded deafeningly across the city, waking it instantly to a wild babel of cries, a confused, rising uproar. And at the same moment there shot down upon Corla a great fleet of dark airboats from the upper night.

The others sprang to their feet with him. "An attack!" cried Murnal. "It's the Cosps—the spider-men—they're raiding the city!"

4. Spider-Men and Poison-Spray

"HOLK! Jurui!" Murnal shouted. "Order all our light-guns into action—they've caught us by surprize!"

But already the two Corlans and the others of the Council were facing toward the lift-chamber, Murnal and the girl Narna and Jhalan alone remaining in the great room. And already across the great city the light-guns were firing up at the dark craft of the invaders. The guns were soundless but Merrick could see the shining charges of deadly force flashing up from them all across the city.

Here and there invading airboats were hit and blasted by the shining charges, but the others dived unheedingly downward upon Corla's pyramids. From long tubes they rained down a fine spray and as it struck men on the pyramids and streets they fell into withered, distorted heaps. The light-guns, though, were vomiting shining charges upward with increased intensity, the whole terrific battle being almost soundless save for the wild babel of cries.

Merrick, stunned by the transformation of the quiet city into this field of terrific battle, saw the Cosp airboats diving recklessly in all directions. As one shot past their window he glimpsed its occupants and shuddered as he saw them. In shape they were like huge six-foot spiders, but with a near-human head set upon their bulbous central bodies. Clinging to the deck of the long airboat, they were directing their poison-sprays, one of their number guiding the craft from the prow.

In that first moment the battle had been almost even between Cosp and Corlan, light-gun and poison-spray striking up and down with equally deadly effect. But now from the swooping ships great fields of darkness were suddenly projected here and there over the city, areas of absolute lightlessness into which the Cosp ships unhesitatingly dived.

"The darkness-projectors!" Murnal cried. "It is always the same—we can not fight against them and the Cosps overcome us, being able in some way to see in the darkness!"

"But order all your light-guns to fire straight upward, then!" Merrick cried. "If they do that the Cosp ships can't land on the pyramids whether in darkness or not!"

Murnal's eyes lit. "We will try it, O Chan!" He sprang toward the lift-chamber.

Merrick, Narna beside him, looked out now across a scene that seemed out of nightmare, the spectacle of Corla struggling with the raiding spider-men. The huge city of black pyramids was a wild chaos of flashing light-guns and down-swooping Cosp airboats, blotted out here and there by the lightless areas of the darkness-projectors. Over it all swung the four great moons, three of crimson and one of vivid green.

Cosp ships were swooping into the darkness-areas, a few already rising laden with captives and loot. But abruptly the tenor of the battle changed. Wreckage of Cosp airboats drifted in masses out of the dark areas, and other craft of the spider-men that tried to dive into the darkness they created beneath them were met by up-bursting hails of charges from the light-guns. The darkness-areas were vanishing, the Cosp ships recoiling——

"They're beaten!" Merrick cried. "They're rising!"

"Truly they rise!" Narna exclaimed. "Your order has repulsed them, O Chan!"

"Beaten!" Merrick exulted. "And once we find a way to neutralize those darkness-projectors——"

"Chan Merrick! Jhalan signals to the Cosps!"

At Narna's cry Merrick whirled. He had forgotten Jhalan and now saw that the big black-bearded Corlan, at one of the other great windows, had pointed his light-gun up and fired four shining charges up into the darkness. In answer to them a Cosp airboat was racing down toward them. Jhalan signalling to the Cosps—it crashed to Merrick's brain that this attack was no fortuitous one but had been arranged with the Cosps in some way by Jhalan in the depths of his hate for the earth-man!

Merrick leapt toward the other, jerking the long light-sword from his sheath more by instinct than by design. Jhalan, his light-gun sheathed, whipped his own sword out in time to meet him. The two blades glowed as one with white light as the deadly force of the hilts was released into them. Then Merrick felt his blade click against his enemy's as they closed. He knew that the charged blades could not harm each other but that a touch of either meant death to the person touched.

Jhalan handled his deadly weapon like a master, its shining length cleaving the air around the earth-man. But Merrick was for the moment his equal, old fencing lore coming swiftly back to him in this strange duel where a touch was death. Up and down—right and left—back and forth—the two shining light-swords wove like twin shuttles of death as the two rushed, stabbed, parried.

Over the white heat of battle Merrick heard a cry from Narna, and as he whirled he saw something that froze the blood in his veins. The Cosp ship had swooped to hang level with the room's windows and a half-dozen great spider-men poured into the room. Jhalan called something to them and Merrick in a glance saw that they had seized the girl Narna and were hurrying her onto their craft's deck!

Maddened by the sight, Merrick flung himself with desperate recklessness upon Jhalan, but the Corlan had called again and Cosps were rushing toward them. Poison-sprays were lifted toward Merrick, but there came a sudden interruption. Men were pouring up out of the lift-chamber with light-swords in hand, Murnal and Holk and Jurul and others! Jhalan leapt back and as Merrick sprang after him a whirled tube in the grasp of one of the Cosps struck his head and sent him reeling back. Jhalan was on the airboat with the spider-men, and with Narna held upon it it darted rocket-like up into the night.

MERRICK rushed to the window with Holk and Jurul. The whole fleet of the Cosp raiders was moving southward, recoiling from the attack and vanishing swiftly in the weird moonlight, leaving the city in wild uproar behind them.

"Narna!" cried Merrick. "Jhalan has her—he and the Cosps!"

"Jhalan a traitor!" Murnal exclaimed. "To think that any Corlan should ever join forces with the Cosps as he has done, from jealousy and rage! He must have been in communication with them, and arranged this attack that he might carry away Narna!"

"But I'll find him—I'll bring her back!" Merrick swore.

Murnal shook his head sadly. "Impossible, O Chan Merrick. Jhalan has taken her with the Cosps southward, to the great Cosp city far beyond the mountains. None on Kaldar has ever entered that great city of the spider-men and returned."

"But I'll enter—and return!" Merrick asserted. A cold purpose was replacing his first wild rage. "And not for Narna alone but for Jhalan. If he lives to aid the Cosps their attacks will be strengthened by all the information he can give them, and they will end by destroying Corla."

"It is true," Murnal said, and the others murmured assent. "But why go yourself, O Chan? Why not send some of your warriors to attempt this venture?"

"Because this lies now between Jhalan and myself," Merrick answered. "Also, would I be fit Chan of Corla if I sent others where I dared not go myself?"

The eyes of Holk lit. "Truly you are Chan!" the big veteran exclaimed. "And I for one follow when you start for the Cosp city! Jurul here, too, though he's too shy to say so. Why, a dozen of us can fight our way into the spider-men's city and out again, if need be!"

THE next hours passed for Merrick in a whirl of activity. While the fifth moon of Kaldar still hung in the west like a crimson wafer, the huge red sun was rising eastward to look down on a Corla different far from that of the day before. Already the Corlans were repairing their city's injuries, recovering quickly from the night attack of the spider-men. Murnal reported to Merrick that while the city was joyful over its repulse of the Cosps, it was saddened by the news of Jhalan's treachery and the abduction of their last Chan's daughter.

Merrick had decided that for his venture to the Cosp city a single airboat would hold the necessary party. No large force that he could take could battle successfully the overwhelming forces of the Cosps, and by limiting his companions to a dozen and taking but one craft their chances of reaching and penetrating the Cosp city were far greater, it being by stealth only that they could reach their goal.

He inspected the airboats and on the recommendation of Holk and Jurul chose one of fifteen-man size and of unequalled swiftness among the ships of Corla. It was the first close glimpse of the craft that Merrick had had, and he found the airboats simple in design, long, tapering metal craft like racing-shells, but broader of beam, decked, and with low surrounding rail. They moved in the air by projecting ahead of them a shaft of the annihilating force of the light-swords and light-guns, which ceaselessly destroyed the air just in front of the craft and thus forced it on by the pressure of the air behind. The changing of this invisible force-shaft's direction controlled the boat's direction of flight, and the changing of its intensity regulated speed.

The simple controls were at the prow, while at the stern and along the sides were light-guns of medium size mounted on swivels.

For the remainder of that day, while the airboat was being made ready, Merrick slept, exhausted. When he woke he found awaiting him Murnal, who was to act with the remainder of the Council of Twelve as ruler of Corla during the absence of its Chan. It was night again, and on one of the great pyramid's upper terraces the chosen airboat waited, the ten Corlans of its crew ready in it. Holk and Jurul were waiting with Murnal beside him.

Murnal pointed down to the thronged streets as Merrick buckled on light-sword and light-gun.

"The people wait to see you go, O Chan," he said. "They know now that you are truly Chan and they are sad to see you start to what seems certain death."

"Certain death for Jhalan, perhaps," Merrick answered grimly. "As for me, I'll be back with Narna. While I am gone see that the scientists try that way of neutralizing the darkness-projectors I mentioned to you. Those projectors give off light-damping vibrations of some sort and could be neutralized and made ineffective by the proper opposing vibrations."

"We will try," Murnal nodded, "and it may be that your way will give us victory again. Until you return, then, Chan Merrick."

Merrick rested his hand for a moment on the other's shoulder, then strode out with Holk and Jurul onto the terrace. Night lay over Corla, and in its streets great throngs watched in death-like silence as the three stepped onto their airboat and it shot up over the city. In moments the mighty black pyramids of the city had dropped behind and beneath, and Merrick and his companions were gazing ahead into the darkness as their craft shot southward through the night toward the distant stronghold of the Cosps.

5. Over the Fungus Forest

AS THEIR craft flew southward Merrick crouched with Holk and Jurul at its prow, the latter having the controls in his grasp. The airboat flew almost soundlessly, with only a low purring from the squat mechanism at the stern that produced the force-shaft which moved them onward. The ten Corlans of their crew crouched and lay along the craft's sides.

Merrick, peering ahead, could make out in the distance the dim black rampart of the great mountain-ring toward which they were flying. It grew rapidly colder about them as Jurul slanted the airboat upward as they approached the huge mountain wall. At last in freezing cold air they were racing over the huge range, gazing down in awe upon it.

Merrick could see in the light of the two risen red moons that the giant peaks of the range were of a height unknown on earth, and that the great range itself was surprizingly regular in its circular shape. In the clefts between the mountains was white snow, but there was none on the great peaks, for they and the gigantic chasms and cliffs gleamed as though glassy-smooth, black and awesome masses.

"They look as if they were of black metal," Merrick commented to the men beside him, and was amazed at Holk's answer.

"They are metal, O Chan. That black metal exists in tremendous masses in Kaldar's interior, and crops out here and there as huge mountain ranges or ledges. We and the Cosps and all other races use it for our airboats and buildings and almost all else."

"Metal mountains!" marvelled the earth-man.

By the time that the great range dropped behind, all five of Kaldar's moons were in the night heavens, bunched together in seeming for the time as they followed their separate orbits around their world. The sight of the stupendous, lonely black metal mountains in the light of the red and green moons was one that remained long in Merrick's mind.

As the metal mountains receded behind them Jurul slanted the craft downward and the air grew warmer again about them. They flew on at smooth, unchanging speed, noting below them the lower hills and scarps of the great metal range. Beyond these the moonlight disclosed smooth and rolling plains, over which they flew for hours. At last these gave way to a dark mass of vegetation that extended ahead and to either side as far as the eye could reach.

As they arrowed above this, Merrick tried to estimate the length of the day and night of Kaldar, coming to the conclusion that they were not greatly different from those of earth. The period of Kaldar's rotation, as he was later to learn, was some twenty earth-hours, so that he was not far wrong in the estimate he made when the huge crimson sun lifted from the horizon to their left.

The coming of day disclosed the extraordinary nature of the forest over which they were flying.

It was a vast fungus forest. As far as the eye could reach in all directions stretched the mass of great crimson growths, most of them twenty feet or more in height. They were monstrous of form, great central trunks with projecting arms, quite leafless, which gave them a grotesque appearance. They were crowded together in an unending sea swept by tides and currents of movement. Merrick thought at first that the things were swaying in a wind, but closer inspection showed him that the great growths were rootless and actually moving, crawling to and fro by their great groping arms, brushing and crowding against each other.

From Holk and Jurul he learned that this fungus forest was of vast extent and feared by all on Kaldar. For the great growths did not, like ordinary fungi, prey upon other plants, but upon animals. Any luckless Cosp or Corlan or living thing of any kind that fell into the forest was doomed, since before he could move the great growths would have grasped him, suffocating and crushing him, and battening upon his body as ordinary fungi do upon plants.

For all of that day their craft flew steadily south over the unending, crawling crimson masses of this forest of horror. His companions assured Merrick that it extended to the very edge of the city of the Cosps, and was one reason why that city of the spider-men was never attacked by land, and almost never by air, few venturing over the fungus forest, a fall into which meant death. Night closed down with the limitless expanse of fungi still beneath them.

At reduced speed they flew on through the night, Merrick and his companions peering intently ahead.

"We must be near the Cosp city now, I think," Holk declared. "But it may be that we have missed it—we Corlans know little of its location because few of us have ever reached it and returned."

"We'll reach it," Merrick said, his jaw setting. "And we'll——"

Jurul's cry stabbed their ears. "A Cosp airboat—attacking!"

At the moment he cried out Jurul had whirled their craft over, and as it heeled dizzily in midair there shot soundlessly down past it a long craft on which were a score of the hideous spider-monsters, the Cosps! Their poison-sprays were belching the fine rain of death that had missed the Corlan craft only because of its lightning turn.

"The light-guns!" Merrick cried. "Get it before it can reach us again!"

The Corlans of their crew leapt to the guns, and as Jurul sent their craft on a slant toward the other a half-dozen shining charges of force clove soundlessly toward it. But the Cosp craft had whirled upward in a turn as quick as their own and was rushing back on a level with them, the long tubes of its poison-sprays outstretched toward them.

The thing was instantly a wild, whirling duel of the two craft, Cosp and Corlan airboats grappling in the night with light-gun and poison-spray, with three of Kaldar's great crimson moons looking down from above and with the fungus forest below. The two airboats circled like fighting falcons, evading each other's sprays and charges and striving for an advantageous position. Had the Cosp craft one of the darkness projectors they would have had short shrift, Merrick knew, but even as it was, the darting, deadly sprays of the spider-men were each instant harder to evade.

THE wild duel seemed endless to the earth-man, but in reality it was over in moments. Jurul, seeing that the poison-sprays were certain to catch them in a moment more, shot their craft downward as though to a lower level to escape, and as the Cosp airboat dived hawk-like he slanted it up in a giddy curve, giving their gunners a momentary chance at the craft beneath. Down hailed the shining charges, two striking the Cosp craft near its stern, blasting the metal there into a distorted and twisted blackened mass, sending the craft whirling downward.

Merrick saw it crash in the fungus masses a thousand feet beneath, and in the clear moonlight could see the Cosps leaping forth. But as the great spider-men did so they were caught by groping arms and disappeared from view beneath the huge fungi, which were crawling from all directions toward them as though informed by some instinct what had happened. Merrick felt sick as their own craft whirled up and onward.

"A Cosp patrol-boat!" Holk was exclaiming. "That means there must be others out, too!"

Jurul nodded quietly. "We'll have to fly higher," he said. "That ought to take us past the Cosp patrols—the spider-men don't like the cold of the upper air."

"Always passing up a fight," the great Holk grumbled. "For anyone who fights like you, avoiding a battle is a waste of talent."

"Jurul is right," Merrick declared.

"We've no time for these encounters—our only objective is the Cosp city."

"And when we get there?" asked Holk. "I suppose you know that there isn't a chance in a thousand of getting out of there once we enter."

Merrick smiled. "Leave that to take care of itself," he said. "Jhalan is in there—and Narna. Once I find them it'll be time enough to worry about getting out."

Holk grinned his approval. "Jhalan has always been thought one of the greatest fighters on Kaldar," he said, "but I think it will be interesting when you and he meet again."

While they talked the airboat had been flying steadily southward, carrying up to a greater height. Soon the wind was cold again about them and the fungus forest a dark plain far beneath. In the west two red moons were setting while eastward the green moon rose. Made tense by their recent battle, Merrick and Holk and Jurul watched alertly for Cosp craft. But in the next hour they saw none, evading them by their greater altitude if any others were actually near.

Holk stared ahead, his weather-beaten face a mask in the mixed light, Jurul watching as silently as ever at the controls. It was Jurul who gave word at last that they were nearing their goal.

"Look!" he said simply, pointing ahead and downward.

"The city—the city of the Cosps!" Holk exclaimed.

Merrick peered with narrowed eyes. At first he saw only a darker bulk against the dark fungus forest far ahead, one that glinted in the moonlight at points. It was only when after minutes of onward flight the dark bulk slowly grew that he appreciated its enormous size. Fascinated he watched.

It largened slowly and Merrick almost forgot their errand in the wonder of the sight. The Cosp city lay before them! And it was a city of but a single structure —a gigantic, irregular-shaped mass of metal with countless flat smooth sides, miles upon miles in extent. And it was as bored with tunnel-openings and honey-combed passages as some colossal black metal cheese. Around its giant metal mass rose a metal wall hundreds of feet in height, against which the crawling fungus forest pressed and crept.

"The city of the Cosps!" Holk repeated. "Long ago the spider-men found here that giant outcrop of solid metal, and hollowed out in it their cells and tunnels until now it holds all their countless hordes. The wall around it keeps out the great crawling fungi of the forest that surrounds it."

"Then those tunnel-passages——" Merrick began.

"Run through the whole huge city in a labyrinth," the other answered. "Somewhere deep down in that mighty honeycombed mass lies the hall of the Cospai, the ruler of the Cosp race. It is near there, I think, that Jhalan would be with Narna, but how are we to reach it?"

"There's but one way," Merrick said decisively. "The city seems sleeping, and two of us might penetrate into it and get back, where all of us would inevitably be discovered. You will land Jurul and me between the wall and city and we'll try it. You can hover high over the city, and if we get out again we'll fire our light-guns as signal to drop for us."

"And leave Jurul to have the fun of it while I lie up in the cold?" Holk asked belligerently. Jurul was laughing softly.

"Yes. As Chan I order it," Merrick told him. "You'll have fighting enough before we get out of this, Holk."

"In that case, well enough," Holk grinned.

He took the controls and while Merrick and Jurul looked to their weapons sent the airboat downward. Some of the tunnel openings were lit, and there were what seemed lit guard-towers on the great wall, but no airboats were in sight, and silently as some ship of the dead their craft sank toward the sleeping city of the spider-men.

6. *In the Cosp City*

MERRICK expected each instant a challenge or alarm from the guard-towers on the great wall, but none came. Long ages of immunity from attack had made the Cosps negligent in their guard, and without accident the Corlan craft came to rest on the black metal plain that lay between the surrounding wall and the city's huge honeycombed mass.

At once Merrick and Jurul were leaping from it. "Hold her high above," Merrick whispered to Holk, "and when you see our light-guns firing down here drop like lightning for us."

"If it's firing you can't keep me from it," Holk grinned, and set the craft darting up again into the darkness.

Merrick and Jurul, their hands on the hilts of their light-swords, set off instantly toward the looming bulk of the city whose honeycombed metal cliffs towered a half-mile away. The metal floor over which they hastened gleamed in the light of the moons. No Cosps were in sight, though they saw dark spider-forms against a few of the dim-lit tunnel-openings from time to time.

They headed toward one of the openings on a level with the floor, the upper ones being reached by projecting holds in the cliffs unusable by any but the many-limbed spider-men. Merrick had in mind the suggestion of Holk that it was only deep down toward the center of the great city, where the Cosp ruler was, that Jhalan and Narna would most likely be found. He realized the slenderness of their chance of finding them, but was carried on by the very unreality of the adventure and by a strong memory of the Corlan girl.

They slowed as they neared the tunnel opening, and peered stealthily into it. Dim-lit by feebly glowing plates inset in the walls, it curved out of sight before them, quite unoccupied. Merrick and Jurul stepped cautiously into it, stooping because of its low height. They passed doors as they went on in it, opening one or two and finding beyond them storerooms filled with unused mechanisms and weapons.

They went on and soon found that other tunnels crossed their own. Merrick took the first one leading downward and inward. Its downward slant was steep and the metal floor slippery to their feet. They shrank back once as a sound of oddly hissing voices came to them and two spider-men crossed their tunnel just ahead. The two great Cosps, hideous spider-bodies made more ghastly by their hairless and human-like heads and features, were discussing some matter, talking in the tongue Merrick had learned was common to almost all Kaldar's races. They passed, and Merrick and Jurul crept on.

They found themselves passing other doors and when they peered through one found the room inside full of sleeping Cosps, each resting on a square raised platform. They crept quietly past these, following their tunnel that wound ever downward. Moving around one of its sharp turns, they ran squarely into three Cosps coming around the turn. Before the spider-men could recover from their surprise, Merrick and Jurul had their light-swords out of their sheaths and had sprung forward. Merrick's shining sword touched one of the great spider-men and before he could realize it the Cosp was a scorched and distorted lifeless heap, blasted by the sword's terrible force. Jurul accounted for a second in the same instant, and as the third spider-man turned to flee Jurul's blade touched and blasted him also, the light-swords being automatically recharged from the hilt at each release of their force.

For a moment Merrick and Jurul stood, panting and wild of eye, shining swords ready, but no more of the Cosps appeared for the moment.

"We can't stay here long," Merrick whispered. "Some of them are sure to stumble upon us."

"Back, Chan," warned Jurul. "I hear others——"

They shrank back into the darkness of one of the transverse tunnels, more dimly lit than their own, dragging the three twisted forms of the slain spider-men with them. Five Cosps were approaching along the tunnel they had been following, and as they came around the turn Merrick saw that they were armed with black-tubed poison-sprays. He heard them talking as they came on.

"——and why he should receive him so I can not guess. There has never been anything but war to the death between Cosp and Corlan and there never will be. Why, then, should this one be received in honor with his prisoner?"

"You forget," another answered, "that this Corlan hates his people now as much as we do. This Jhalan can help us to make a final conquest of Corla."

"Also," a third spider-man put in, "the Cospal will know how to deal with him when we have conquered his race."

"It may be so," the first replied, "but in the meantime it irritates me to see him a guest in the chambers of the Cospal himself."

Merrick, listening, hardly realized their danger in his interest until the five Cosps came level with the cross-tunnel in which they crouched. Were they to turn down it discovery was inevitable, but fortune favored the two and the spider-men went on along the brighter-lighted way. When their voices had receded Merrick plucked at Jurul's arm.

"You heard?" he asked excitedly. "Holk was right—Jhalan and Narna are in the Cospal's chambers!"

"But how to get into them?" Jurul said doubtfully. "They'll be guarded, remember."

"This lighted tunnel must lead to them, for those five were apparently just coming from the Cospal's chambers," Merrick pointed out. "And once we find them we'll find some way of getting in."

THEY started along the lighted way again, made more cautious by their two narrow escapes, shining light-swords in their hands. It came to Merrick as they crept forward how vast must be the sleeping honeycombed Cosp city that lay around and above and beneath them, a limitless labyrinth of tunneled ways holding in its cells and chambers all the countless sleeping spider-men. He crept on with Jurul.

They crossed other tunnels, but the lighted one led surely onward and downward. At last they were brought up short as they rounded a curve in it by glimpsing ahead a portal-like door across it, guarded by four spider-men with poison-sprays. At sight of the Cosp guards the two shrank back.

"Guards of the Cospal," Jurul whispered. "We're near—but how to pass them?"

"Our light-guns?" Merrick asked, and the other thought and nodded.

"Our only chance, it seems. Before we could get near them with swords they'd kill us with the sprays."

Sheathing their swords, therefore, the two drew their stubby light-guns and crept silently to the curve's edge. Then, raising them, they pressed the inset firing-plates on the stocks. Merrick was aiming at the Cosp on the extreme right and saw him fall in a blasted heap as the shining charge flashed soundlessly from the gun and struck him. One on the left had fallen at the same instant beneath Jurul's fire, and as the two remaining Cosps darted forward with poison-sprays upraised they were met by two more charges that cut off their rising cries of alarm by instant death.

Merrick and Jurul, trembling with excitement, dragged the slain guards back into another of the transverse tunnels and then went on through the portal. Along the tunnel now were designs worked in white metal on the black metal walls, showing Cosps battling with Corlans and also with beings unlike any Merrick had ever seen, that he realized must have been inhabitants of some part of Kaldar.

But the pictured walls meant little to Merrick in the excitement that now urged him on. He had not realized how much his quest for Narna meant to him until now when he came within reach of the Corlan girl. He and Jurul glimpsed far along lit corridors spider-guards here and there, but were able by following branching ways to avoid them. They were in a great maze of guarded corridors and ante-rooms that must surround the inner retreat of the Cospal, he knew, and he halted at last in doubt.

He was turning to Jurul, when from both came whispered exclamations. Some one was following the transverse tunnel some distance ahead, and as he crossed their own they saw that it was the great figure of Jhalan!

Merrick almost leapt forward as he saw him but checked himself in time. His heart pounded madly as they watched the great Corlan cross ahead. Black-bearded and still in his black metal garment, Jhalan still wore his light-sword and light-gun, and his possession of weapons in this city of the Cosps was in itself ample proof of his treachery. They crept silently after him, and as they followed him down the dim-lit cross-tunnel saw him pass two spider-guards, exchanging a word with the Cosps as he did so. Merrick and Jurul made a quick detour through divergent tunnels to avoid the guards and again a moment later were dogging the traitor Corlan's heels.

In both their minds, as they followed like stalking beasts of prey, was the same thought, that by following Jhalan most surely would they be led to Narna.

They dared not keep too close to their unconscious quarry, though, for ever and again he cast a glance around and behind him. So it was that after trailing him through several tunnels in which, luckily for them, were no more guards, they saw Jhalan turn a curve ahead. Before they reached it they heard the clang of a door and when they hastened around the curve found the corridor beyond it empty. Along it were a dozen doors, through any of which the Corlan might have gone. They halted, tense, Merrick sick with doubt.

"We'll have to try all these rooms," he whispered. "He must have gone into one of them."

Jurul shook his head. "Suicide to do that," he declared. "There may be a half-hundred Cosp guards or even the Cospal himself in those rooms, even if Jhalan is in one."

Merrick saw all the force of the other's words and stood for a moment in despair. Their whole venture seemed black, when from the second door there came out a sound that startled them. The scream of a girl!

7. *Flight and Battle*

"NARNA!" cried Merrick as the scream struck his ears. He leapt to the door.

"Wait!" Jurul exclaimed. "There may be Cosps inside too!"

But Merrick was for the moment beyond control of reason. He tugged fruitlessly at the handle of the locked door and then whipped out his light-sword and drew its shining blade around the handle. Beneath the sword's force the metal of the door twisted and melted instantly, and as the door gave before him Merrick burst inside, shining rapier in his hand.

The scene inside was one that fanned his quick rage to flame. The room was a small one, with strange metal furnishings, and at one side of it Narna was struggling in the grasp of Jhalan. No fear, but loathing, was in her eyes, and they lit instantly as she and Jhalan turned and saw Merrick burst in.

"Chan Merrick!" cried the girl.

"One side, Narna—quick!" Merrick exclaimed.

For Jhalan, behind the girl, had recognized Merrick and had instantly whipped out and levelled his light-gun. Instead of springing aside, though, Narna struck up the weapon and the charge that flew from it blasted the wall over Merrick's head. Rather than waste time Jhalan dropped the weapon and ripped out his light-sword. Merrick's weapon clashed against it as he leapt forward, and then the interrupted battle they had fought in Corla was resumed.

O. S.—**8**

Again the shining slender blades clicked against each other like needles of death as Merrick and Jhalan circled each other in the chamber. Once Jhalan raised his voice in a hissing cry, but Jurul had closed the door to prevent the fight from arousing the spider-men. Merrick knew as he stabbed and feinted that his ally dared not use his light-gun in the little room lest he annihilate friend and foe alike.

Whatever Jhalan was, he was a supreme swordsman. But the long slender light-sword in Merrick's hand was so like a fencing-foil in weight that it was as though he were engaged in a friendly bout rather than in one where a touch was the end. He pressed Jhalan fiercely forward, but as the Corlan gave way slipped suddenly. Instantly the other's blade leapt toward him but Merrick threw himself aside in time, was on his feet again. A cold rage filled him now and he pressed Jhalan irresistibly.

The Corlan was maneuvering around the room and in a moment more his plan made itself evident. For as he neared the door he flung it open with a swift motion of his left hand, and as he leapt for the opening hurled his light-sword in Merrick's face!

The sword, as it left Jhalan's grasp, went dead and forceless, and Merrick's own blade, striking it in his instinctive parry, sent the weapon flying back to strike the head of Jhalan just as he leapt through the door-opening. Without a sound the great black-bearded Corlan sank to the floor, stunned by the blow.

Merrick, panting, stepped to the unconscious man and extended his shining blade toward him, then suddenly drew it back.

"I can't do it!" he panted. "In fight, yes, but I can't kill an unconscious man."

"Then I will!" Jurul declared. His

light-sword leapt forth, but Narna interposed.

"No, the Chan Merrick is right. No
Corlan strikes a prostrate foe." Jurul
drew back and the girl turned to Merrick.

"Did they capture you also, O Chan?"
she asked. "Have you escaped them?"

"They never captured me," Merrick
told her. "I came with Holk and Jurul
and others to find you—our airboat waits
above."

"You came—for me?" she marvelled.
"Why, scarce a Corlan in history has ever
dared approach this Cosp city. Truly you
are our Chan, when for a single one of
your subjects you dare what no Corlan
has ever dared before!"

"It was not that," Merrick began, feeling in some way clumsy in expressing himself, but Jurul interposed.

"If we're to get back up to the surface
we'd best be going," he warned. "It
must be near day now and all this Cosp
city will be waking soon."

They left the unconscious Jhalan where
he lay and started back through the corridors they had followed in coming.
Narna, though, showed them another
way which she declared was a shorter
route to the surface, being the one by
which she had been brought down captive by Jhalan and the Cosps, and running
past the inmost hall of the Cospal.

They followed it as hastily as possible,
detouring through adjacent tunnels now
and then to avoid guards, knowing that
a single cry would bring the sleeping
hordes of spider-men around them into
wakefulness. Soon they were following
a wider tunnel, one side of which was
open, giving view of a great dim-lit hall
along whose side high up their passage led
like a balcony. Merrick peered down into
the hall as they crept onward.

It was of enormous size and he could
see drawn up around it rank on rank of
armed Cosps, great spider-men standing
as motionless as though carven. In a cup-
like depression at the hall's center rested
a single Cosp at least three times as large
as any Merrick had seen, a huge spider-
monster twenty feet across with enormous,
bulging head. It was the Cospal, he
knew, the strange ruler of the spider-race.
It seemed sleeping, perhaps only thinking, but motionless as the guards around
it. The strangeness of the sight remained
with Merrick long after they had crept
past the hall and on up the tunnel.

They moved onward, upward, sometimes in dark tunnels where only Narna's
soft grasp of his wrist told that his companions were beside him. Hope rose in
Merrick as they climbed steadily up and
outward through the Cosp city's vast
labyrinthine mass. At last the dim-lit
tunnel ended in a dark circle ahead, dot-
ted with stars. Merrick turned with a
whisper of exultation on his lips, but as
he did so a single long, rising, hissing cry
trembled up from deep in the city's mass
behind them, taken up and repeated by
dozens of similar voices instantly.

"Jhalan!" cried Jurul. "He's come to
and given the alarm! I knew it was
wrong to let him live!"

"We can still make it if Holk is watching!" Merrick cried, all effort at stealth
gone now as the city woke around them.
They raced up toward the star-dotted
mouth of the tunnel.

"Cosps ahead, O Chan!" Narna cried
suddenly, but Merrick had seen the dark
spider-shapes appearing in the opening
ahead.

As one he and Jurul aimed their light-
guns in racing forward, and as the shining charges flicked and flashed from them
the Cosps ahead reeled back and down in
scorched heaps. In all the tunnels behind
and around them, though, Cosps were crying to each other, searching through the

ways toward them as up from beneath poured pursuing guards. They burst out of the tunnel's mouth onto the black metal plain and Jurul's light-gun shot its charges rocket-like up through the night in shining signal. From the wall ahead and from the city's mass behind Cosps were pouring, poison-sprays in their grasp.

Merrick yelled, stopped with Jurul and Narna. A great shape was swooping like a dark hawk out of the night, an airboat whose guns were hailing charges on the rushing Cosps. As they recoiled from its unlooked-for attack the craft swept low and Narna and Jurul leapt to its deck, Merrick felt Holk's great arms pulling him after them as the craft darted upward again.

"Out of here!" Merrick cried. "There'll be a hundred airboats after us in a minute!"

T HE craft shot like a thing alive up into the night with great poison-sprays from wall and city wheeling to dart their deadly jets toward it. Behind, they glimpsed Cosp ships beginning to rise from the city's top and the metal around it. But the whole panorama of the aroused city of the spider-men vanished behind them as their craft shot at immense speed northward through the darkness.

"We have escaped!" Narna cried. "The first Corlans ever to win clear of the Cosp city once they had entered it!"

"Yes, but I thought there was going to be some fighting to it!" Holk complained. "All my life I've been hoping for a raid down here and when I finally get here all I do is wait up there in the cold like some bird!"

Narna and Jurul laughed at him, but Merrick, who had been peering back as they flew on, dawn beginning to rift the darkness eastward, turned an anxious face to them.

"You may have your fighting yet, Holk," he said. "Look back there— what are those?"

A wide string of dark dots was becoming visible far behind, extending across the reddening dawn sky and moving after them. Holk gazed, Narna looking back anxiously at Merrick's side, and then the big veteran nodded grimly.

"Cosp airboats! They're not going to let us get away so easily, it seems."

"It is Jhalan," murmured Narna. "He will never see me escape."

"I begin to think that Jurul was right about killing Jhalan," said Merrick grimly. "Well, they'll not catch us without a chase—head straight north for Corla."

When the huge crimson sun flamed up eastward it disclosed the fact that the Cosp craft far behind were massing more closely and had settled down to a relentless chase. They seemed of no greater speed than the Corlan craft, though as the next hours passed it seemed that some of them were drawing closer.

For all of that day, while the great sun wheeled across the sky, the Corlan craft and its pursuers fled on high over the vast fungus forest. By sunset it was plain to all that the Cosp craft were much closer, though whether they could overtake their prey before reaching Corla remained doubtful. They would pursue, Merrick knew, to the city itself, being more than a hundred strong and no doubt having their great darkness-projectors on some of their craft.

With the coming of night, the great moons of Kaldar lifting one by one as though to view the chase, the Cosps drew still closer. Through the night as through the day the pursuit held grimly after them. And when Merrick woke from an hour's exhausted sleep on the airboat's deck to find dawn blood-red in the east, it was to find the spider-men's ships a bare half-mile behind. Ahead by then loomed the great wall of the black mountains, beyond which Corla lay, but rapidly now the Cosps were drawing closer.

Merrick could make out the erect figure of Jhalan on one of the foremost airboats and he cursed his squeamishness in sparing the traitor. At the same time he was aware that he would do the same again in like case, and as he caught Narna's eyes he saw her smile bravely at him.

He waited until the Cosp ships were hardly more than a thousand feet behind before ordering the Corlans of his crew to open fire. With Holk directing them, Jurul at the controls, they poured back for a few moments a deadly fire of shining charges that confused and slowed the Cosp pursuit, sending a half-dozen craft whirling down. The others then split into two portions, long lines, one of which swept to either side to pass and surround the fleeing Corlan ship and hold it in their circle. They were passing over the great mountains by then, low over the giant metal peaks, and Merrick saw at last the two lines of Cosp craft joining ahead, a great circle of them holding the fugitive Corlan ship.

"They've got us," Merrick said quietly to Narna. "We have brought you from the Cosp city only to death, it seems—better had our rescue failed."

She shook her head quietly. "Better here with you, O Chan," she said.

Merrick turned to Holk and Jurul. "Hold all our charges until they close in on us," he told them. "Just before they get into range with the poison-sprays let them have it—I just want to get Jhalan before they end us."

They were still flying forward, the circle of the Cosp ships contracting now upon them. They might destroy a dozen of the spider-men's craft, Merrick knew, but the others would in that time have their deadly sprays in range. It seemed a strange end—Narna's calm eyes and the tense figures of Holk and Jural and the others, and the black range beneath and huge red Antares above, a kaleidoscope of impressions as the moment approached. The Cosp ships were nearer, poison-tubes raising, and he had on his lips the order to fire when from Holk burst an inhuman, exultant yell.

Airboats in a great mass were rushing toward them from ahead, and instantly their guns were raining deadly charges on the ring of Cosp ships!

"Corlan ships!" Merrick cried. "They may save us yet!"

Jurul shook his head sadly. "They can not fight the darkness-projectors of the Cosps," he said. "See——!"

For the Corlan airboats, rushing fiercely upon the craft of the spider-men, had so surprised them that for a moment the battle had been a mere wild chaos of struggling craft in which deadly sprays and shining charges thronged thick the air. Outnumbered, the Cosp ships were blasted in dozens in that first shock of battle, but in a moment had recovered from their surprize and darting back had brought their darkness-projectors into play. Great areas of black lightlessness engulfed the Corlan craft, the spider-men turning their sprays upon these instantly.

But, astoundingly, after that first instant of darkness the lightless areas seemed to waver, to be broken by darting rays, and then to vanish! And as the Corlans again swooped toward their enemies, the Cosps, astounded at the failure of the weapon that for ages had given them supremacy, became a confused, stunned mass of ships into which the others poured a deadly fire. Merrick glimpsed the craft of Jhalan at the center of that terrific inferno of blasting death, saw it whirl down with dozens around it. Then the remainder of the shattered Cosp fleet had turned, was racing away in mad flight southward, half the Corlan ships in hot pursuit.

"Beaten!" Holk bellowed. "The first time in history that Corlan has met Cosp on equal terms, and we've beaten them!"

Narna's eyes were shining. "Look, Murnal's airboat coming toward us!" she cried.

Merrick saw the craft driving level with their own, and then from it the white-bearded Murnal stepped to their own. His face flamed with the victory, and as he saw Narna beside Merrick his eyes widened.

"The victory is yours, Chan Merrick!" he cried. "Your suggestion for neutralizing the darkness-projectors worked perfectly, and with some airboats equipped with neutralizers we were starting south to see if we might find you.

"Corla will be mad with joy," the old noble added, "not only that we have shattered the supremacy of the Cosps, but that its Chan has returned safely and brought with him her for whom he went."

In moments the Corlan ships, their own in the van, were flying back over the metal mountains, swift scout-boats going ahead to give to the people of Corla the great news. When at last their fleet dipped down over the city of mighty black pyramids they found streets and terraces jammed with madly rejoicing throngs. The great plaza was packed solid with hoarse-voiced humanity, and it was down among them and beside the dais of the Chan that their airboat landed.

A deafening thunder of voices greeted them when Merrick and Narna stepped from the airboat, Holk and Jurul and Murnal behind them. And when Merrick stepped up onto the dais there was an in-

tensifying of the deafening storm of acclamation. Merrick, with Narna's shining eyes upon his, raised his hand and the massed humanity about him grew silent.

"People and nobles of Corla," he told them, "for ages have Cosp and Corlan battled, but never until today on equal terms, the spider-men having always the advantage. But today, with that advantage gone, we have fought them and have beaten them, have sent their shattered fleet reeling back to their city in defeat and have broken their power for ever! And what we have done to the Cosps today we can do again. We can meet and beat our enemies until on all Kaldar no race shall dare attack Corla and its people. Chan of Corla, I say it!"

There was silence still for a moment, and then out from the countless masses about him there crashed up to him a terrific shout of "Chan!"

But as it sounded there was a thunder-out roaring in Merrick's ears and he seemed shaken in every atom by awful force. As swift memory came to him in that moment he cried out and saw Narna, white-faced, run with Holk and Jurul and Murnal toward the dais. But for the merest instant only he saw them, since in the next they and the city around him and the huge red sun above vanished from around him as he was whirled into lightless blackness.

8. Epilogue

MERRICK whirled out of that black unconsciousness of instants to find himself staggering suddenly in a room, a long, white-lit, roofless room at whose center upon a square metal platform he stood. Dynamos and other apparatus were throbbing about him and elderly men were crowding excitedly toward him. He stood dazed for the moment, a strange figure among them in his black metal tunic with light-sword and light-gun swinging still at his side.

"You made it!" they were crying. "What did you find there?"

"Three days!" The cry broke from Merrick as he remembered. "Three days!"

"Yes," they nodded excitedly, "the three days are up, and at two exactly we turned on the projector's force and drew you back across to earth."

Merrick was stunned. In the wild rush of events on Kaldar, his strange kingship, Narna and Jhalan and the attack of the Cosps, his venture to the spider-city and desperate flight from it, he had forgotten wholly his agreement to return to earth in three days. And chance had made him take his place on the dais where first he had found himself on Kaldar, at the exact moment when the projector's force stabbed across the void to that one spot to draw him back to earth!

"I've got to go back!" he cried. "I never meant to return to earth—it was only accident. I tell you I have a people out there—you've got to send me back now!"

They were astounded. "Impossible," said their spokesman. "It will take weeks to charge the condensers again with enough force to operate the projector."

Merrick was dazed, the nine scientists bewildered. "But we can send you back then if you want to return," they told him.

"You'll send me back, then?" Merrick cried.

"If you want to go, surely. But where did you get those things?—what is that world like that you reached?—what did you find there?"

Merrick for the moment did not answer their excited questions. He was gazing up through the room's open top to where among the brilliant stars great Antares swung. His mind, travelling back out across the gulf toward the huge sun, seemed to have before it again its world of Kaldar. Kaldar—with Corla and its people, *his* people—with Holk and Jurul and Murnal, with Narna—Narna—with all of Kaldar's great unhuman races and unending war and strange monsters, with all its mystery and horror and unearthly beauty. The men around Merrick saw him smile.

"I found—my world," he said.

GIFTS

By HUNG LONG TOM

Great gifts to man are these—
The laughter of a happy child,
Fragrance of myrtle growing wild,
A vase of porcelain, a cup of jade,
A skylark singing in the trees,
A bit of song new made.

THE SOUK

ENTHUSIASTIC comment has greeted the first issue of the MAGIC CARPET Magazine under its new name and broadened scope. We have room here to quote from only a few of the letters received, but these are typical of the rest.

"I have just seen the new edition of the old ORIENTAL STORIES," writes Hugh B. Cave, from his home in New England. "You certainly do start things out there in Chicago! But it looks good. It looks mighty good. Every magazine that ever amounted to anything in this famous Land of the Spree and the Home of the Rave started out by being new and different. Keep it up. And here's luck. Good luck. The very best there is."

H. Bedford-Jones writes: "Have seen your new issue. Fine! A good title and striking cover. You'll go over with it and the program laid out. You're not afraid of being original. All the other boys holler for something different and don't know it when they see it. One of these days an adventure magazine will bust out and knock the rest off the boards; good stuff only, and different. Your magazine may be it. Watch and see. Good luck to the MAGIC CARPET."

E. Hoffmann Price, master of Oriental fantasy, writes: "The MAGIC CARPET arrived today, and boy, it's an Ispahan! A mighty good cover line-up. That smaller picture, with the view concentrated on a nice eyeful—catchy stuff. And then that imposing array of names, starting off with H. Bedford-Jones, with title and a few words to catch the eye—Chinese mystery—slave mart of Mecca—adventure in Borneo—far east detective story—adventure in Kurdistan—new Arabian Nights. The magazine came in the morning's mail, and I've been looking it over, drooling eggs and apricots all over my new kaftan as I sought to consume a frugal meal and look at the pictures and the Souk. I sincerely hope it goes across with a big bang."

Robert E. Howard, whose historical tales of Genghis Khan, Tamerlane and the Crusades have been so much admired, writes to the editor: "Congratulations on the quality and appearance of the MAGIC CARPET. There is a freshness and vigor of imagination about the magazine that is rare in this day of standardization. I wish it the best of luck. As usual, Price turned in a fine job with *Ismeddin and the Holy Carpet*. Ismeddin is my favorite Oriental character, worthy to take his place beside Sinbad and the Kalif Haroun."

"Congratulations on the MAGIC CARPET Magazine," writes Bruce Bryan, of Los Angeles. "It is a fine magazine in these days when others are going crash. I think it is an even better magazine than ORIENTAL STORIES, though I liked the latter first-rate. All the stories in the MAGIC CARPET were well-written and interesting."

"You are filling a long-felt want by readers of the 'different' with your new magazine, the MAGIC CARPET," writes M. M. Graham, of San Jose, California. "Every story is an outstanding feature. *Ismeddin and the Holy Carpet,* by E. Hoffmann Price, is a real classic. Give us one in every issue if possible."

Writes Richmond W. Haustein, of San Diego, California: "The best story in the January issue is *The Dragoman's Pilgrimage.* The three next best are *The Master of Dragons, Kong Beng,* and *Ismeddin and the Holy Carpet.* One trouble with this number which I can not overlook, however, is that I found no story by Dorothy Quick. Her stories get my vote in your last two ORIENTAL STORIES.

Earl Erimil, of Cleveland, Ohio, writes to the Souk: "Everything in the MAGIC CARPET Magazine was good, especially the stories by Grace Keon, Hugh B. Cave and Otis Adelbert Kline. When I read your magazine I said to myself, 'Here's a magazine I am going to read all the time.' I enjoy the MAGIC CARPET Magazine very much because it is so different from other fiction, and you just seem to be in the stories yourself when you read them."

"I, for one, am much pleased at the change that has taken place with the current issue of ORIENTAL STORIES—pardon me, the MAGIC CARPET," writes R. Arnold, of Springfield, Massachusetts. "For one thing, the new title is much more appealing to the imagination. The new realms open to the magazine's scope present great possibilities, provided a certain limit is maintained. The combination of the glamor of the Orient and the veiled mystery of far planets is a unique and irresistible idea. There is no reason why such seemingly diverse fields of writing should not be brought together to produce a truly unusual atmosphere, if the idea is handled correctly, and I am sure you can be trusted for that. I am glad to note that Adolphe de Castro has contributed a story to the MAGIC CARPET. I recall him as the author of *The Last Test,* that extremely powerful story in WEIRD TALES."

Writes C. H. Bolen, of Newark, New Jersey, "One of our Syrian agents brought a copy of the MAGIC CARPET to our office last week, and passed it among the boys. It finally was thrown on my desk with a note that it was good stuff. The boys picked the following stories in order of their popularity: 1, *Ismeddin and the Holy Carpet* by E. Hoffmann Price; 2, *The Master of Dragons* by H. Bedford-Jones; 3, *The Dragoman's Pilgrimage* by Otis Adelbert Kline. After reading the magazine through, I added my vote. However, if E. Hoffmann Price is merely a pen name, and if he really is a Syrian, my first choice is *The Dragoman's Pilgrimage.* If Mr. Price is not a Syrian, the palm surely goes to him; for our Syrian friend says that Ismeddin is faithful Oriental atmosphere. These unusual stories have intrigued us, and our newsboy has been asked to bring copies of the MAGIC CARPET along with other magazines on his trips to our office." [No, E. Hoffmann Price is not a pen name, and he is not a Syrian. He is a graduate of West Point, an acetylene gas engineer, and former soldier of fortune. He is an Orientalist by avocation, and his hobby is the collecting of Oriental rugs, which he calls 'carpets', by the way. It has been our pleasure to know him for several years. It is quite a treat to hear him ordering quaint Arabian dishes in Hassan's Syrian restaurant, calling out his commands in

Arabic. Saracenic eyebrows meet at the top of his nose, giving him a somewhat Oriental aspect, which is quite what one would expect of this writer of superb orientales.—THE EDITORS.]

"I think Allan Govan is your best bet, in his new *Arabian Nights* stories," writes J. O. Santesson, of West Newbury, Massachusetts. "He is delightfully hilarious, and when he comes to a situation that might become risqué he makes it so ridiculous that a plaster saint would crack his sides with mirth. *Kong Beng,* by Warren Hastings Miller, was good stuff. The atmosphere and the problems of the white man in dealing with the inferior race are well handled; it gets under one's skin. The suspense, characterization and everything else that a story should have are all there."

Mr. Santesson may be interested to learn that *Kong Beng* is founded on fact. Warren Hastings Miller writes in a letter to the editor: "For many years all that was known about the giant black boar of Borneo was conjectured from a single skull in the museum in Charlottenburg. When I was out East in 1921 I met Fletcher, the big game hunter of Calcutta, who gave me the first details of the animal, which I forwarded to Doctor Hornaday at the Bronx zoo. Fletcher had shot the first one, in East Borneo, in the Kong Beng region. Lumholtz is convinced that the fabulous Neduma of the Dyaks is none other than that same black boar. Neither they nor their dogs will follow its track. Fletcher had to bring his own *shikaris* from India. I wove it all into this story. The gods in Kong Beng were reported by a Dutch archeologist about 1902. Few white men have ever visited the cave."

Readers, what story do you like best in this issue? Your favorite story in the January issue, as shown by your votes and letters, is *Ismeddin and the Holy Carpet,* by E. Hoffmann Price. This story is closely pressed for first honors by H. Bedford-Jones' story, *The Master of Dragons,* which is trailing by only four votes as this issue goes to press.

My favorite stories in the April MAGIC CARPET are:

Story	Remarks
(1)_____	_____
(2)_____	_____
(3)_____	_____

I do not like the following stories:

(1)_____	Why? _____
(2)_____	_____

It will help us to know what kind of stories you want in the Magic Carpet Magazine if you will fill out this coupon and mail it to The Souk, Magic Carpet Magazine, 840 N. Michigan Ave., Chicago, Ill.

Reader's name and address:

_____

_____

_____

Mr. Jimson Assists

By AUGUST W. DERLETH

An incident of the Japanese invasion of Manchuria—Mr. Lu-Gen sends a package of cigarettes to a friend in Peiping

NO ONE would have guessed that the shabby beggar squatting in a squalid side street of Mukden was in reality Mr. Lu-Gen, sometimes also known as the Mandarin Ming, that enigmatic personage whose phantom-like fingers were too much present in all political and economic upheavals in China. He chose to squat in the sunlight because then he would be seen, and no further attention would be paid to him. "Thus," he mused as he sat there, "I can see without being molested. I need not fear discovery because I am without doubt observed. And being observed in this perhaps offensive guise, I am disdainfully passed over and not counted."

He did not like to think that he was sitting there in that shabby disguise because every road out of Mukden was being closely watched by certain people very desirous of putting hands upon the person of Mr. Lu-Gen, whose meddlings had become in the last two weeks fully as dangerous in their opinion as those of the unknown Mandarin Ming, all of which, while causing Mr. Lu-Gen vast amusement, yet irritated him not a little.

Yet the temporary necessity of disguise did not bother Mr. Lu-Gen nearly as much as the fact that he must deliver a certain document to a Chinese in Peiping. It was absurd that he knew no one to be trusted in this hour of need, but the situation existed and must accordingly be faced. He was beginning to feel very low-spirited when his slanting eyes caught sight of a lanky American sauntering casually down the street. At the

250

same moment he recognized the shock of black hair, and smiled to himself.

The American came on down the street and passed very close to the squatting beggar, who extended a sudden forceful foot and struck his ankle such a blow as to bring out an explosive and thoroughly American oath.

Without looking up, the offensive beggar at once began to speak, having accomplished his primary object of bringing the American to a stop. "Please pay no attention to my humble person, Mr. Jimson."

The American, hearing his name uttered with such apparent familiarity by the beggar, started in surprise, but continued to stand at attention, which was all that Mr. Lu-Gen desired.

"You will recollect meeting humble Lu-Gen in Shanghai on business two months past," continued the beggar imperturbably, "in the office of the American consul, Mr. Peterkin."

"The Chinese merchant," murmured Mr. Jimson, his voice betraying his surprize.

"Quite so. Please do not speak. Attention may be attracted. So sorry. I continue. I am no longer a merchant, as you see. Am merely humble beggar. However, surface appearances often deceive. Pray do not be deceived. I am not actually in monetary distress, though I may say I am in some measure of physical distress which you are powerless to dispel. There is, however, a certain mental distress which I believe you can and will alleviate, especially since I can promise you that a check of comfortable size will await your disposal at the consulate in Shanghai should you be so good as to assist me in a very minor matter and carry your assistance through successfully.

"You are perhaps willing to undertake this errand for me? It will take perhaps two days."

"Yes."

"I am much pleased. On the pavement before me you will observe a pack of cigarettes which I believe you have dropped."

"On the contrary——" began Jimson, whereupon he received another blow on the ankle. With a wry smile he bent and picked up the package of cigarettes, apparently unopened, and slipped it into his pocket, Mr. Lu-Gen meanwhile observing with satisfaction.

"Sorry blow was necessary," continued Mr. Lu-Gen composedly, "but Chinese are funny people. Deeply sorry. To go on. Cigarettes are of rare Russian brand not often brought into Manchuria. I have promised them to Mr. Ki Su-Hsiang at the Restaurant of the Roses in Peiping, but I am unfortunately detained by circumstances beyond my control. I desire you to bring those cigarettes to him before forty-eight hours pass—if you will humor this fancy."

Jimson considered. "It won't be too easy getting out of Mukden," he said. "The Japanese guard all the roads."

"Of this I am well aware, but I hoped an adventure would be more to your liking." Mr. Lu-Gen paused suggestively, and Jimson flushed.

"Very well," said Jimson curtly. "I'll go."

"In seven days' time, call at the American consulate in Shanghai, and be so good as to accept with my compliments the check which will be waiting for you there. And allow me a further suggestion. Perhaps it would be well for you not to carry more than one pack of cigarettes."

JIMSON went down the street, and Mr. Lu-Gen once more gave thanks to his ancestors. He continued to sit in the somnolent sunlight, blinking his eyes and exercising exceeding great patience with the Japanese whose efficient surveillance made outgoing paths so impossible for his person. However, if all went well, the Japanese would presently withdraw, and he might go on about his business. Once again Mr. Lu-Gen gave thanks to his ancestors and prayed that the mantle of fortune might descend upon the broad shoulders of the excellent Mr. Jimson.

Jimson, meanwhile, went blithely on his way and presently found himself at the railroad station, where he bought a ticket to Peiping. He had reckoned his time right; the train was just about to leave. Boarding the train, however, was somewhat more difficult, for he was promptly stopped by two Japanese soldiers who persisted in holding him by the arms until a military inspector got around to questioning him with profuse apologies for indignity thus bestowed.

"You are an American," said the Japanese in understandable English. "You are going to Peiping. We must know your business there."

"I have no business there," replied Jimson. "I have only a few hours in Peiping on my way to Shanghai."

"And your business in Shanghai?"

"Is concerned with the American consulate," snapped Jimson. "I hope you will not find it your duty to investigate our consulate?" Jimson's voice was deliberately sharp, and its effect was not lost upon his interrogator.

"We are sorry," said the Japanese at once. "We did not know you were connected with the consular service."

Jimson saved himself from grinning just in time.

He was released and allowed to board the train. Not far out of Mukden the train was halted and the passengers again checked over. Jimson was beginning to feel very irritated. However, he did not for an instant suspect that all these elaborate precautions were taken to assure the Japanese that Mr. Lu-Gen was not leaving Mukden, where by some miracle they had learned that personage was in hiding. Nor did Jimson know that all lines of communication were being tapped to avoid the possibility of Lu-Gen's getting in touch with the world beyond Mukden.

IN DUE time Jimson reached Peiping. He got himself a luncheon and then set about searching for the Restaurant of the Roses, which was in no directory of the city, as a hasty glance at an ancient and torn volume had assured him.

He encountered more trouble than he had supposed he might. It appeared that not only was the restaurant difficult to find, but it was evidently extremely difficult to gain admittance. Jimson made inquiry, but was met with unblinking stares and curt statements that the Restaurant of the Roses was not for such as he.

He had asked his tenth likely person in vain when he was unexpectedly accosted by a beggar, who while extending his palm for alms, whispered, "What do you want at the Roses?" in broken English.

"I have urgent business there," replied Jimson, dropping a coin into the extended palm.

There was a momentary air of uncertainty about the beggar as he stood there. Then he said, "Follow me." He turned and shuffled away, and Jimson followed, it seemed, through interminable streets

(Please turn to page 254)

COMING NEXT ISSUE

CLEGHORN turned into the passage, passed the door of the girl's cabin, shoved open his own door, and reached for the light. His figure was illuminated by the light in the passage; the cabin was pitch-black. As he put out his arm, something moved before him. Every sense alert, he ducked, and swerved quickly to one side.

A furious blow glanced from his head—had he not ducked, it would have brained him. Half stunned, he hurled himself to one side, and collided full with an unseen figure. His hands shot out. A grim and furious satisfaction seized Cleghorn as his fingers sank into the throat of a man, sank in with a terrible grip.

Another smash over the head, and another.

Blinded, he sank in his fingers the deeper. The two struggling figures hit against the door, and it slammed shut. Now there was perfect darkness. In his ears, Cleghorn heard the hoarse, frenzied panting of a man, felt the smashing blows of the other's fists and of some blunt weapon. He had not the slightest idea who it could be, and cared not. This fellow had been waiting here to get him, and had come within an ace of it.

That man, gripped about the throat by those fingers of iron, gasped terribly, struggled with blind and frantic desperation to loose the grip, and could not. His strength began to fail. Again Cleghorn caught a terrific smash over the head, and this fourth blow all but knocked him out.

He lost balance, but did not lose his grip. He dragged down the other with him; they fell heavily, rolled against the closed door, and lay there sprawling. Flashes of fire beat before Cleghorn's eyes. He tried to rise, and could not. He felt his senses slipping away. With an effort, he held himself motionless, let all his strength, all his will-power, flow into his hard-gripped fingers.

Even when everything went black before him, there was no slackening of his frightful hold. . . .

Don't miss this vivid thrill-tale of a desperate voyage on the China sea, with murder striking from the shadows again and again, and a beautiful girl on board—all bound for a coral reef off the Manchurian coast, where a treasure-ship lay wrecked. This stirring novelette will be published complete in the next issue of the MAGIC CARPET Magazine:

PEARLS FROM MACAO
By H. BEDFORD-JONES

—ALSO—

THE SAMARITAN
By Warren Hastings Miller

The story of a ship's officer who tried to help an American girl in the *souks* of Tunis, and plunged into a wild and dangerous adventure.

THE LION OF TIBERIAS
By Robert E. Howard

The Magic Carpet takes you back to the stirring days of the Crusades, when Zenghi, Lord of Mosul and precursor of Saladin, rode up the glittering stairs of empire to his doom.

THE BRIDE OF GOD
By Seabury Quinn

This thrilling episode in the life of Carlos de la Muerte—the second story in the series "The Vagabond-at-Arms"—is crammed to the brim with action—the bite of sharp sword-blades and the tang of exciting adventures in the valiant days of yore. Each story in this series is complete in itself.

THE JUMPING-WELL
By Geoffrey Vace

A story of eery adventures in Delhi, that begins in Mitro's hop joint and ends in the mysterious house of mirrors—a tale of Chowkander King.

THE FORGOTTEN OF ALLAH
By E. Hoffmann Price

The story of a doughty sultan in Kurdistan—a tale of the Pious Companions and red feats of valor.

The Next MAGIC CARPET On Sale April 15th

(Continued from page 252)
and alleys, emerging at last in a nearly deserted quarter of the city, where once in the days of the great Empire the mandarins had held court. They came to a building set away from the street by high walls, passed beyond them, through court after court, and arrived at last before a door upon which the beggar beat a quick tattoo.

At once a panel slid back and an inquiring bronze-skinned Chinese face was thrust into the space thus disclosed. A word was spoken in dialect, to which the beggar replied in kind, and stepped aside, motioning Jimson to come up.

"Your business?" asked the face in the door in crisp English.

"I wish to see Mr. Ki Su-Hsiang."

The eyes of the face in the door betrayed the faintest flicker. Then the voice came again. "Personage can not be disturbed at every notice. Can you say why you came?"

"I have a message for him."

"I will take same."

"I must deliver it in person."

"That is not necessary," said the face firmly. Then abruptly the slanting eyes narrowed, and in a lower voice the man behind the door asked, "From whom do come?"

"I come from Mr. Lu-Gen."

From beyond the face in the door came a single explosive word—"Ming!" Then the door swung back, and Jimson was confronted by a servile Oriental who took him at once along a corridor and into a long room where a small Chinese, obviously of high caste, sat cross-legged on a dais, his body clothed in the richest mandarin's robes, his mask-like face made striking by his black glasses.

"I am the person you seek," he said in a soft voice, addressing Jimson at once.

STATEMENT OF THE OWNERSHIP, MANAGEMENT, CIRCULATION, ETC., REQUIRED BY THE ACT OF CONGRESS OF AUGUST 24, 1912,

Of Oriental Stories, published quarterly at Indianapolis, Indiana, for October 1, 1932.

State of Illinois } ss.
County of Cook }

Before me, a notary public in and for the State and county aforesaid, personally appeared Wm. R. Sprenger, who, having been duly sworn according to law, deposes and says that he is the Business Manager of the Oriental Stories and that the following is, to the best of his knowledge and belief, a true statement of the ownership, management (and if a daily paper, the circulation), etc., of the aforesaid publication for the date shown in the above caption required by the Act of August 24, 1912, embodied in section 411, Postal Laws and Regulations, printed on the reverse of this form, to wit:

1. That the names and addresses of the publisher, editor, managing editor, and business manager are:

Publisher—Popular Fiction Publishing Company, 2457 E. Washington St., Indianapolis, Ind.

Editor—Farnsworth Wright, 840 N. Michigan Ave., Chicago, Ill.

Managing Editor—None.

Business Manager—William R. Sprenger, 840 N. Michigan Ave., Chicago, Ill.

2. That the owner is: (If owned by a corporation, its name and address must be stated and also immediately thereunder the names and addresses of stockholders owning or holding one per cent or more of total amount of stock. If not owned by a corporation, the names and addresses of the individual owners must be given. If owned by a firm, company, or other unincorporated concern, its name and address, as well as those of each individual member must be given.)

Popular Fiction Publishing Company, 2457 E. Washington St., Indianapolis, Ind.

Wm. R. Sprenger, 840 N. Michigan Ave., Chicago, Ill.

Farnsworth Wright, 840 N. Michigan Ave., Chicago, Ill.

George M. Cornelius, 2457 E. Washington St., Indianapolis, Indiana.

George H. Cornelius, 2457 E. Washington St., Indianapolis, Indiana.

P. W. Cornelius, 2457 E. Washington St., Indianapolis, Indiana.

3. That the known bondholders, mortgagees, and other security holders owning or holding 1 per cent or more of total amount of bonds, mortgages, or other securities are: (If there are none, so state). None.

4. That the two paragraphs next above, giving the names of the owners, stockholders, and security holders, if any, contain not only the list of stockholders and security holders as they appear upon the books of the company, but also, in cases where the stockholder or security holder appears upon the books of the company as trustee or in any other fiduciary relation, the name of the person or corporation for whom such trustee is acting, is given; also that the said two paragraphs contain statements embracing affiant's full knowledge and belief as to the circumstances and conditions under which stockholders and security holders who do not appear upon the books of the company as trustees, hold stock and securities in a capacity other than that of a bona fide owner; and this affiant has no reason to believe that any other person, association, or corporation has any interest, direct or indirect, in the said stock, bonds, or other securities than as so stated by him.

5. That the average number of copies of each issue of this publication sold or distributed, through the mails or otherwise, to paid subscribers during the six months preceding the date shown above is————. (This information is required from daily publications only.)

WM. R. SPRENGER,
Business Manager.

Sworn to and subscribed before me this 28th day of September, 1932.   RICHARD S. GOULDEN,
[SEAL]   Notary Public.
My commission expires May 3, 1934.

"You come from my great and good friend, Mr. Lu-Gen?"

"I've brought you the cigarettes he promised you."

"Service gives me infinite pleasure," he murmured. "May I have them?" His voice was eager.

Jimson delivered the pack of cigarettes, and the Chinese said, "Now it would be best for you to leave Peiping at your earliest opportunity and to follow any further directions Mr. Lu-Gen might have given you." Whereupon the personage rose and disappeared into an adjoining room, drawing curtains to behind him.

Immediately some one appeared at Jimson's elbow. It was the servant who had brought him to the room. His bland face was creased by a smile.

Jimson was conducted from the house and away, while Mr. Ki Su-Hsiang occupied himself with breaking the cigarettes in the package and taking from each one a carefully folded piece of paper, until he had before him twenty such pieces, which when painstakingly arranged resolved into a map of Manchuria done with infinite care. Mr. Ki Su-Hsiang chuckled low in his throat and murmured, "Oh, excellent Lu-Gen, admirable Lu-Gen, may your progeny be many."

A T THE appointed time Jimson walked into the American consulate at Shanghai, where he was greeted by Mr. Peterkin, a white-haired man who had held his post for many years.

"Well, well, Jimson," said the old man. "We were just discussing you. A check has just arrived for you from no less a person than Mr. Lu-Gen."

"Indeed," said Jimson. "I was expecting it. How much does it amount to?"

"About five hundred dollars, I should say. You must have done a pretty job for Lu-Gen to earn that."

Jimson hoped that his face betrayed none of the excitement he felt. He took the check, looked at it once or twice, trying to appear very unconcerned, and put it carefully away in his wallet. Then he sat down to chat with Mr. Peterkin.

"Just come from the north?" asked the consul abruptly.

"Not exactly. I've been at Nanking for a day."

"The latest is a smashing defeat for the Japanese. It makes interesting reading."

Jimson took up the English daily, scanning the headlines. *"Four Major Japanese Positions Surprized by Night—Chinese Obtain Secret Knowledge of Japanese Fortifications—General Fu Routs Japs from Mukden."* He ran his eyes down the page, pausing for a moment on the somewhat indistinct picture of General Fu, whose likeness was grinning toothily. Jimson did not recognize in General Fu the high-caste Chinese, Mr. Ki Su-Hsiang.

Then his eye caught a smaller head. He read it over to himself, then read it aloud to the consul. *"Mysterious American Believed to Have Carried Secret Information to General Fu."* Dropping the paper, Jimson added, "That's bad. Any American with sense ought to know better than to get mixed up in a business like this. He'll be the loser in the long run."

"I quite agree with you, Jimson," said Mr. Peterkin gravely, looking quizzically at the younger man, "if you really believe it."

"Of course I believe it," said Jimson, somewhat nettled. He really did. As he left the consulate, whistling, he was wondering why the Chinese paid such an infernal attention to trivial details—such as a casual promise to deliver a pack of cigarettes.

O. S.—8

www.ingramcontent.com/pod-product-compliance
Lightning Source LLC
Chambersburg PA
CBHW080816250626
47159CB00010B/3408